THE STEPNEY TAKEOVER

Carol Hellier

The Stepney Takeover - Text copyright © Carol Hellier 2024

All Rights Reserved

The Stepney Takeover is a work of fiction. All characters, places, and events are from the author's imagination. Any resemblance to persons, living or dead, events or places is purely coincidental.

The author respectfully recognises the use of any and all trademarks.

With the exception of quotes used in reviews, this book may not be reproduced or used in whole or in part by any means existing without written permission from the author.

Warning: The unauthorised reproduction or distribution of this copyrighted work is illegal. No part of this book may be scanned, uploaded, or distributed via the Internet or any other means, electronic or print, without the author's written permission.

DEDICATION

As always, a big thank you to my children and grandchildren, for keeping me on my toes. I love you all.

A special thank you to everyone who has bought, downloaded, and read my books. Your support is, as always, very much appreciated.

Thank you to my friends who have supported me in my quest to become an author; I know I can be difficult.

And lastly, a big thank you to the Rothcock Charity Festival. These guys raise money every year for a different charity. The 2024 charity was for PAPYRUS – PREVENTION OF YOUNG SUICIDE, in aid of my niece, Lauren Ashley Rose Hellier, who sadly took her own life in 2022. They did an amazing job and served her memory well. Once again, thank you Julie, Craig, Sarah, and Andy. You really are amazing people.

For anyone struggling and in need of help, you can contact these organisations:

SAMARITANS HELPLINE: 116 123
CAMPAIGN AGAINST LIVING MISERABLY (CALM): 0800585858
PAPYRUS – PREVENTION OF YOUNG SUICIDE: 0800 068 41 41
SOS SILENCE OF SUICIDE: 0300 1020 505

A woman's loyalty is tested when her man has nothing. A man's loyalty is tested when he has everything.
    -Unknown

HEAVY IS THE HEAD THAT WEARS THE CROWN

PROLOGUE

November 1976

The house was in total darkness. Millie sat in the lounge waiting silently for Paul. The bodies would have been disposed of by now. All evidence gone. In her mind, she couldn't shake the words Ronald had said.

'It was never about you, it was about him. He slept with my Rita.'

It was the look in his eyes. The look that said he was telling the truth. Had Paul betrayed her? As sure as she had been that he would never do such a thing, now she doubted even her own judgement. They say love is blind.

Love makes you weak.

She turned her head towards the window. The glare of headlights illuminated the room. This was the hour of reckoning.

THE STEPNEY TAKEOVER

The rattle of the key in the door, then the hall light switched on. Paul's footsteps grew nearer.

"Mil?" he half whispered.

"I'm in here," she answered.

"Why are you sitting in the dark?" he asked as he flicked the switch.

The light blinded her briefly.

Staring into his eyes, she asked the question that could end their marriage. "Did you sleep with Rita?"

CHAPTER 1

January 1977

Millie sat at the kitchen table, yawning while rubbing her growing belly. She was now four months pregnant and had a tiny bulge that she was in awe of. The morning sickness, which seemed to come and go as it pleased, had made sleeping impossible, so she had risen early at four-thirty a.m.

"I wish you'd go back to bed, Mil, you need to rest," Connie said. She'd popped over because the lights were on.

"I'm fine, Mum." It still seemed strange calling her Mum.

Having grown up in a children's home, she wasn't used to having a family unit, and although she'd gone searching for them, it was still a shock finding out Duke and Connie Lee were her parents. She had struggled. Duke was a gypsy and Connie a gorger, but they lived the gypsy lifestyle. Living in a caravan, or trailer, as they called it.

Was that why she had found it so hard with them or was it because her first husband, Levi, who was also a gypsy, had beaten her black and blue? The whole gypsy heritage thing that Duke was so proud of, she herself had hated. It hadn't helped that Paul hated gypsies, and the feud that had taken place when they'd first met had made it even harder for her.

However, her parents had stood by her in the darkest of times, and she appreciated that. That was what made them family, that and loyalty, which Paul seemed to have neglected.

"Here, drink this while it's still warm." Connie pushed the cup of tea towards her.

"You fuss too much." Millie smiled.

"Maybe so, but that's what you need right now," Connie said.

Millie knew what she was speaking of. It had been two months since she had split from Paul, the betrayal of him sleeping with Rita too much for her to take. Not that Paul would accept the end of their marriage. Every day he turned up with flowers, begging for a second chance. But how did you recover from a broken heart, caused by the person you loved more than life itself? Paul thought it was her pride, he didn't understand how deeply it cut. The thought of the old hag blackmailing him into bed made a mockery of their marriage. And all because he wanted the scrapyard. Forging Ronnie Taylor's will was never going to end well. Hadn't he considered that, or didn't he care?

Selfish, that's what you are, Kelly.

"So what have you planned for today?" Connie enquired, breaking into her thoughts.

Today she was going to see Rosie, her best friend. She had been taken to a special hospital after trying to take her own life. It had been a rough couple of months, but finally she was on the mend. "I'm out this afternoon visiting Rosie, Scott's driving me... I thought we could go to the market on Saturday and get some more baby bits, if you're free?"

"I'm always free for my daughter. Right, I best get home, your dad will be up shortly. I'll pop in later." Connie stood. She lovingly gazed down at Millie. "Don't overdo things today."

"I won't. See you later." Millie watched her mother leave, her thoughts then turning to Paul and how he'd react when she told him she wanted a divorce.

***

Paul sat on the end of the bed. He had been staying with his mum and dad for the last couple of months. It wasn't ideal, especially sleeping in a single bed, however, there was no way he would buy a flat, even if finances would allow it, when he was certain they could patch things up. After all, there was a baby to consider. He took a few deep breaths, preparing himself for yet another lecture from his mother, Bridie. Being Irish Catholic meant there was no question of divorce, so she expected him to go and make things right with Millie. When he had told her what had happened, leaving out the adultery, she had surprised him with a swift clip around the ear, and the verbal abuse, which he deserved, had quickly followed.

He descended the stairs and headed towards the noise of the kettle boiling and cups clinking. Opening the kitchen door, he was greeted with her stern face.

"You should be at yours making amends with Millie, not—"

"Not now, Mum, I don't need to wake up to a lecture every morning," he warned in a low voice. As much as he loved her, she could moan for Ireland, and while she was partly right, he had to give the love of his life a bit of space. Millie was a thinker, she needed to be left alone to think things through. He would go and see her later, with flowers and yet another sincere apology.

So much had happened in the last six months. He had gained full ownership of the docks after Millie had Duke kill Ronnie, and now owned the scrapyard after he had forged the will.

Was it worth it? No.

If he could, he would have gone back in time and changed everything. He blamed Rita, but deep down, he knew it was his own greed. Why hadn't he called her bluff instead of climbing into bed with her? Why hadn't he killed her sooner? Now he was paying the price.

A cup was placed in front of him accompanied with a loud tut. He ignored that and instead decided that by the end of the day, if he wasn't back with Millie, he would find alternative accommodation until he was.

***

Millie climbed out of the motor and stared up at the massive house. It looked like a stately home; it was magnificent. All red brick and tall windows, with a long, winding tree-lined drive. Rosie had been moved here a few weeks ago as her mental health had improved. It was a lovely area in Surrey, and the grounds were something out of a novel, with a picturesque landscape. It had cost a small fortune, but as far as Millie was concerned it was worth every penny. Soon she hoped Rosie would be ready to return home and continue her care in Stepney with her.

Scott appeared at her side with a large bouquet. He was smiling, but Millie could see he was anxious. She also felt the same every time they came to visit.

They walked to the entrance and rang the doorbell. Even though this was not a high-risk psychiatric hospital, it was still high security, you couldn't walk in and out as you wanted. There was a barrier to stop unwanted traffic and a security man who would only let you through if your name was on his list.

The door opened, and they were greeted by a tall slim man by the name of Christopher. He was friendly, and Millie had warmed to him instantly, the first time they had met.

"Good morning, Millie. Scott. Rosie is in the day room. I'll take you through," Christopher told them and led the way.

Rosie sat at a table in the day room. It had tables and chairs dotted around for the visiting families. She appeared to be gazing out of the window.

Millie eagerly joined her. "Hey, Rose."

Rosie jumped up and hugged her friend and then her brother, Scott. "I'm so pleased to see you both. It gets a bit boring here after a while. They wanted me to do some arty-farty stuff." She lowered her voice to a whisper. "I told 'em to get lost. Wasn't good at it when I was at school and I certainly ain't good at it now." She turned away and scanned the room. Resting her gaze back on Millie, she continued. "When are you breaking me out?"

Millie glanced at Scott; that question had thrown her. "I'll talk to Christopher in a bit and see what I can find out. First I want to know how you are?"

"Are those for me?" Rosie grabbed the flowers and sniffed at them. "Thanks, bruv." She waved them at a nurse who sat by the door. "Can you put these in a vase, please?" she shouted.

Millie watched with interest. Rosie seemed a bit erratic. Had they changed her medication? "Rosie, how have you been since we last visited?"

"Bored, so can you talk to Christopher now, please, Mil?"

Millie smiled and gave a small nod. "Okay, I won't be long." She stood to make her way back to the reception area. It was at the bottom of a grand staircase that split at the top, going in different directions. She could just imagine royalty having lived here a hundred years ago. The place had a regal feel to it. It would have been bustling with activity, servants running around cleaning and bringing cups of tea when ordered.

She glanced at the stony-faced receptionist and smiled. "Can I see someone about Rosie, please? I'd like to know how her treatment is going and when she'll be ready to come home?"

"The doctor will be about thirty minutes. I'll come and get you when she is here, Mrs Kelly," she replied in a stern voice.

She reminded Millie of a headmistress.

"Okay. Thank you." She returned to the day room.

Rosie and Scott were laughing. As she neared them she could overhear the conversation. They were chatting about the children's home where they'd all grown up. It was strange to think that when times were hard they all reverted back to those days. Although they'd all felt abandoned, it was the one place they had any security. The one place they'd felt safe.

"That was quick," Scott said when he noticed her approaching.

"The doctor's not here yet, they're gonna get me when she arrives." She sat next to Rosie and studied her face. "You seem so much better; hopefully you'll be home soon."

"No. I need to go home now," Rosie snapped.

"You know they have to discharge you first, sis, we can't just take you," Scott added.

"You don't understand, they're—" Rosie stared over Millie's shoulder, her eyes growing wide.

The colour drained from her face. She looked scared.

"Whatever's wrong?" Millie asked, her stomach sinking.

"Mrs Kelly, would you like to come through to my office, we can chat in there?"

Turning, she looked at the doctor. She didn't like her, there had been something off from day one, but because Rosie had seemed to improve under her care, she had put her feelings to one side. "I won't be long."

Rosie's eyes darted between the doctor and Millie. "Mil. Please. Don't listen to her. It's not safe here."

CHAPTER 2

The journey home had been stressful. Scott had questioned her for most of it. She didn't have answers, she was as confused as he was. Was Rosie suffering from psychosis as the doctor suggested, or was something more sinister going on? The way Rosie had clung to her when she'd left and whispered, "Mil, I'm not safe here." The pleading in her eyes made Millie doubt the doctor.

Fuck.

She picked up her keys and left via the back door. She was having dinner with Duke and Connie. Not that she wanted to, not after today, but then again, maybe she could talk to them, see what they thought about Rosie and her situation.

It was now dark. She hated the winter for this very reason. Dark mornings and even darker evenings. She made her way down the garden. It was handy having her parents living in the field behind her house. The mobile home they lived in was like a bungalow, not that she would say that to Duke. Every inch the Romani that he was, he hated the thought of living in bricks and mortar.

'I was born on the open road, Millie, and that's where I will die' he had said.

She laughed inwardly. Living in a mobile on the bit of land he had bought was not the open road.

Leaving the gate open behind her, she headed for the door, knocking before letting herself in.

"Come in and warm yourself, girl, it's bloody cold tonight," Duke said from the lounge.

She sat and gazed at the fire. It was roaring away, the flames licking the glass. "It's certainly toasty in here." She watched Duke down a can of beer then turned her attention to Connie. "Can I help with anything?"

"No. You sit there and keep your father company." Connie disappeared into the kitchen.

"We've got a nice bit of Irish stew and crusty bread," Duke said as he crushed the can and threw it into the bin. "So how's your friend Rosie doing?"

"Actually, I wanted to talk to you about her… She seemed so much better today and then she…" Millie stood and studied the Crown Derby proudly displayed in a cabinet. "You bought some candlesticks, they look lovely."

"Don't change the subject; and then she what?" Duke sat forward on the edge of his seat.

"She reckons she's in danger, something bad is happening there." The thought of what Rosie had said now seemed mad. Jesus, was she mad to even consider it? "Take no notice of me, Rosie is in there for a reason."

"From what I've heard, bad things do happen in those places. Not all, but some. What does your gut tell you?" Duke asked.

Millie turned and stared at him. She hadn't been expecting that. "My gut tells me to not trust the doctor, I've never liked her from day one. But for a start, Rose couldn't elaborate on what she meant, she said it was more of a feeling. Is that possible?"

"Do you have to make an appointment to see her?" He stood and walked towards her. "Because if you don't, maybe we should go and visit her tomorrow."

"We just phone and say we're coming. Scott will have to come, too, as he's next of kin."

Duke's face dropped. "Oh great, Kelly's lackey." He sighed. "Well, if he has to come, so be it. I'm not having you stressing while you're pregnant."

"Scott might work for Paul, but he's family to me. He won't tell Paul anything private," she assured him.

He rubbed the back of his neck. "Okay. We go tomorrow and suss this situation out. Maybe Rosie will be able to tell you more."

***

Paul parked on the driveway. He hated January, it was the worst month of the year. It seemed to go on forever, and the dark mornings and dark evenings brought his mood down. Add the fact that he was estranged from Millie, and he found he was having trouble controlling his temper. All his men at work were treading on eggshells around him, but he didn't care. He needed her by his side. She was his, she would always be his, unless he decided differently. It irritated him that she couldn't see the bigger picture and annoyed him more that she was calling the shots.

Glancing at the house, he sighed. It was in total darkness. He let himself in. "Mil, you home?" No answer. Where had she gone? He wasn't happy; he would need to put a tail on her so he knew her movements. Flicking the light on, he sat at the kitchen table, still holding the bouquet, and waited. He stared at the clock: it was now eight p.m.

The kitchen door opened, and he was met with a sour-faced Millie. "Paul."

It wasn't the kind of greeting he'd expected. He thought she may have missed him by now, even wanted him back. Standing, he thrust the flowers towards her. "I got you these, babe. How's bump?" He looked down and smiled. Not that he could see anything, she was as slim as ever in her clothes.

"Thanks, but flowers aren't gonna change the situation." She placed them down and sighed.

"We belong together, Mil, we're gonna be parents... Are you really gonna let one discrepancy ruin that?"

Millie laughed. "A discrepancy is when the accounts don't add up. Not when you stick your dick in another woman."

"We've gone through all this, you know why I did what I did. It—"

"Was because of your greed," Millie added. "We had everything, Paul. The club, the docks, and the girls, all making us a more than comfortable living. Did you really need the scrapyard, too?"

"You like the money as much as I do, so don't blame me for trying my best to give you everything," Paul replied, trying to hold his temper.

"I never asked you for anything. I did, however, expect loyalty," she countered.

"Yet you don't mind living in my house, while I'm slumming it at my parents'." He regretted his words immediately; he would hardly win her back like this. "I didn't mean that."

"Yes you did, and you're right, this is your house, and I should leave." She marched past him and up the stairs.

Paul followed. When they reached the top, he grabbed her arm and twisted her round to face him.

"You're staying here, this is yours and the baby's home... Mil, I was out of line. I just get so angry going round and round all the time. We don't seem to be getting anywhere."

"I don't think I can forgive you, Paul. You broke my heart, and I'm not gonna give you the chance to do it again."

"For fuck's sake, you know why I did it. Christ, I even killed the old tart so I didn't have to do it again. I can stand here now, with my hand on my heart, and promise you that will never happen again."

Her face seemed to soften. Was she considering it?

"Mil, I love you."

Her stomach did a little summersault before she came back to her senses. "I'm tired, you should go." She tugged her arm away and entered the bedroom.

Paul stood for a moment as if wondering what he was supposed to do now, follow her or give her more time? "I'm not giving up on us." He turned and descended the stairs quickly.

Millie listened out for the click of the front door then relaxed when she knew she was on her own. She couldn't carry on like this. He wouldn't accept that the marriage was over. The crack about her living in his house had been another nail in the coffin. The main reason he wanted her here was so he could keep tabs on her. As far as he was concerned she was his property, just like the house and businesses.

But you went weak when he said, 'I love you'.

"That's why I need to go." She flopped down onto the bed, put her head in her hands, and sobbed.

Her life was in tatters.

***

Paul unlocked the back door of the club and made his way to the office. He would stay here. It was private, he wouldn't get any more lectures from his interfering mother, and he could come and go as and when he wanted. This would do until he was back in his own gaff with Millie.

He sat back on the sofa and let out a loud sigh. He missed her, more than he ever thought possible. Although to be fair, he never thought they would split. He went through their conversation again, in his head. It was a form of torture; he had done the same thing every night since that night she had questioned him. At the time he'd convinced himself he was doing it for them. Just the thought of sleeping with Rita turned his stomach.

You fucking prick.

He reached across to the desk and grabbed the photo that held pride of place. It was of their wedding day. They both wore great big smiles. Millie's eyes sparkled, lighting up his world. He felt a stirring in his loins. Unzipping his trousers, he reached for his cock and gave it a stroke.

After cleaning himself up, he laid out a blanket and pillow and undressed. Pouring himself a large scotch, he necked it in one. The burn hit his throat immediately. He poured another and then another until the bottle was empty. He glanced around the room with drunken eyes. Why should he have to sleep here when he owned a large four-bedroom house? A house that he'd paid for. There was enough room for them both to live there, and maybe if she saw him every day, they would get back together sooner. Mind made up, Paul settled back on the sofa. Tomorrow he'd return home, and Millie would have to like it or lump it.

***

Rosie lay staring at the ceiling. A sliver of light shone through the crack of her partly open bedroom door. Everyone would be tucked up in their beds, soundly sleeping. But not her. Oh no, her mind was in overdrive. Had Scott or Millie believed her? She doubted it. Why would they believe the ramblings of a madwoman? Was she mad? No. She was one hundred percent sane, and the things she had noticed had happened. She had to believe that.

A squeaking noise piqued her interest. She climbed from the bed and walked towards the door. She crouched, spying through the crack. A trolley was wheeled past, one of those clumpy metal things they carried in ambulances. The noise lingered in the distance until silence.

She got back into bed and had just settled back when a muffled scream came through the wall. It was Remi, a young woman she had befriended upon arriving here. She had a drug problem and had been disowned by her family. Rosie felt she had a connection with her straight away. Was it because her parents had abandoned her, too? Maybe, but she was lucky to have her brother, Scott, and Millie who she thought of as a sister.

A loud bump made her sit up.

What the fuck was that?

Leaving the bed once again, she walked slowly towards the door and spied through the gap. A trolley passed, and on it Remi lay, strapped down. Was she unconscious? Rosie opened the door and came face to face with a man she hadn't seen before.

"What's going on?"

The doctor appeared from behind him. "Remi was feeling unwell. She's being taken to hospital to get checked out. There's nothing to worry about, now back to bed."

"What's wrong with her?" Rose asked as she was pushed back into her room by the man.

The door shut, and the key turned in the lock.

CHAPTER 3

Millie wrapped her coat around her and stood at the window waiting for Scott. Hearing a motor pulling in, she wandered into the kitchen and grabbed her handbag. Surprised when the front door opened, she rushed to the hallway where she was greeted with a smiling Paul.

"I've been thinking, babe, there's more than enough room for both of us here, and as I'm paying the bills—"

"No, Paul. Absolutely not." Millie gasped. "You promised you'd stay away."

Before Paul answered, a knock came from the front door and, pushing past him, she opened it.

"Morning, Mil." Scott stared over her shoulder. "Mr Kelly."

"What the fuck are you doing here?" Paul snapped.

"He's here to drive me. Now if you don't mind, I haven't time for this. Scott, I'll meet you outside."

"Using my car to drive you around. Do you mind telling me where you're going as I'm footing the bill?" Paul demanded.

"Yes, I do, as it's none of your business," she said, her chest tightening. This wasn't good for the baby.

"Then Scott can't drive you. He works for me, remember," Paul snarled.

"I quit," Scott announced. "There's the keys, Mr Kelly."

"Well done, Paul, you've been here two minutes and upset everyone. Scott, follow me." Millie headed towards the kitchen, turning when she reached the doorway. "I'll collect my stuff later."

Millie continued down the garden and out of the gate onto Duke's ground. He would have to drive them. She hoped he'd had the heater fixed, because last time she had been in the Transit it was warmer outside than in.

"Dad?"

"I was just about to come round." Duke frowned. "What's happened?"

"Scott's cars broken down, can you drive?" Millie asked.

"Okay. Let me get the keys."

Scott looked at Millie and raised an eyebrow. "Broken down?"

"He mustn't know what just happened. I can't deal with those two going head to head, and besides, Rosie is what we need to concentrate on. If she is in danger we need to get her out."

***

Paul sank back into the sofa. She was right, he had promised to give her space and let her work through her feelings. Every day he had been here, begging and pleading, and now he'd ruined everything by moving back in. He ran his hand over his face. "Fucking idiot."

Duke's Transit roared as it started up. Just where were they going?

"Only one way to find out." Grabbing his keys, he left the house.

***

Duke slammed the motor into gear and drove out of the lane. He glanced at Millie. "Everything okay?"

"Apart from worrying about Rosie, yes." She smiled.

Duke wasn't daft, he could tell a false smile when he saw one. "Paul hasn't been bothering you?"

"No, and anyway, I can handle Paul."

Duke decided to leave the interrogation for now, he'd let Connie quiz her later. She was better with that kind of thing. All he wanted to do was punch him in the face and make him suffer, just like he had his daughter. Connie had to keep reminding him Paul was the baby's father, but as far as he was concerned, he didn't deserve to be. Millie and the child deserved better. Much better.

He glanced at her again. She sat stony-faced.

The atmosphere in the cab had taken a turn for the worse.

"Shouldn't take too long before we get there," Scott informed them. Was he hoping the change of subject might help?

"Depending on the traffic, hopefully only a couple of hours," Duke said. "This is the way we go to the Derby." He took a quick peek at Millie.

"What did they say when you phoned to say we're coming to visit?" she replied while riffling through her handbag, obviously uninterested in that bit of information.

"Same as usual, they'll let her know, blah, blah, blah… You know, I thought the place was great at first, but now…" Scott glanced down at his shaking hands.

"Hey." Millie grabbed his hand and gave it a gentle squeeze. "Rosie is gonna be okay, we'll make sure of it."

Duke nudged Millie. "Is that Paul's motor behind?"

"I can't see from here. Scott, can you see?" she asked.

Scott leant forward and checked the wing mirror. "Yeah, that's his car."

"Un-fucking-believable." Duke started to slow down.

"No. Keep going. If he wants to know what we're doing so badly, let him waste his time. He won't be allowed in anyway." Millie clenched her hands in her lap.

It was Scott's turn to comfort her.

***

Paul stared at the giant house. It was like a bloody great palace. Large stone pillars either side of steps which led to the entrance. He glanced at Duke's Transit as it sailed through the security gates and laughed.

THE STEPNEY TAKEOVER

I bet they're gonna love seeing that old thing pull up.

He wouldn't be able to follow, but he didn't want to. His scar on his left cheek rose and itched. He was angry.

Doing a U-turn in the tree-lined lane, he decided to head back. He recognised the name of this place from a bank statement. This was costing him over a hundred and fifty quid a week, and Millie didn't think he deserved an explanation. Putting two and two together, he realised this was for Rosie.

"Got ya." He grinned.

He needed to unpack, after all, and when Millie returned home, he would have it out with her. As much as he loved her, he wouldn't be taken for a mug.

CHAPTER 4

Millie smiled at Christopher as he greeted them. "How's Rosie today?"

"She was a little unsettled after you left yesterday. The doctor gave her something last night to help her relax. Actually, the doc would like a word with you. I'll show you in and then go find her."

She followed him into the day room. Rosie sat by the window, staring vacantly into space. "Rose?"

"What have they done to her?" Scott asked. "She looks spaced out."

Millie knelt in front of her and smiled. "Rose, hey."

A glimmer of recognition appeared on her face. "Mil... hey." Her words were slurred and slow.

Scott knelt next to her. "What happened, you were fine yesterday?"

"They... gave me... something... this morning," Rosie replied.

"Are you sure it was this morning?" Millie glanced at Duke. "Christopher said they sedated her last night."

"Mrs Kelly, the doctor will see you now," a miserable-looking woman called.

"Dad, come with me. Scott, you stay here, see if she remembers anything else." While they followed the woman through to the doctor's office, she whispered in Duke's ear, "This feels wrong."

He nodded in return. "Don't worry, we'll get to the bottom of this."

"Mrs Kelly, lovely to see you again so soon." Her eyes widened when her gaze fell on Duke.

"This is my dad, Mr Lee." You couldn't mistake him for anything but a gypsy, which in this instance pleased Millie. Placing her hands on the desk, she leant forward and glared at the doctor. "I want to know why you've drugged Rosie."

***

Paul hung the last of his suits back in the wardrobe. He'd had a shower and decided to sit and wait for Millie. Heading downstairs, he made his way to the front room. He needed a drink to calm his nerves. The anger had now subsided, and he was left with a knot in the pit of his stomach. She had a habit of making him feel like this lately. He knew he'd fucked up. He also knew he deserved to be punished, but surely two months was long enough. Pouring the drink, he necked it, savouring the soothing effect it had on him. He couldn't get drunk, he needed a clear head, but one more wouldn't hurt. He grabbed the bottle and sat on the chair by the window. Now all he could do was wait.

***

Millie's mind raced, her temper building with each passing mile. The doctor was lying, she had to be. When Millie had told her she wanted Rosie moved nearer to Stepney, she had flatly refused, saying it was a bad idea as they were making progress.

Ha, fucking progress, drugging her up, making out it was last night when it was this morning. Rosie had told Scott enough for them all to know she had to be moved. But were people really going missing, or was she really suffering from psychosis?

Rosie had explained that she had made a couple of friends. They sat and chatted together in the evenings. It was a few days ago the first had disappeared. Literally vanished overnight. Last night, Rosie had heard Remi being taken out. Her door was left open, and she'd watched through the crack. A trolley was wheeled along the hallway, empty, then returned ten minutes later with Remi strapped to it. Rosie had asked what was going on, was lied to and then locked in her bedroom. Then this morning, when she'd asked about Remi, she'd been given an injection to calm her.

What unsettled Millie the most was the doctor had told her there was no one called Remi there. There never had been.

"Is she safe in there?" Millie sighed.

"I dunno… What if she's having a relapse?" Scott asked. "People say strange things when they're drugged up. I mean, this is a posh place, recommended by the psychiatric hospital. Surely they wouldn't—"

"You spoke to her, what's your feeling?" Duke interrupted.

"I don't know, it sounds too far-fetched, like something out of a horror movie," Scott answered.

"I think we should believe her," Millie said. "The doctor's a not right, and even if Rosie is wrong, which is a strong possibility, she needs to see we're on her side."

Duke sighed as he pulled up on his piece of land. "So what do we do?"

"If they won't let us take her, can't we break her out?" Millie asked.

"This is a high-security place, it's not gonna be that easy," Duke reasoned.

"And that's another thing, why is it high security when all the patients are low risk and recovering?" In her mind there were so many things that didn't add up. "Let's sleep on it. Things may be clearer in the morning."

Millie made her way back home, more annoyed than ever. If she hadn't been so eaten up with her own problems, maybe she would have spotted things sooner. Letting herself in, she threw her bag on the table and kicked off her shoes.

"Mil?" Paul's voice drifted from the front room.

THE STEPNEY TAKEOVER

"Great," she whispered while heading towards him. "What are you doing, Paul?" She spotted the almost empty bottle of whiskey on the coffee table. He looked half-cut.

"I want to talk, babe, work things out. We can't throw away our marriage—"

"Shouldn't you have thought about that before you did what you did?" she snapped.

"We're having a baby, and that baby needs a mum and a dad." Paul reached for the bottle and poured another large glass, draining it completely.

"Our baby will have a mum and dad, just not living together. I want you to leave."

Paul laughed. "I paid for this house, I'm not going anywhere, and while we're on the subject, why am I paying for your mate's stay in that swanky fucking psychiatric home?"

"I was gonna leave, remember, but you told me to stay here, so you left, but that's fine, I'll pack now," Millie answered, swerving the question about Rosie.

"If you leave me I'm gonna cancel Rosie's payments." Paul stood and swayed. "I'm not gonna be mugged off, not even by you."

Millie stared at him, her heart breaking a little bit more. "Fine, I'll stay for now, but remember one thing, I never mugged you off, Paul, you did that to me when your dick slipped into Rita."

CHAPTER 5

Millie drew back the curtains and sighed. Rainwater trickled down the window, making it difficult to see out. No doubt she would get soaked running to Connie's—soaked and muddy. She'd been spending her days with her mum, just to escape Paul.

"Another day in paradise," she mumbled while rummaging through the wardrobe.

After she grabbed her clothes, she dressed quickly, then tiptoed down the stairs, ready to rush out the back door. But when she got to the kitchen, Paul sat at the table, sipping tea and reading the paper.

"Morning, babe." He didn't glance up. "I've poured you a cuppa."

"Thanks." She took a seat opposite him. The tension in the air was so thick, it was making it difficult for her to breathe.

"So what are your plans for today?"

"I'm going to see Rosie… Why are you wearing old clothes, are you not working today?"

THE STEPNEY TAKEOVER

He always wore a suit and tie, gold cufflinks and tie pin. It seemed strange seeing him so... scruffy.

"It's a surprise." He folded the newspaper and placed it on the table. "Here, take that, in case you need anything." He pushed a wad of notes towards her.

"What are you playing at?" She placed it back in front of him; she wouldn't take it.

"I'm making sure my wife has everything she needs, is that a crime?" He shoved the money back.

She glanced between him and the cash. It was clear he was playing a game. "I don't need any money, but thanks anyway."

"Put it somewhere safe, we can use that to buy baby bits. Right, I need to get on. You have a good day." He stood and walked around the table.

Millie stiffened when he bent down and placed a kiss on her cheek.

***

Paul returned home with two of his men and gave them strict instructions on what to do. He handed one the paint and the other the brushes. "Don't make a fucking mess either. You've got two hours to get this done before the carpet is being laid."

He went back downstairs and waited for Tony, who was bringing the cot and other bits he had bought a few days ago. He knew he had to pull out all the stops to win Millie back, but it didn't mean he had to get his hands dirty. She only had to think he had.

***

Duke studied his cassettes while Millie sat freezing her tits off.

"Dad, can you start the motor so it warms up a bit?"

"Umm..." He took a cassette out and shoved it into the player. "There, let's have a bit of Patsy on the way home."

"Who's Patsy?" Scott asked.

Millie rolled her eyes. "Patsy Cline. It'll make a change from Dean Martin, I guess."

"These are all the great country singers, Scott." As the music blasted out, Duke broke into song. "Crazy... Crazy for feeling so blue..."

"Oh God." Millie huffed. "Can we just get going, I wanna see what Paul's been up to."

She knew he was up to something. That morning had unnerved her. The wad of cash, the old clothes. He was up to something all right, and she wasn't sure she was going to like it.

***

Paul stood back and admired the room. He was pleased with himself. If this didn't make her realise what she meant to him, then nothing would. The nursery was done. The cot was in pride of place, and he had bought a gigantic teddy and sat it on the armchair.

After his men had left, he splashed some paint on his clothes and a dollop on his chin. He had to make it seem like he'd done a hard days graft. Then he went downstairs, poured himself a drink, and waited.

***

Millie opened the back gate and slowly headed up the garden. She was dreading going indoors. He would be there, expecting her to be all normal and shit. Well, this wasn't a normal situation. If it wasn't for Rosie's fees she would have left. She needed space, space and time, but no, Paul wouldn't allow that.

Opening the kitchen door, she popped her head in. All seemed quiet. Maybe he was at the club. She locked the door behind her and decided to head up for a bath. She always felt grotty after visiting Rosie. She didn't know if it was the place or the traveling.

"Is that you, Mil?"

Oh fuck.

Before she answered, he appeared. "I've got a surprise for you. Now just remember, I'm not a decorator but I've done my best." Grabbing her hand, he led her up the stairs towards the nursery. "Open the door."

When she pushed the door open, her heart did a little flutter. "Oh, Paul."

THE STEPNEY TAKEOVER

"Do you like it?"

"I love it... did you do this?" Her eyes flicked around the room and settled on the giant teddy. "I don't know what to say."

"You don't need to say anything. I did this for you, and our baby."

"It makes it seem real, seeing the cot." She stepped closer to the teddy and lifted it. "This is almost as big as me." She placed it down and turned to him. "You've done a really good job. Thank you."

"I'd do anything for you..."

Millie smiled. He'd do anything other than be faithful. "I need a bath and an early night. I'll see you in the morning."

Paul blocked her way. "Is that it?"

"Paul, don't." She took a step back, her heart sinking.

"I did all this." He waved his hand at the nursery. "And I get nothing in return. What more can I do?"

"I told you, I need time."

"And I need my wife." He grabbed her arm and dragged her towards the bedroom.

Millie's heart beat wildly as she struggled to free herself. "Paul, no, please."

He shoved her back onto the bed then lunged, pinning her down.

She smelled the alcohol; it was thick on his breath. "Paul, you're hurting me." She wriggled underneath him, trying to get away. It wasn't until she screamed that he seemed to come to his senses.

Paul stood, staring down at Millie. He could see real fear in her eyes. He had caused that, he had scared her.

"Jesus." He ran a hand over his face. "I'm so sorry, Mil, I..."

Her sobs echoed in his ears. Closing his eyes, he crumpled to the floor while repeating the word sorry, over and over again.

She pushed herself off the bed. "I can't stay here, Paul."

He glanced up and nodded. Her eyes were red, her cheeks wet with tears.

"I love you, Mil, don't ever forget that."

She walked out of the room, leaving him on the floor. He finally knew what it was like to have a broken heart.

CHAPTER 6

Paul sat in the VIP area of the club. He had driven there after Millie had left. He would have sworn on the Bible that he'd never hurt her, and here he now sat, having almost raped her. Just what was he thinking?

"Tone, I need to go away for a bit, just a week or two. I'll be leaving tonight." He needed to put a bit of distance between them. Give her time to forgive him; he was sure she would. Eventually.

***

Millie stared at the fire, losing herself in the dancing flames. It was hard to believe she was back staying with her parents. It was even harder to stare out of the window and see the home that she had shared with Paul. The thoughts flew through her mind.

THE STEPNEY TAKEOVER

Had she done something wrong… led him on… did she deserve it?

Connie and Duke had both questioned her when she'd run in, but she wouldn't tell them what had happened. How could she when she found it hard to believe he was capable of acting that way?

Maybe she should have been more grateful. He had worked so hard on the nursery. *Did she deserve it? Was it her fault?*

Duke watched her closely. She appeared drained, emotionless. "Have you heard from Finn lately?"

Finn was Millie's old boss who'd given her a job and a home when she'd escaped her dead husband, Levi's, mother. A big six-foot Irishman with a rough exterior but a heart of gold. When a gold digger appeared last year, set fire to the pub while Finn was sleeping, putting him in hospital and then pretended to be Shannon, his long-lost daughter, it was Millie and Paul who had sorted her out.

"No, he's due home next week. I wonder if he found Shannon."

"I'm sure he'll tell you all about it. How long has he been away, four weeks?" Duke asked.

Millie nodded. It would be good to see him. He hadn't wanted to go; the thought of leaving her when she'd needed him had made the decision hard. But as she had insisted, he'd taken the chance and left, leaving Millie overseeing the running of the pub. She had told him she needed something to focus on, other than Paul, which seemed to do the trick.

The phone rang and startled Millie. Her heart sank at the thought of who could be calling so late at night; she was certain it would be bad news. Duke got up and answered.

"Who was that?" Connie said with an air of caution.

"Eddie Smith. Patience has passed away." Duke began to relay the message.

That was the moment the floodgates opened, and Millie sobbed. Patience was a seer, she had the Romany gift of sight. A strange old girl Millie had found comfort with when she'd stayed with Duke and Connie on a gypsy site in Essex. She was the one who'd told her she was pregnant. She had also told her someone close to her was going to die — thankfully, that hadn't come true.

Duke wrapped his arms around her while Connie went to put the kettle on.

"She was old, Mil," Duke's voice was gentle, no doubt in an effort to comfort her. "She had a long life, and no one lives forever."

Pushing him away, she sniffed and wiped her eyes. "It doesn't matter how old someone is, if you like them, you like them." She didn't only like the old woman, she loved her. The story she had told Millie of her life was a sad one. Because she had the gift of the sight, she had spent her life alone. Many people were scared of her, of what she might tell them.

"I wonder what will happen to her wagon?" She sniffed again.

"Her family will have it to burn, in her honour, at the wake." Duke handed her a tissue. "She was a character." He smiled.

"When will the funeral be?" She reached up and grabbed the cup Connie offered her.

"In a couple of weeks' time or so." Duke took his and sat back. "Eddie's gonna let me know when and where."

"I think I'm gonna take this to bed with me. I'm feeling exhausted." Millie stood and glanced at Duke and then Connie. "Thanks again for letting me stay."

Sitting on the edge of the bed, she placed the cup on the side table. She could have done with a brandy, but being pregnant put a stop to that. Paul, Rosie, and Patience. They say trouble always comes in threes. Was that it, or was there more heartache to come?

***

Stomach pains woke Millie in the dead of night. The bed was wet. She moaned as another pain hit her. "Mum!"

"What is it?" Connie ran into the bedroom with Duke behind her. Connie's face went white when Millie pushed the bedcovers back. The sheets were blood-soaked.

"We need to get her to the hospital." Connie panicked. "Get the Transit started, while I help her out."

Millie held her stomach as Connie helped her up. "I can't. It hurts too much," she cried. "What's happening?"

"We need to get you to the hospital. Duke, help!" Connie called.

Duke rushed in and swooped Millie up. He carried her to the Transit and placed her in. "Get in the other side, Con, I can't move her over, she's in too much pain."

"You need to call Paul," Millie yelped. "Please."

"Shh, I'll call him from the hospital," Duke promised. "We need to get you there first." Without another word, he roared off down the lane.

CHAPTER 7

Connie and Duke sat at Millie's bedside. She knew neither had a clue what to say, while she lay staring at the ceiling, unblinking. She was numb. No feelings left inside her. Through the night she had experienced every horrible emotion possible. The worst one being grief. Her baby was gone. Had she caused that?

***

Finn dropped his case on the bed and slumped down beside it. His flight had been delayed, and now he was knackered.

The Old Artichoke public house had been a welcome sight when the taxi had stopped outside. The chap he had in managing it had said the takings were up. That was the type of news he liked to hear. But it worried him that Millie hadn't been in for the last few days.

She would normally do the banking. Grabbing his car keys from the bedside cabinet, he made his way downstairs.

"I'll be home in an hour or two," Finn told the barmaid before heading outside.

The air wasn't exactly fresh, after all, this was Stepney, but it smelled good to him. The trip to Ireland had been a waste of time. There were no clues as to where his daughter might be. Probably that fraud, Barbara, had lied about that, too. But one thing was for sure, she must have met her to get so much info on him.

Pushing the thoughts from his mind, he set off for Millie's.

***

Millie sat up in the bed and stretched. Still numb, she glanced at Connie who now dozed in the chair. Duke was nowhere to be seen. The smell of disinfectant was making her nauseated. She needed to get out of there, go home and work out what she was going to do with her life. She hadn't allowed herself to think about Paul since they'd split. She knew she would never take him back after his infidelity, but last night she had needed him, wanted him even. But no, he hadn't shown.

"Look who I found." Duke entered the room.

There behind him was Finn.

Before she could blink, his arms were wrapped around her. "I'm so sorry, Millie."

"Everyone's sorry," she said, a bit too quickly. "Sorry, Finn, I…"

"You have nothing to be sorry for. Why don't we have a catch-up. Maybe Connie and Duke could go and get a drink and bite to eat while I keep you company."

"No, I'm not leaving her," Connie argued.

"Con, come on. You need to keep your strength up. We'll be about forty minutes." Duke aided Connie up and practically dragged her from the room.

"So," Finn began. "Shall we start at the beginning?"

"With Paul?" she asked and was met with a nod.

"You already know what he did. Yesterday he decided to move back in, so I moved out. I'm staying with my parents for now. It's not ideal when I keep looking at the house where I lived. It's just another reminder of what he's done." Millie paused; the next bit was painful.

"It was early hours of the morning I woke up in pain. They rushed me here. I wanted Paul. Duke phoned him four times, but he wasn't home. I needed him, Finn."

Millie let out a loud sob. "They wouldn't let me see the baby, but they told me he was a boy." After reaching for a tissue, she blew her nose. "Is this my fault, am I being punished?"

The question wasn't for Finn, it was something she'd been thinking about all morning.

"You haven't done anything wrong, child." Finns hand wrapped around hers.

It was of no comfort.

"Tell me about your trip, any success?" Millie asked as she took her hand away.

"No. No luck, but I did get to see a few family members while I was over there," Finn replied. "I wish I hadn't gone, Millie, I…"

"You had to go, otherwise you would've wondered for the rest of your life." She sighed. "Maybe people like us ain't allowed happy ever afters."

***

The old Irish pub, on the outskirts of Kinsale, was dimly lit, the air thick with the smell of tobacco, spilled beer, and the lingering sound of fiddle music. It was well past midnight, the kind of hour where the honest man had gone home to bed.

Paul paid for the drinks then took a seat with his cousin, Aiden. They sat in a corner, were he was able to keep an eye on the other punters. He wished Millie was here with him. He had promised to bring her here before…

"Slainte," Aiden announced while holding up his pint. It was the traditional Irish toast meaning 'health'.

"Cheers," Paul countered before taking a large mouthful of his whiskey. "When's Conner and Sean getting here?"

"Any minute now. Relax, you're on holiday." Aiden grinned. "I've got to say, I'm surprised Millie let you come on your own."

"She doesn't know I'm here…" Paul let the words hang in the air for a minute. "We're having a few problems, that I caused, before you ask."

THE STEPNEY TAKEOVER

"Jaysus, I'm sorry, Paul." Aiden grabbed his shoulder and gave it a squeeze. "Silly question, but shouldn't you be at home trying to sort it out?"

"No. She needs some space, and that's what I'm giving her."

"Ahh… Absence makes the heart grow fonder."

Before Paul could answer, a fight broke out the other side of the pub. It looked like a free-for-all. Tables were upturned and glasses shattered. "This is just what I need. A distraction." He took off his jacket and threw it over the bar. "You coming?" He grinned, then turned and ran into the affray.

The first punch came fast towards Paul's head, a meaty left hook which he managed to duck. He countered by driving his shoulder into the man's gut, sending him stumbling back into a table. He glanced at Aiden who was just about to slam his knee into some bloke's ribs. Paul was sure he heard the crack of breaking bones. He turned just as a fist connected with his cheek, knocking him back against the bar. The sound of glass shattering and the metallic smell of blood made him realise he had been hit with a bottle. He turned and delivered a vicious uppercut to the perpetrator, knocking him off his feet. He looked down as the man lay on the floor, unconscious.

"Paul!"

He turned to see Conner and Sean rushing in. "Yous boys have missed all the fun."

"You're covered in blood. Feck, Paul, we'd better go before the Gardai get here." Sean grabbed Aiden.

The flashing lights strobed through the window.

Paul smirked. "Think they're already here."

CHAPTER 8

Paul emerged from the cell. Lucky to only get charged with being drunk and disorderly, he was released along with Aiden. The gardai had patched them both up and sent them on their merry way. Although neither felt very merry, they had the hangover from hell.

"I need some grub," Aiden complained, rubbing his stomach.

"I need a drink. Come on, hair of the dog will have you right in no time."

They headed off to find the nearest pub.

***

It had been two days before they would let Millie out of hospital. In the end, she had threatened to discharge herself. The doctor, wanting to keep an eye on her, allowed her home with a district nurse coming to check on her for the next few days.

Duke and Connie had gone shopping after the nurse had called. Millie had been given the all clear and wouldn't need to see her again. Today was the first time she'd been left alone in four days. It was almost like being released from prison, or that was how she felt. She had done well putting on a brave face, telling everyone she was fine, when in reality she didn't think she would ever be fine again. But she wouldn't think about that. She couldn't, it was the only way she could protect herself.

"Knock-knock." Scott entered the mobile. "You're looking better, Mil."

"Morning, I'm fine. I'm coming to see Rosie with you."

"And what does Duke and Connie have to say about that?" He sat on the edge of the seat and glanced around everywhere but in her direction. A nervous tinge had edged his voice. He was worried what her dad would say.

"I need to get out of here, it's driving me mad being under lock and key."

"Well, if it's okay with them then it's okay with me." He smiled.

"Also…" she began.

"Also what?"

"I want you to find out what Paul's up to. I haven't heard from him, not even with me losing…" She couldn't bring herself to say it. It made the pain too real.

Scott stood and walked towards her. "I know, Mil."

He wrapped his arms around her, but she found no comfort.

Pushing him away, she smiled. "I'm fine." She wasn't and she doubted she ever would be.

***

Paul threw his keys on the side and walked through to the lounge. Even though it was good to be home, he needed a drink. He picked up the bottle and poured a large measure, then sat back on the sofa and closed his eyes.

He had only decided to come home that morning. He could no longer run from his problems or Millie. Tomorrow he would go and see her, ask to talk. He had to consider the baby, they both did. Glancing into the hallway, he spotted the answering machine flashing but chose to ignore it. It was late, he was tired, and all he wanted was a shower and bed.

***

Rosie barricaded her door. She had done the same thing every night since Remi had disappeared. She then climbed into bed and allowed herself to relax. Her thoughts turned to poor Millie. She had lost her baby. It put things into perspective in a sad way. Here she was, because she had lost Bobby — although he hadn't died, it had felt like she was grieving him. She had caught him in bed with another woman. Their bed, that they'd shared every night.

"Bastard."

She wasn't grieving now, she was angry. All she wanted to do was get out of this place and get revenge. One of the so-called shrinks she had spoken to had said she needed to focus on something else, well, this was it. Payback. Her thoughts were cut short when the squeaky wheels of the trolley rang out.

Her heart sank. Were they coming for her?

CHAPTER 9

Paul finished his cuppa, grabbed his keys, and headed to the front door. He pressed the answerphone and listened to the messages while he laced up his shoes. The first two were work related. He would sort that later. The third was his mum asking how Millie was. Standing, he listened to the fourth.

'Paul, Millie's been taken to hospital, she needs you.'
The fifth.
'Where are you? Millie's asking for you.'
The sixth.
'Paul, you need to get here now, hurry.'

Grabbing hold of the side to keep himself upright, he wobbled, his legs buckling. He ran his hand over his face. Millie, he needed to get to Millie. The messages were a week old. "Shit."

Paul ran to the kitchen door and headed down the garden and, pulling open the gate, he ran to Duke's mobile and banged on the door.

He was met with Duke's glaring face. "What do you want?"

"Millie, where is she?" Paul demanded.

"Don't you think you're a bit late?" Duke spat.

Millie appeared at Duke's side. "I need to talk to him, Dad. Paul, I'll meet you at the house in ten minutes."

"Are you okay?" he asked frantically, looking at her from head to toe.

"Ten minutes, Paul." Then she closed the door.

Duke paced around the front room. "You're not going over there, Millie."

"I need to tell him." She placed her hand on his arm. "Even he deserves to know."

Duke opened his mouth, but Millie shushed him. Without another word, she grabbed her coat and left.

The walk seemed to take forever, even though it was only minutes. In her head she was trying to find the right words. She didn't want to hurt him any more than she was about to.

He didn't give a shit about you.

"But he didn't lose our baby," she whispered in reply to the little voice in her head.

She knocked on the kitchen door and waited, her heart thumping. The door opened.

"You don't need to knock. This is your home." Paul stood back, his face taut with worry.

"Take a seat, Paul."

He sat, then she sat next to him.

"Am I going to need a drink?" he asked shakily.

"Where were you? Last week?"

"I went over to stay with Aiden. I thought it best after... you know, give you the space you wanted. Why?"

"Last week I was rushed into hospital with severe stomach pains," she began.

"But you're all right now?"

"Please let me finish." She took a deep breath before continuing. "I was having a miscarriage. I'm sorry, Paul, the baby's gone."

Silence.

"Well, say something," she pleaded.

The colour drained from his face.

"I've gotta get to work, can we speak later?" Paul stood. "I don't mean to rush you, but time and money wait for no man."

"But…" Millie stood and stared at him.

His face had hardened.

"Have you nothing to say?" she asked.

"I told you we'll talk later."

***

Rosie glanced around the day room to see who'd gone missing this time. She couldn't ask. They would know she was onto them. They were already keeping a close eye on her.

"All right, sis, look who's here," Scott said.

She turned and spotted Millie. "Mil." She flung her arms around her. "I'm so sorry."

"Shh, I'm fine." Millie pushed her away. "Let's take a seat."

Rosie glanced at Scott. He looked worried, too. "How are you feeling?"

"I should be asking you that. How have things been here?" Millie asked.

Before Rosie answered, a well-dressed man interrupted. "Miss, you haven't happened to see Gareth, have you? He's late for our game of chess."

"That's it, that's who's missing," Rosie blurted out.

"What?" Scott asked.

"Oh, umm, Gareth must have forgotten. Go and ask the nurse over there, she may know." Rosie watched closely.

The nurse seemed on edge, but whatever she told the man it seemed to placate him.

"Can you please tell me what's going on?" Millie sat forward and grabbed her hand. "Well?"

"I told you, people are going missing. Remi and now Gareth. I heard that same trolley last night, and now he's missing. See, I'm not mad," she informed them.

"We never said you were," Scott said, a little surprised.

"I could see it in your eyes, bruv, so don't lie," she chastised.

"Oh, there you are, Gareth," the man said.

Rosie looked up, and there he was. "They're playing games with me."

"Nurse." Millie motioned. "We would like to take Rosie out to the garden. Can you get her coat, please?"

"Mil, it's fucking freezing outside," Rosie moaned.

"Shh, fresh air will do you good. Come on."

The three walked into the garden, the air crisp and fresh.

"See? No prying eyes or ears. Now. Start at the beginning, and I want to hear everything."

"What I told you about Remi was true, she was the second to go missing. Since I caught them they've been pushing that squeaky trolley past my room every night... I barricade my door, you know, that's how scared I am." Rosie shuddered. "They're playing games with me. They could slit my wrists and tell you I had a relapse. Who you gonna believe, me, a headcase, or a doctor?"

"Rose." Scott took her hand. "I won't let anything happen to you."

"But you can't stop it, you're not here at night..." She brushed away her tears.

"That's it. You're coming home. I'll go see the doctor." Millie went to walk away but then paused. "I believe you, Rose, something's not right with this place."

***

Paul sat in the VIP area of the club. He had been drinking most of the day with the odd line of coke thrown in. Numbing his thoughts and feelings. He'd felt guilt, and that was a feeling he wasn't used to. Why was it, even when he did what he thought was right, it was wrong?

He hadn't asked how Millie was, but then she had lost the baby, not him. She had one job, just one fucking job, and she'd fucked that up. If she had stayed at the house like he'd wanted then things would've been different. This was her fault.

With the paranoia setting in, he decided Millie should be punished.

"Tone, who's the new barmaid?"

"That's Nicky, right little sort, but she's married," Tony said in warning. "What's happening with you and Mil?"

"I don't want to hear her name, not tonight. Get another bottle of scotch and invite Nicky up for a drink."

***

Millie perched on the edge of the sofa after helping Rosie settle into the spare bedroom in the mobile. It was getting late. The drive back from Surrey hadn't been too joyous for her. With thoughts of Paul crowding her head, she had found it hard to concentrate. Did he blame her?

Rosie came and sat next to her, her smile real for the first time in months. "It feels so good to be free, Mil. Whatever you said to the doctor worked."

Connie clattered the cups and saucers in the kitchen. Millie didn't need tea, she needed something stronger.

Duke stood in the doorway, frowning. "So what did you say?"

She knew he was worried, could see it in his face. "I told the doctor I'm a very rich woman who is also friends with councillors and politicians. I have the means and power to get an investigation into the goings-on at that place, and if Rosie wasn't released there and then I would proceed with the threat."

"Bloody hell, Mil." Rosie gasped.

"For fuck's sake," Duke added. "You could have put yourself in danger."

Millie rolled her eyes. "Next time I'll take—"

"There won't be a next time," Duke said. "You will not leave my sight until you can act like a sensible adult and stop putting yourself in harm's way."

***

Paul cleaned himself up in the small bathroom behind the office. Tony had said Nicky was a right little sort, what he didn't tell him was she was a right little goer. She could fuck for Britain, that one. This had turned out handy, a shag on tap. He had made sure to wear protection, he wasn't going to get caught out, that had happened once already.

"I'll get you a cab home, don't think your old man will appreciate another man dropping you off, even if I am your boss."

THE STEPNEY TAKEOVER

"It's okay, my old man's in prison," she said cooly. "Why don't you come back to mine, we can continue the party."

Paul grinned. He didn't need asking twice.

CHAPTER 10

Millie sat at the table. This was the third time she had read the letter. It was from Paul's solicitor demanding she sign all the businesses over to him. This would have broken her but for the fact she was already broken. How could he do this?

She placed her own letter into her bag and stood. "You ready, Dad?"

"Yeah, let me just get me coat," Duke said. "Go wait in the motor, its open."

He waited for her to leave then turned to Connie. "Has she mentioned the baby?"

"No, nothing... It's like it never happened. I'm worried about her." Connie glanced out of the window. "She's waiting, you'd better go."

THE STEPNEY TAKEOVER

"I'll see if she'll talk to me. We'll be straight there and back." He kissed her on the cheek then joined Millie.

The journey there was short. Duke wanted to go in with her, but she was adamant he stay outside. "I won't be long."

Millie marched into the solicitor's holding the letter. She didn't speak to the receptionist but instead stormed past and shoved open the door to his office.

"Mrs Kelly. I-I wasn't expecting you," he stammered.

"I thought I would surprise you, just like this shitty letter surprised me." She tossed it on the desk. "I also have this." She handed him her own letter. "It states all the dodgy dealings you and Paul have made, times, dates et cetera. This is my insurance. You see, I've made five copies of this, and they are on their way around the country to various gypsy camps, where they will look after them and, of course, if anything happens to me, they will be going to the Old Bill, who, without a doubt, will lock you both up." She grinned as the colour drained from his face. "Do you reckon you'd cope inside, Mr Barrett?" She waited for an answer, but none came. "Well, seems like we have an understanding. Tell your client to think very hard before sending me any more of this crap."

She turned on her heels and left, slamming the door for good measure. Her dad was standing outside waiting.

"You all right?" Duke asked while opening the door for her.

"I feel better than all right, I feel stronger. I'm taking control of my life. Did you arrange for Granny and Grandfather to come over?" She hoisted herself up into the Transit and clipped the seat belt on.

"Yes. Are you going to tell me what's going on?" Duke pushed her door closed and sauntered round to the driver's side. He opened his door and got in before continuing. "Only, I'm feeling a little in the dark here, Mil."

Millie explained while they drove home. He handled the news better than she thought he would.

"So you want these letters taken to different camps?"

She nodded. "He's not calling all the shots anymore... Dad?"

"What?"

"Promise you won't go after him," Millie begged. "I need to do this my way."

"Okay, but if he hurts you in any way, shape, or form, I will kill him."

***

After inspecting the scrapyard, Paul headed to the Portakabin. "Pour us a drink, Tone, me throat feels like fucking sandpaper."

He took a seat, placing his arms behind his head and his feet up on the desk. "This is the life, Tony boy. The money's flooding in and life is good."

Tony eyed Paul. How could life be good, he'd just lost a baby? "There's more to life than money, mate, it's not the be all and end all."

Paul laughed. "Yeah, but it's better to be rich and have problems than poor."

"Maybe—" Tony stopped when the phone rang.

Paul answered it. "You fucking what... I'm on my way." He snatched up his keys. "Gotta go, solicitor's had a visit from Millie."

Tony sat and sipped the scotch while Paul rushed out. He liked Paul, they'd been friends for years, but he'd fucked up with the Rita malarky and now he was acting out of character. Millie was nice, maybe a bit whiney at times, but she had a good effect on Paul, it was like they were made for each other. Tony had always got on well with her, and all this with that bird, Nicky, was going to end in tears. Her old man was not going to take Paul screwing his missus lightly.

***

Millie waved to her grandparents, Duke's mother, Darkie, and father, Nelson, who left with the letters. They were on their way to Duke's brother's, then from there they would be handed to various trusted family members.

"I expect I'll be getting a visit from Paul soon," Millie told Duke. "Please don't get involved."

"I'm not gonna let him touch you," Duke said.

"I know, but it won't come to that. He's gonna have to tread carefully with this or he will end up losing everything," she reassured him. "Speak of the devil."

Paul came stomping through the gate.

"That reminds me, I'll get that closed tomorrow," Duke whispered.

"I think we need a chat, don't you?" Paul demanded.

"What do you want to chat about?" Millie said cooly.

"Don't play games, I'm not in the fucking mood." His eyes shone with malice.

There was no trace of the man she'd once loved. Just the man who had let her down so badly. "Start talking then."

"Not here, in the house, my house." Paul was waiting for a reaction.

She wouldn't give him one.

"No. If you want to talk to me, do it through your solicitor, like you did before."

Millie turned to walk away, but Paul grabbed her arm. She spun around to face him, smelling the alcohol on his breath as he spoke.

"You can't blackmail me, you're a killer, too, you and your dad." Paul smirked. "Remember Ronnie Taylor?"

Millie laughed. "Who's gonna believe you, a gangster who's done a lot of bad things, or me, your wife, who you're trying so hard to get rid of... I never thought I'd say this, Paul, but I hate you. Now fuck off back to your tart."

"I will, the sex is amazing, and I bet she wouldn't lose a baby."

Paul ended up on his arse. Duke lunged at him before Millie could intervene.

"Dad, no. Let him go, he's not worth it."

"Get off of my fucking land and don't come back," Duke warned. "Cos next time, you'll be leaving in a body bag."

CHAPTER 11

The church was quiet, apart from the murmur of whispered prayers and the gentle creak of wooden pews as the mourners settled into their seats. Stained-glass windows cast a golden glow over the congregation. At the front, Patience's coffin rested, adorned by an array of wreaths made from wild flowers. It seemed fitting that someone who'd spent her life so close to nature be surrounded by it at the end. Candles flickered solemnly either side. It was almost too much for Millie to take as she sat there holding the rosary beads that Patience had given her.

Beside her sat Duke, Connie, her brothers, Aron and Jasper, and Jasper's wife, Sherry. She still had no time for Sherry; she was a jealous little moron, Millie had decided. They sat listening to the eulogy for Patience. The place was packed with more standing outside. It warmed her cold heart that so many had turned up in true gypsy style.

She had struggled to listen at first because her thoughts were on Paul. The main thing that had crept into her mind was his words. Although she knew he was trying to hurt her, what he'd said was unforgivable. 'I bet she wouldn't lose a baby.' How had he moved on so quickly?

"Okay, Mil, we need to go outside," Connie said, nudging her. "Are you sure you're okay?"

"Yes. I'm fine. Stop fussing," Millie whispered. She left the pew, tripped and stumbled, nearly landing flat on her face. When she looked up, John Jo Ward was holding her upright. "Sorry," she mumbled.

"How are you, Millie?" a voice behind him asked.

It was Gypsy Ward, John Jo's wife. Millie glanced at her stomach; she was pregnant. A lump caught in her throat, and she wished she could run.

"I'm fine, I-I just need some fresh air." She pushed away from his grasp and practically ran to the exit. Leaning back against the wall, she took in a couple of deep lungfuls of air.

"Are you sure you're all right?" Gypsy asked again. She even sounded concerned.

Millie nodded. "The floor's uneven in there, and I wasn't paying attention. Thank your husband for saving me the embarrassment of falling over." She smiled. "That would have given everyone something to laugh at."

"Right time, right place, as the saying goes... I was sorry to hear about you and your husband splitting up, especially after all that to do with the stalker."

"These things happen, I guess. Anyway, how have you been?" Millie tried to change the subject. She was fine day to day, not having to talk about it, but when she was forced to it made her feel uncomfortable and then she'd want to cry.

"We're okay. Having a bit of trouble with the ground we bought. The council wants us off."

"Can they do that?"

"If gorgers complain they can. I best go find John Jo, I'll see you at the wake." Gypsy headed off, leaving Millie on her own.

***

The Old Artichoke brimmed with punters. The smell of hops and tobacco smoke filled the air. Finn grinned. This was the life he loved, bums on seats and money in the till. He glanced at Paul's sour face and placed the scotch down in front of him. "How's things going?"

"My wife wants all my money. Other than that, everything's great," Paul said flatly.

"Millie wants all your money... Come on, Paul, Millie's not a money-grabber," Finn reasoned.

"Isn't she? You ask her, next time you see her then, if it's true that she's blackmailing me to keep her name on everything." Paul necked the scotch and slammed the glass onto the bar. "Same again."

"You know, getting drunk every day isn't gonna solve your problems." Finn looked up, surprised when Paul threw the glass across the pub. "That woman has lost a baby."

"So have I, or doesn't that count?" Paul asked.

"Did you know she had to give birth to him? She went through all that pain knowing he was dead?" Finn rubbed the back of his neck. Paul Kelly was feeling sorry for himself and needed telling a few home truths.

"Him?" Paul asked.

"Yes. It was a boy. Now like I said, this isn't gonna solve your problems."

"I don't need to be told what is or isn't gonna solve my problems as I only have the one. That tramp you brought into my life when you gave her a job."

"I think you best leave, Paul, before we both say things we'll regret."

Finn sighed. Paul was in a bad way and on the path to self-destruct. It wasn't easy to watch.

***

Having laid Patience to rest, it was one more sad memory Millie would keep in her heart. She still held the rosary beads in her hand, she didn't know why as she'd never been religious. Why would she be with all the shit she'd lived? Where was this so-called God when Levi was beating her? Where was He when Levi's mother had forced her to sleep with men, and where was He when she'd lost her baby boy? Shaking her head, she then took another sip of her wine.

THE STEPNEY TAKEOVER

She had relaxed a little since going to the wake. This was her third wine, and she now no longer cared about anything. She hadn't been to a pub for a while, not that she cared. Would she ever care about anything again?

"I think you should get something to eat." Duke led Millie by the arm to the tables laden with food. "Soak up some of that wine."

"Relax, will you, I haven't had a drink for four months." She placed her glass down. Four months of being pregnant.

Why couldn't you have made it to nine months?

The thought hit her so hard she thought she was going to throw up. "I need some air." Practically running, she made her way through the crowd of mourners and outside, once again taking deep breaths.

"You aright darling?" an Irish accent wafted over her shoulder.

She turned to see a tall Irish traveller with the bluest eyes and cheekiest smile.

"I'm fine, thank you." She knew her face had heated up. Why did people always find her at her worst? Wishing he would piss off, she focused back on the ground.

"I see you run out, I thought you was a damsel in distress." He beamed. "I'm Tommy Lee," he added while holding his hand out.

Glancing back up, she placed her hand in his and almost choked when he kissed the back of it. "I'm Millie, now if you don't mind, I need to find my family."

The rest of the evening passed by without Millie getting drunk. She mingled with the people she knew and had more than one chat with Tommy Lee. He seemed to home in on her whenever she was on her own. As lovely as his company was, and it did give her confidence a boost, especially after what Paul had said, she had just lost a baby, and her marriage had ended. She had already decided she would never consider allowing another man in her life, no matter how handsome he was.

CHAPTER 12

Millie sat in the pub with Finn. She had joined him for lunch and to have a proper catch-up. She felt safe here, away from Paul. Safe and at ease.

"Any luck finding somewhere to live?" Finn asked. "Only, you could always move back here."

Millie smiled. "Thanks, but I need a fresh start, somewhere I won't be reminded of Paul, and the fact that he drinks in here won't work. My dad's even thinking of selling the ground so I can stay with them, but I'm an adult, I need to stand on my own two feet."

"Okay, but just remember the offer's there," he said.

Finn was like a hero to Millie, the way he had helped her when she had nothing. She would be forever grateful.

It had been three weeks since she had last seen Paul. They'd had no contact. She had heard he was with another woman. She wouldn't admit it, but it had hurt at first. Him moving on so quickly had cut deep, but equally it had made her stronger. She would never trust a man again.

"He still hasn't signed the divorce papers. Says the only way he would sign is if my name's taken off all the businesses. Reckons if I sign them all back to him he'll pay me an allowance." Millie laughed. "That is until I meet a new man, and then, and I quote: 'It will be his job to look after you'. He must think I'm daft, he could make out I've got a new bloke just to stop paying."

"You've seen him then?" Finn sounded surprised.

"No, I received a letter from his brief." She chewed at her nail and frowned. "I don't know what to do. Should I sign and cut my losses?"

"Are you after his money?"

"What!" That question hurt. Finn knew her better than that. "I know that's what Paul's telling everyone, but I'm not like that. I take no money for myself, in fact, my dad is feeding me and putting a roof over my head. But other than that, as far as I'm concerned I secured the docks, saved his life, and supported him in all the crap decisions he made. I know we weren't married long, but I had a home and a job when I met him. Now I have nothing. He owes me for taking that away from me. If I was after money, I would let the courts sort it out. At least that way I'd get something."

"Why don't you work out what you would be happy with and put in your own proposal?"

"Paul wouldn't part with anything he's got. As far as he is concerned, everything is his and I should get nothing." Millie knew Paul inside and out. He was stubborn and selfish. Whatever she had seen in him had withered and died when she'd lost the baby.

"I need to go. Thanks for lunch." She pecked Finn on the cheek and left.

Millie stood at the bus stop. She needed to restart her driving lessons. That would be something good to focus on. She mulled over Finn's words. What would she be happy with? That was easy enough to answer. A home and an income. She shook her head. There was no way Paul would part with anything, unless…?

***

Robbie McNamara looked at the bent screw and sneered. "What d'ya fucking mean, she's shagging some bloke?" He was a force of nature, not to be messed with. His time inside had been easy due to his reputation of being a nutter, which was easily proven when you glimpsed his teeth. They had been filed into points. When he smiled, he resembled something from a horror movie.

"That's all I was told, your Nicky's been seen with him, flaunting it, she is." The screw glanced around, afraid. It would do him no good if he was overheard giving prisoners outside messages. "You're out in three months. Stay calm." Daryl put his finger to his lips. "They said they will let me know when they have more info." He could kick himself now for having taken the bribe, but his wages were shite for the work that he did. Normally he would smuggle a bit of weed in, this time, however, it was information. Information that could see him getting his throat ripped out.

Robbie ran a hand over his face. Nicky was the one who kept him going in here. Not in a million years did he think she would do that. This prick she was seeing, whoever he was, must have hounded her. Well, he'd pay once Robbie was released. "Tell them I want to know everything, name, address, the lot. Now fuck off."

***

Millie sat at the table, pen in hand, ready to write to Paul's solicitor. She had thought long and hard about what she would write and had decided that it was the best outcome.

She would accept the house and the brothel as her divorce settlement. That way she would have a home and an income. Paul would keep the nightclub, docks, and scrapyard; they all brought in much more revenue than the girls. Once finished, she stuck the envelope down, addressed it, and licked the stamp.

"Are you sure that's what you want?" Duke asked.

"Yes. This way we get divorced, and he can sail off into the sunset with his tart. Also, you won't need to sell up. It's a win-win for us all." Millie picked up the letter and placed it in the pocket of her coat. "I'll post it now. D'ya want anything from the shop while I'm out?"

Duke shook his head.

"Okay, won't be long." Millie stepped outside and took a deep breath of the crisp winter air. It was now February, and she was looking forward to the springtime. Only a couple of months to go. This winter seemed to have lasted ten years, or that's how it felt.

THE STEPNEY TAKEOVER

Marching along the lane towards the road, she spotted Paul's Range Rover, and he had a woman in the front seat next to him. She stood back partly covered by a bush while he drove onto the driveway of their house.

"Bastard," she mumbled. Had he no respect? She turned and stomped back to the trailer.

"Dad, I want to hand-deliver this, can you drive me, please?"

"Yeah, but why the change of mind?"

"It's more urgent than I realised, and I need to go to the bank." She planned to open another account and start putting money into it. If Paul was going to play dirty, which now she realised he would, she needed to be ready.

***

Tommy Lee wiped the last mouthful of bread around the plate before shoving it into his mouth. "Thanks, Gypsy, it's nice to get a home-cooked meal."

"Get yourself a wife then, boy, best thing I ever did," John Jo said.

"I'm not the marrying kind, and who you calling boy? I'm two years older than you, little brother." He laughed. "Besides, why would I marry when I can come here and eat like a king?"

Tommy Lee Ward was twenty-six years old and had served time in the British army. Upon leaving, he'd done three years as a mercenary and was definitely a hardman. He owned land dotted around the country, all bought from his, some would say, illegal earnings, but as far as he was concerned, he had earnt his money fair and square.

"I'm going to the launderette, is there anything else you want before I go?" Gypsy asked.

"No, darling." John Jo stood and pecked his wife on the lips. "See you later."

Tommy Lee waited for her to go then turned to his brother. "Remember Patience's funeral, the woman I was talking to, Millie, what do you know about her?"

"Stay away from her," John Jo said with no further information.

"What if I don't want to?"

"Jaysus, Tommy Lee, you don't half know how to pick them… Her old man's a gangster, I've done a bit of work for him. He don't mess about, he carries a gun. Why her, of all the women who fall at your feet, why her?"

"I heard they're not together anymore." Tommy Lee reached for his beer and took a sip. He wasn't a big drinker, he preferred a nice cup of tea.

"They're not, she's living with Duke Lee, but Paul Kelly is the type to think he owns her." Shaking his head, John Jo sighed. "Please stay away."

Tommy Lee smiled. He might pay Duke a visit. After all, Millie was the first woman to make an impression on him, and he was the type who always wanted what he couldn't have.

CHAPTER 13

Music blared out from the house, so much so Millie had trouble sleeping. She threw the covers off and sat on the edge of the bed, fumbling for her dressing gown.

Once she had tied it around her middle, she headed towards the kitchen. She filled the kettle and popped it on the stove, then made her way to the front room. Pulling the blind aside, she stood on the sofa so she could peek out over the fence. All the lights were on in the house. She could just about make out the outlines of people through the windows, dancing and drinking.

"What's going on?" Duke asked.

Millie jumped. With her heart now thumping, she turned and slumped onto the seat. "Looks like he's having a party. Maybe he's accepted my terms for the divorce."

THE STEPNEY TAKEOVER

"No. He's trying to wind you up, wind us all up so we do something stupid. Well, it's not going to work." Duke sighed. "I'm going to kill him."

"No, I've got a better idea." She grinned.

"Let's hear it then."

"I think it's time we invited the family to come and stay." She was pleased when Duke's face broke into a smile.

"You are a clever girl, you must take after me. I'll let everyone know in the morning."

Connie appeared through the doorway. "I'll make the tea. Looks like we're in for a long night."

***

Paul was in the bedroom. He sniffed another line of coke. He felt fantastic. After receiving a call from his solicitor, he had hatched a plan to fuck Millie over, and that bunch of pikeys she called her family, once and for all. He moved over to the window and stared out. Lights were on in the trailer. "Good. They're awake."

"Who are you talking to?" Nicky said from the doorway.

"No one," Paul said.

He was getting fed up with her hanging off his arm all the time. She was a useful distraction and an okay shag, but he needed to pull himself together. For what he had planned, he'd need all his wits about him.

"Babe, are you coming?" Nicky was loving the unlimited supply of booze, coke, and attention. A big posh house to move into also. All she had to do was get knocked up and she would be set for life. The only black cloud on the horizon was Robbie. He was due to be released in a couple of months. Then what, would Paul get rid of him?

***

"Music's stopped, thank God," Connie whispered to Duke.

Millie lay on the sofa, her eyes closed, but she wasn't asleep. She listened instead to their conversation.

A loud sigh came from Duke. "I can't let this go on, Con, he's taking us all for idiots."

Millie knew he was struggling. He was head of the family, and it was his job to protect them all, but she wouldn't allow him to get into any trouble because of her.

"Millie's suggestion was good. Bring all the family here, Duke. We don't need a war. That won't be good for any of us."

"I know. I don't want you or her to worry. Get yourself to bed, I'll sit here until she wakes."

Millie cursed Paul. Why would he act like this? Three months ago they were very much in love and having a baby, and now they hated each other. Life was cruel. Millie moaned and opened her eyes. "I must have dropped off."

"Get yourself to bed. Your mother's just gone."

"Are you going, too?" she asked.

"Yes, I'll turn the lights off first." Duke rose and pulled her up. "And another thing, I don't want you to worry."

***

After tossing and turning for two hours, Millie finally gave up the idea of sleep. She had a quick wash and dressed, then went to make a cup of tea. Duke was already up, sitting at the table.

"You not sleep either?" she asked.

"No, and I didn't want to wake your mother," Duke replied. "And if he starts that again tonight, I'm going around there and sorting him out once and for all."

"Don't let him get to you, Dad. He likes playing games."

"I've just made a fresh pot," he said. "Get a cup."

She did as she was told and let him pour the tea. "I'm a bit worried—"

"Don't you worry about him."

"Let me finish. I was going to say I'm a bit worried about Rosie. She's still talking about people going missing. What if it spirals out of control? Scott said she was talking about it again yesterday when he took her out. She won't let it drop."

"We'll just have to keep an eye on her... You know you can't fix everyone, Mil, especially when you have your own problems."

THE STEPNEY TAKEOVER

"I know, but Rosie is family, and I owe her. She looked after me and took me in after the crash. She didn't have to," Millie said.

"You concentrate on Paul and the divorce, and in the meantime, me and Con will keep a close eye on Rosie. She seems to be doing okay; she slept though that racket last night anyway."

"She has sleeping pills, they're to help her relax."

The noise of a motor pulling up had Duke on his feet and at the door in seconds. "Who the fuck is this?"

Tommy Lee approached the open door. He could see Millie sitting on the sofa.

Duke stood and greeted him. "Well, to what do we owe the pleasure of this visit?"

"Thought I'd pop in while I'm in the area on business." Holding his hand out, Tommy Lee gave a firm shake, then entered.

Before Duke answered, the sound of another motor pulling in the gate rumbled. "Looks like our guests are starting to arrive. Millie, make Tommy Lee a cuppa while I sort them out." With that, he disappeared.

"Sugar?" she asked.

"No thanks." He followed her into the kitchen. "So, how have you been?"

"Okay, how have you been?" Her voice was tinged with awkwardness.

"I've been okay, too… I enjoyed chatting with you, at Patience's wake." He smiled.

She was blushing again. "Listen, I'm married, so can you stop flirting with me?"

"I didn't realise I was." He placed his cup down and sighed. "Shall we start again?" He held his hand out. "I'm Tommy Lee, it's nice to meet you."

"Millie. Nice to meet you, too." She gripped his hand. "What brings you to Stepney?"

"Business. I'm meeting someone about a job."

"So you'll be working here?" She sounded intrigued.

"It's overseas, normally three or six months at a time." He couldn't tell her too much, despite wanting to. "If I take the job, would you like to come out and celebrate with me?"

She frowned as if thinking.

"Just a meal, no partying," he added.

Millie's first thought was Rosie, her second Paul and the tart he was sleeping with. "Depends when. I'm busy tonight, with my friend."

"I'll be in the area for a few days. Give me your number and I'll let you know."

"Okay." Millie's heart raced. This would be one in the eye for Paul. She didn't feel good about using Tommy Lee to make herself feel better, but why not, wasn't that what Paul was doing?

***

It was just after two p.m. when all the guests had arrived. The trailers were pulled into place, and everyone was settled. Millie sat alone, biting her nails, waiting for Rosie to come back from a job interview. She thought it was too soon for her to be working, but Rosie wanted to pay her own way. Maybe it was time for Millie to find one, too.

Connie and Duke were out chatting with her granny and grandfather. She stood and walked to the window, her insides like jelly.

"Mil, they're back," Duke bellowed.

She ran to the door and noticed the smile on Rosie's face. "Well?"

"You are now looking at a Woolworths employee." She beamed. "I start on Monday."

"That's great." Millie hugged her. Something had finally gone right. Was this the start of better things for all of them?

"Let me get changed out of this skirt, I feel like a dog's dinner." Rosie disappeared through to her bedroom.

"What's happening with you and Paul?" Scott asked, bringing her mood down once again.

"I really don't know... I've given him my terms for the divorce, now I just wait and see what he comes back with." Millie glanced at Scott. "Have you heard anything?"

Scott rubbed the back of his neck; he was clearly uncomfortable.

"You don't have to tell me," she added. "I just thought you might have heard something from one of the men you worked with."

"Mil, he's losing the plot. Drinking heavy, taking God knows what and acting out of character. If I were you, I'd cut my loses and run. We all know he's big on retaliation."

THE STEPNEY TAKEOVER

A knot formed in Millie's stomach. Of course he would retaliate. That's what he lived for. Winning.

CHAPTER 14

It was now March, and two weeks had passed with not a word from Paul. Rosie, on the other hand, had not shut up about the patients who had gone missing from the psychiatric hospital. Millie was at her wits' end. The only respite she'd had was the dinner with Tommy Lee. He surprised her in many ways. He was easy to talk to; she wasn't sure if it was because he was a stranger to her life or because he had the gift of the gab. He was an Irish traveller, born in Essex, hence being able to join the British army. He had served in Northern Ireland and told her stories of his time there. The evening had been a happy release from her day-to-day troubles, and the evening ended with a shag in his hotel room. She wasn't particularly proud of herself, but as she wouldn't see him again, why not? They'd both left happy. He on his way to…? He'd never actually said. And her on her way back to her life of problems.

The vision of his face popped into her head. Those twinkling blue eyes, that cheeky smile.

"Mil. Are you listening?" Rosie asked. "You look a million miles away."

"Sorry, umm, a job?" She glanced at Rosie then glanced down, her face heating up.

"Yes, I need a better-paying job so I can pay a private investigator to find out what's going on. As much as I love Woolworths, it's not leaving me enough money at the end of each week."

"You do realise they cost a small fortune, and what if you're wrong? What if this was hallucinations from the drugs?" Millie placed her hand on Rosie's.

She pulled her hand away. "Why won't you believe me?"

"I didn't say I didn't believe you… Let's have a think about the best way forward. In the meantime, find a better job, and if I get my divorce settlement from Paul, I'll be able to help. Okay?" Millie replied.

"Okay. Sounds like a plan." Rosie nodded. "Scott's taking me out Wednesday to get some new clothes."

"Ahh, that's nice, you can spend some quality time together."

Where was Scott getting his money from now he wasn't working for Paul?

"Mil, can you get the phone?" Connie called from the bedroom.

Reaching for it, Millie smiled when she heard a familiar voice.

"Millie?"

"Tommy Lee. I thought you were leaving last week?" She smiled wider.

"It's been delayed till this Friday. I was hoping to see you again before I leave?" he asked.

Say no. It was meant to be a one-off.

"Wednesday?"

"Great, shall I pick you up?" he offered.

"No, I'll meet you, same place at one p.m." Millie replaced the receiver.

You're going to regret this.

"Who was it?" Connie walked through with a handful of washing.

"Just a friend. Do you need a hand before we go out?" she asked, quickly changing the subject.

***

Paul sat in the office at the docks, contemplating his life. Having knocked the drink and drugs on the head, he was able to think more clearly. He had also distanced himself from Nicky, getting Tony to give her the boot from the club.

His focus was on Millie. There was no way he would part with anything he had worked so hard for, but he'd have to give her something. She had him over a barrel with this blackmail letter, and unless he could get hold of all the copies she'd made, he was well and truly stuck. He still found it hard to believe she would do such a thing. They had been good together. Had everything. But as things stood, it suited him to stay as they were; she took fifty quid a week from their shared bank account. Compared to the money he had coming in, it was pennies. Maybe he should put that to her? Picking up the phone, he dialled the number.

***

Millie entered the restaurant, spotting Paul waiting at a table. He stood when he saw her approach.

"Mil," he greeted. "You look more beautiful every time I see you."

"Paul." She grabbed the chair opposite and was amazed when he pushed her seat in for her.

Once he'd sat, he waved to the waiter who bought over a bottle of champagne. Millie studied him with interest. What was he playing at?

"We can't go on like this—" he started.

"Agreed."

"I still love you."

She didn't know whether to laugh or cry. Was he being serious? No. This was a game to him. "Why did you want to meet?"

"You're still my wife. I want to make sure you're all right." Paul's eyes burned into hers.

"No, I'm not all right. My husband cheated on me, broke my heart, and while I was losing our baby he was on his jollies, which broke my heart again. So why don't you tell me what you really want." Millie glanced at the champagne. She could just gulp the bottle down in one; she needed to stay level-headed, though. Paul was too good at this game, she knew she wasn't his equal when it came to manipulating.

"I want my wife." Paul held his hand up to stop her from interrupting. "Just hear me out. I want us to give it another go. I'll sleep in the spare room until you're ready. You will have the lifestyle you had before, money to do what you want with and —"

"And what if I'm never ready? What if I can never forgive or forget?" she asked.

"I'll do whatever it takes."

"You said that last time, said you'd give me space, but every day you were there, in my face, hounding me." She picked up her glass and took a large mouthful. None of this added up. He was playing with her, seeing how easy she would be to manipulate. "We're supposed to be getting divorced, and that is because of your actions."

"If I could go back and change things, I would..."

God, he was good. He sounded so sincere, but there was something off here, something that didn't add up. "You took your tart to the house, no doubt in our bed. Do you really think I could sleep in that again?"

"I'll buy a new bed, a new house. Whatever it takes."

"Theres something else you should know. I've slept with another man."

His scar rose. He was angry.

"Does it make you feel good, putting it about like a slag?" Venom dripped from each word.

"And there we have it, Paul. I sleep with one man once and I'm a slag. You, on the other hand, slept with an old lady, just so you could keep the scrapyard, and then some tart, in our bed, and obviously more than once." Millie stood and looked down at him. "I think we should go through our solicitors from now on, and think twice before you throw any more all-night parties as we now have half the gypsy population living on Duke's ground."

Paul stood quickly, his chair tipping back, making a loud crash. "You're not having the house or the girls, you won't get a penny. Whoever this fucking bloke is, he can keep ya."

Millie smiled. "I'll be sure to tell him."

CHAPTER 15

"Fuck, fuck, fuck." Millie lay face down with her head in the pillow.

"Mil, talk to me. Please," Rosie begged.

Rolling over, Millie swiped at her eyes with the back of her sleeve. "I should never have met Paul, I've fucked up."

"So what did he want?"

"Me. Or at least to play mind games with me." Millie stared at the ceiling. "He wants us to try again. What fucking planet is he on?"

"So you told him no?" Rosie handed her a tissue. "Wipe your eyes in case Connie comes in. She was already suspicious last night when you got back, wanting to know where you'd been."

"He wanted me until I told him I'd slept with another man," Millie said.

"Why would you lie about that?" Rosie's eyes widened; it dawned on her it hadn't been a lie. "No way."

"Shh." Placing her finger to her lips, Millie glanced at the door. "Yes way."

"Who?"

"I can't tell you here. I'm meeting him today, or I'm supposed to, but I've got a feeling Paul will have me followed."

"Jesus, Mil, don't you think it's a bit soon to be moving on?"

"It was a bit of fun, nothing more. He's going abroad to work, so I won't see him again, and anyway, at least I waited for my marriage to be over before doing anything, so I don't need you judging me."

"I'm not, I just don't want you getting caught on the rebound." Rosie laughed softly.

"What's so funny?"

"I bet Paul was fuming. Another man touching his property... But seriously, he won't take that lying down. You'll need to watch your back."

"You'll have to go to the hotel and let Tommy Lee, shit, I shouldn't have said his name... let him know I can't make it, tell him I'm ill." Millie shook her head. "Why does everything have to be so bloody complicated?"

"I've got a better idea." Rosie's eyes creased with amusement. "Come with me and Scott and then you can sneak off. He won't know where you've gone, and I'm sure Scott will spot a tail, so we can keep an eye on whoever's following you."

"I don't know. I don't want anyone else involved in this war. It's not fair, and if Paul finds out Scott has covered for me, then Scott will be in the firing line." Millie jumped when a loud knock came from the bedroom door. "Who is it?" she asked, nervous at how much of the conversation they may have overheard.

Duke popped his head around the door. "I think we need a chat, don't you? Rosie, can you leave us?"

***

Duke sat on his step, sipping a beer, while his anger subsided. It was coming up to four hours since Scott had picked up Millie and Rosie, yet still his temper bubbled away, just under the surface. Whilst he wanted to bash Paul Kelly's head in for the way he'd treated Millie, he now also wanted to give her a swift kick up the arse to knock some common sense into her. Just why was it called common sense? In his experience it wasn't that common at all.

Tommy Lee, of all people, a first-class nutter who got off on killing people. Duke had warned her to stay away from him, but would she listen? Probably not.

"Duke, come in, it's turning cold," Connie said from the window.

"I'll be in in a minute." His thoughts returned to Millie.

She needed a fresh start far away from here. He couldn't go to Essex, that was where the Ward boys lived, and now Millie had done whatever she had done with Tommy Lee, he wouldn't chance being that close. Kent sounded the best bet. Jasper and Sherry lived there. She was expecting a baby, so Connie would be happy to be near her grandchild. Aron would go wherever, it wouldn't be long before he was off anyway. Yep, Kent was the perfect choice.

He stood to go inside, happy with his decision, when the sound of Scott's car stopped him. Would Millie be with them? He glanced over, happy that she was there in the back seat. Maybe she did listen after all.

Connie eyed Duke. He had that look on his face, the look that meant he'd made a life-changing decision that they would all have to go along with.

"You're all in time for dinner, come in and warm up," she said to them.

"What did you buy then?" Duke asked Millie.

"Nothing, I don't need any more clothes," she said sharply.

"That's a first, ain't it? Never known you to go shopping and not buy anything," Duke snapped back.

"Would someone like to tell me what's going on?" Connie folded her arms and glared at Duke.

"Why don't you ask our daughter?" He pointed.

"I'm old enough to make my own choices, in fact, I've been doing it all my life, you know, on account of not having any parents." Millie's eyes closed. She knew she had gone too far with that comment.

"Scott, help me put my stuff away." Rosie turned and headed to the bedroom with Scott swiftly on her tail.

"I'm sorry. I shouldn't have said that." Millie slumped onto the sofa.

"No, you shouldn't, but you did anyway," Duke said. "I've told you a hundred times how important you are to me and your mother. I don't want to see you get hurt again, so tell me, truthfully, did you meet him?"

"Meet who?" Connie asked while glancing between her husband and daughter.

"I'm waiting for an answer," he pressed.

"I had lunch with him," Millie said eventually, then turned towards Connie. "I had lunch with Tommy Lee."

Duke sat and put his arm around her, pulling her towards him. He kissed the top of her head. "We all need a fresh start. I'm gonna sell up and buy somewhere in Kent."

Millie pushed him away and jumped up. "No. I'm not leaving Stepney, I've got to see the divorce through."

"You don't need to be here for the divorce, the solicitors do it. Look, we have family in Kent, your brother Jasper, and let's not forget him and Sherry are having a baby, you'll—"

"Duke!" Connie gasped.

"What now, woman?"

Millie swallowed down the sob building in her throat. She didn't want to hear about babies. Hers was dead, she'd failed him. Composing herself, she took a deep breath. "If yous want to move to Kent, then fine. I won't be going, I'll get a place with Rosie." She turned to walk away, then paused. "I'm already fighting Paul, Dad. Please don't make me fight you as well."

CHAPTER 16

Millie sat at the bedroom window watching the rain fall. Along with the noise it made on the roof, she found it soothing.

"Talk to me, Mil," Rosie said softly. "It's been three days, and you haven't told me what happened."

"Nothing much to tell." She grabbed her stuffed white bunny and held it out in front of her. "This is the only thing I have that's truly mine, and yet, at any minute, someone could come and take it, and I wouldn't be able to do a thing about it."

"Why would someone want to take that?"

"Because that's what people do, Rose… They take the things that make people happy."

"You're not making any sense, Mil… You've been sat here brooding for the last few days. You need to get out of here. Why don't you come out for lunch with Scott and me?"

Millie turned towards her. "Did Duke put you up to this?"

"He's worried about you, we all are." Rosie placed her hand on Millie's shoulder. "A change of scenery will do you good."

"Peace and quiet will do me good. I just need some time on my own to think. I can't do it with people around me all the time."

"Okay, I'll be going soon, but if you change your mind, let me know." Rosie left the bedroom, closing the door behind her.

Millie lay back against the pillow and closed her eyes, the thoughts that kept her awake at night all fighting for dominance. Paul. The way he'd looked at her when she'd told him she'd been with another man. The spite in his eyes. The venom in his voice. Had she told him because she wanted to hurt him? Probably. But why, the marriage was over, so why the need to hurt him?

Because you wanted him to feel what you're feeling. Pain.

***

Paul lifted the collar of his Crombie then plunged his hands deep into his pockets. He was not only fucking freezing but also soaked to the bone. It was that weird rain, looked nothing much but drenched you within minutes. The water lapped at the quayside violently while he scanned the horizon. The goods should have been here half hour ago. Worry etched his face, worry and shame.

He hated himself. He hated that he was jealous. The thought of another man touching Millie drove him insane. As if it wasn't bad enough calling her a slag, he then went home, got steaming drunk, and smashed up the house.

The noise of an engine drew him from his thoughts. A boat came chugging towards him. He turned to his men and motioned with his head for them to unload while he returned to the office. Pulling his coat off, he lay it over a chair in front of the heater.

Tony joined him minutes later. "What is with this fucking weather? Thought it would start warming up a bit by now." He sat at the desk, grabbed the paperwork, and glanced at Paul. "I know that look."

"What look?"

"You look like you want to kill someone. Who is it?"

Paul ran his hands over his face and sighed. "Me. I want to kill me, or at the very least give myself a slap… I've fucked up, Tone, and I don't know how I'm gonna make it right."

"Well, whatever the problem is, you're not gonna solve it by sitting here."

***

Millie waited for Duke and Connie to leave the trailer before she left the sanctuary of her bedroom. She glanced out of the kitchen window. Duke's two German Shepherds barked at something in the trees, probably a squirrel. Smoke was coming from her grandparents' little chimney on top of their trailer. There were six other family members staying on the ground. All parked up around the edge, all facing inwards. She was surprised they hadn't built a fire in the middle.

Because of the rain, no one was outside, which pleased Millie. She felt tired, but not in the way that sleep would fix. It was a deep tiredness, her brain needed to rest. She didn't need any more questions, what she needed was answers. Grabbing her coat and bag, she decided it was time to get them.

Within minutes she found herself standing outside her old home. She hadn't set out to come here, but here she was nonetheless. Why?

She ignored the sound of Paul's car behind her and instead focused on the bedroom window above her. That was the nursery. That was why she'd come.

"Mil?" Paul's voice was soft. He stood beside her and stared up at the window. "I haven't been able to go in there since…"

"I want to see it," she said sternly.

"Do you think that's a good idea?" He was met with an icy glare. "Okay."

He turned the key in the lock then stood back, allowing her entry. She slipped off her shoes and ran up the stairs, Paul's footsteps right behind her. She stopped at the closed door, her heart thumping.

Paul reached for the handle and pushed it open. There in the centre of the nursery stood a cot with the gigantic teddy up one end. Sitting there, all fluffy with a big white bow around its neck.

She stumbled in, finding it difficult to breathe. Hand on her chest, she crumpled to the floor. Her sobs filled the air. Paul's arms held her. She glanced at him. Was he was crying, too?

***

Duke stormed out of Millie's bedroom and headed to the front room. "Where the fuck is she? I told you she shouldn't be left alone."

"Calm down, she'll be back, when she's ready," Connie replied. "She needed time on her own, to work things through in her head."

"What. Like losing a baby and not mourning it? She's unstable, Con, sleeping with Tommy Lee. Jesus, woman, she needs watching like a fucking hawk."

Millie listened to the ranting as she made her way inside. "Can you stop talking about me? I reckon the whole of Stepney heard that."

"Where the fuck have you been?" Duke roared.

"Duke, calm down." Connie stood between them. "Millie, we were worried."

"I had some stuff to work through, like my dead baby I haven't mourned, and just for the record, Dad, I'll sleep with whoever I like. I don't need permission."

Connie stamped her foot and glared between them. "That's it. I've had enough. Do you know your trouble. You're like two peas in a pod, both stubborn and selfish. Well, let me tell yous something, while you're both trying to get the upper hand, it's the rest of us who suffer."

"We're nothing alike," Millie and Duke said in unison.

"Really?" Connie rolled her eyes and then stormed out, slamming the door for good measure.

Millie glanced at Duke. He appeared as shocked as she was.

"That's us told," she said.

He sighed. "She might have a point... I worry about you, and that worry comes out in anger because I don't know how to protect you."

"I know. I'm not the easiest person to be around, I seem to fuck everything up." Millie sat on the sofa and dropped her head into her hands.

"Well, you can be difficult." Duke laughed. "Probably like me."

"Most definitely like you... You should go and check on Mum, make sure she's okay. I'm gonna take a bath."

Millie rushed to the bedroom and sat on the bed. She felt better in a way. Better, but she knew more problems were coming, especially with Paul.

Shit.

***

Paul sauntered into the nightclub. He felt more like his old self—no, he felt better than his old self. He grinned as Tony approached.

"Tone, how's it going?"

"You've got a visitor in your office, and just for the record, I didn't let her in." Tony turned on his toes and disappeared into the crowd of people lining the bar.

Paul's first thought was Millie, but she'd said she needed time, and now he was certain she still wanted him, he didn't mind obliging. Especially as it meant there would be no more talk about taking his businesses from him.

So who else would be here this time of night? He glanced at his watch. Nine-fifty p.m. Rushing through to the back of the club, he stood in the doorway and glared at Nicky. She sat on the sofa, stocking tops showing and tits practically falling out. It turned his stomach in a way. She was every inch what she looked like. A slut.

"What d'ya want?" he asked, kicking the door shut behind him. He noticed the startled expression; he preferred that to the desperate one.

"You said you'd phone, you didn't," she managed once she had composed herself.

"Doesn't that tell you something? I'm not interested. Now you can leave of your own accord, or I can make you. What's it to be?" Paul loomed over her, his face set in a sneer.

"Fine." Standing, Nicky sidestepped him. "But you'll be sorry."

Paul lunged at her and shoved her against the wall with his hand around her throat. "I'm gonna say this once and only once. If I see or hear from you again, you'll be the one ending up sorry, that is if I decide to let you live… Understand?"

She struggled to breathe.

Paul smirked and released his grip. "I said, understand?"

***

Millie stood in front of Connie, Duke, and Rosie, holding a pair of white booties and a lace shawl. She had bought them from the market on a trip with her mother months ago. Her body trembled slightly, and it took all her strength to hold it together. These items were all she had left to remind her of her son.

"I want to hold a... a memorial service, for my boy. I thought I could bury these and maybe..." Millie took a deep breath to stop the tears from falling.

"Maybe we could plant something," Duke added.

"I think that's a lovely idea," Connie agreed. "In the corner where the sun shines all day. We could put a seat there, too."

"You don't think it's stupid?" Millie asked.

"No, Mil, I think it's perfect." Rosie smiled.

"We can go and choose a plant tomorrow, if you're not busy," Duke suggested.

"That would be good, thanks, Dad." Millie clutched the items to her chest. "I'm tired, so I'm gonna go to bed. Goodnight."

Rosie followed and sat next to her on the bed. "What about Paul?"

"What about him?"

"It's his baby, too. Did you want him there?" Rosie slipped her arm around her. "It's your decision, no one else's... I'm sure your dad wouldn't mind."

"He can't be there," Millie said.

"Why. What's happened?"

"I've messed up, Rosie, and I'm trying to fix everything, but I can only do one thing at a time, and Micheal comes first."

"Micheal?"

"My son Micheal, he deserved a name." She lay the shawl out and placed the booties on top. "Things with Paul are complicated at the moment."

Rosie studied Millie's face. There was no expression there, no giveaway signs of what might be wrong. What had Paul done? "Oh my God, you're thinking of getting back with him."

"No. I'm not, but he may have got the wrong idea."

"How could he get the wrong idea, Mil?"

"Because I slept with him this morning."

CHAPTER 17

Saturday the nineteenth of March was a glorious sunny day. Everyone had wrapped up and stood around the hole that Duke had dug. Micheal's shawl and booties were placed in an old biscuit tin, and that was then put into the hole. Next Duke grabbed the rose tree and planted it, all under the watchful eye of Millie. Her brother, Aron, stood with his arm around her. He towered over her now at six feet; he was even taller than Duke by an inch.

Once the tree was firmly stamped in, Rosie handed Millie a package.

"What's this?" Millie asked.

"Open it and see."

Rosie smiled as Millie's eyes lit up. It was a small wooden cross with Micheal's name on it.

"Rosie, I…"

"Like you said, he deserves a name."

THE STEPNEY TAKEOVER

***

Robbie McNamara stared at his wife. He was making her nervous. "So, Nicky, what have you been up to while I'm here, banged up?"

He knew, she could tell. But instead of being honest, she decided to bluff it. "Not much. Got a job for a while, but I didn't like the late nights."

"Is that the job where you were shagging the boss?"

"What, where d'ya get that silly idea from?" She placed her hands in her lap and looked down at the table.

"Do you think I'm stupid?" he asked.

"No, Robbie, I don't."

"Then why are you treating my like an idiot? I know everything. You've been shagging Paul Kelly. I take it that's where you were working, Kelly's nightclub. Did he give you a bit more money?"

"No, he blackmailed me, said he would sack me if I didn't do what he wanted. Well, I did what he wanted, and he sacked me anyway… You know I only have eyes for you, but I needed the money." Nicky turned on the waterworks, just for good measure. She knew how to play Robbie.

"Shh, don't cry. I'll sort the prick when I get out, and if I hear of you pulling anymore tricks like this again, I'll be sorting you out, too."

***

Millie sat next to the rose bush. She sipped at her tea, although now it was nearly cold. She had arranged to see Paul tonight. It was time to tell him the truth. There was no future for them together. Too much had happened on both sides. Once she had sorted that, she could help Rosie and the mystery of the disappearing patients, if it was really a mystery. At the very least she would humour her.

"Mil, it's getting cold, come in," Connie said.

"I won't be long, just finishing my tea," she lied.

She wished she had somewhere to live, alone, without being watched all the time. She could no longer leave here, though, not now Micheal's memorial was here.

You could have your own mobile home.

The thought played on her mind. A place for her and Rosie, giving her parents their privacy back and she would regain hers. She would put the suggestion to Duke. After saving money each week she had a bit put by. It was initially to buy a car with, but at the moment a home was more important.

Tipping the rest of the now cold tea away, she glanced at the house. The bedroom light had just illuminated the room. She could just make out Paul. He was getting ready for her. Guilt sat in the pit of her stomach. Why had she slept with him? The answer was pretty easy.

She'd sobbed in his arms as they'd lain on the floor of the nursery. Paul had kissed her, and she had responded. Not because she wanted him, but because she wanted comfort. Wanted to feel something other than pain, loss, emptiness. It was selfish, she knew that, just the same as sleeping with Tommy Lee. She wanted to feel something else.

"Millie. I really think you should come in now," Connie shouted.

"I'll come in when I'm ready." She sighed. Yep. She needed her own space.

***

Paul was buzzing, but not because he was seeing Millie. Her face, her smile, those blue sparkling eyes that could look deep into his soul, didn't affect him in the same way anymore. It was because he was back in control. He sauntered down the stairs with a smile on his lips. He wanted a drink—no, he couldn't reek of booze. Tonight everything had to be perfect. When the knock came from the kitchen door, he waited a minute before opening it.

Game on.

"Mil, you look beautiful, babe, come in out of the cold. You know you don't need to knock, this is your house, too," Paul gabbled. He led the way to the lounge where two glasses of champagne sat on the coffee table.

"Here. To us," he toasted.

Before Millie could respond, the phone rang. Paul excused himself to answer it. When he returned, his face was ashen.

"Paul?"

"It's Gran, she's…"

THE STEPNEY TAKEOVER

"Go, be with your family, your mum will need you," Millie said.

"You're my family."

"I know, but you need to be with them, now go. I'll lock up." Millie took the glass that Paul was still holding and placed it on the side. "This can wait, now go."

"But will you…?"

"Will I what?" She frowned.

"Wait," he said.

"You know where I am. Phone me, let me know how she is and when you're back."

Paul leant in and kissed her. "I love you."

She didn't answer, she couldn't.

CHAPTER 18

Paul had phoned the next morning to let Millie know his gran had had a stroke. She was obviously in a bad way because she hadn't heard anything else for a couple of days. It left her on edge. How could she tell him the marriage was over now? He would want comforting. From her.

Fuck.

"Are you coming?" Duke asked through the open door.

"Yes, I'm just putting my shoes on." Millie rushed out and climbed into the pickup truck. It was a beautiful April day, just right for a driving lesson.

"I reckon you can put in for your test now. Don't see a reason why you wouldn't pass."

"You think I'm ready?" Millie asked. She didn't feel ready.

THE STEPNEY TAKEOVER

"Put in for it now. It'll be a month or so before you get a date, plenty of time to get the reversing right." Duke laughed. "Just don't run anyone over."

"Ha, ha, very funny. He shouldn't have walked behind me. Surely he could see I was going backwards?" She pulled away down the lane. Maybe Duke was right; this driving malarky was a piece of cake.

Connie watched from the window with a smile on her face. It was lovely when Duke and Millie got on. Father and daughter spending time together. She turned and glanced at Micheal's memorial. Millie was spending a lot of time sitting there. Was that healthy? Connie couldn't decide, but at least Millie seemed more balanced now. That had to be a good thing, didn't it?

***

Paul sat holding his gran's hand, the machine next to her beeping. She was slipping away, the nurse had told him. He didn't want to believe that. The stench of disinfectant filled the room. Was that to mask the smell of death?

"You okay, son?" Bridie, Paul's mother, asked, her eyes creased with worry.

"Yeah, come and sit down, Mum." He stood and ushered her into the seat. "I don't think it's gonna be long now."

"You need to remember, she'll be with your granddaddy, so don't be sad."

"I know, but I'll miss her… Why is she breathing like that?" Paul leant over her.

She opened her eyes.

"Gran?"

Her vacant stare hit him in the pit of his stomach. He wiped the tears from his eyes before turning towards Bridie.

"She's gone, boy."

He reached out and hugged his mum, his thoughts turning to Millie. He hadn't seen much of his gran lately, and that was her fault. Another reason to make her suffer.

***

Finn poured the drinks and handed them to Millie, Rosie, and Scott. "Well, it's nice to have the gang back together."

"I'll drink to that." Scott took a huge gulp of his beer.

"It is," Millie added, taking a sip of her lemonade.

"I can't believe you're on the soft stuff. Millie Kelly is teetotal." Rosie laughed.

"I'm not, I just don't fancy getting sloshed, not with everything going on."

"Have you heard from Paul?" Finn called over while pouring himself a pint.

"No, nothing for a couple of days. Maybe she's picking up a bit." Millie shrugged.

"You really don't care, do you?" Rosie whispered.

"Of course I care, she's a lovely old girl, and I know Paul's gonna be upset if anything happens to her, but…"

"But he's not your responsibility anymore. Good, just remember what he did to you," Rosie prompted.

"We didn't come here to talk about him, we're here to talk about the missing patients. I've been thinking about what you said. If you spotted someone being taken away in the middle of the night, and then it stopped because you were onto them, then maybe, and this is a big maybe, they may have started up again. I spoke to Paul's dodgy doctor, and he said if they're going missing, not to be seen again…" Millie glanced around the pub before continuing. "They could be selling body parts."

"What!" Rosie shrieked.

"Shh, stop drawing attention. It's a big if, Rosie." Millie wished she hadn't said anything now. "I don't know how to find out."

"I could go back in there, undercover," Rosie suggested.

"Calm down, Sherlock." Millie turned when a hand rested on her shoulder. She stared into Paul's eyes. Was he angry?

"I've been searching everywhere for you, and here you are, fucking partying."

"No, I'm not. We've come to see Finn… How's your gran?"

"Dead."

"I'm sorry, I know how close you were—"

"Save your fake sympathy. Are you coming home?" Paul's eyes blazed with anger as he clutched her arm.

She shrugged him off. "Not while you're angry. I think I'm safer here until you've calmed down."

He leant in, inches from her face. "This is fucking calm... Enjoy your piss-up." He then marched out of the pub.

"Are you okay, Mil?" Finn asked. "I've never seen him like that, not with you anyway."

"I'm fine, I need to go after him." Jumping off the stool, Millie ran outside, disregarding the protests from Rosie and Scott. She was just in time. Paul started his motor. "Wait." She reached for the door and climbed in. "What the fuck was that about?"

"I've just lost my gran, and the only person I wanted to see was you," he replied.

"That doesn't excuse you from acting like that. I thought we had come to an understanding." Millie flinched when Paul rested his hand on her leg.

"I always used to drive like this, one hand on the wheel, the other on your leg. Don't you like it anymore?" Paul glanced at her.

For the first time, she realised his eyes were red; he had been crying. "It was a shock, it's been a while since I've been in your motor." Turning, she gazed out of the passenger window. The houses all blurred into one as they passed, just like the last few months of her life had.

"Stay with me tonight." Paul squeezed her leg. "Please."

Millie spun around, her eyes wide with shock. "You promised to give me time."

Silence.

"How come Rosie's back?" he asked.

"She wasn't safe in that place. People were going missing. That's why we were in the pub, discussing what to do about it."

Paul sighed. "You ain't doing anything about it. If people are going missing, they won't think twice about getting rid of you."

"Yeah, well, just as well you can't stop me... unless you help?"

CHAPTER 19

The morning was bright when Millie woke. Paul's arms were around her. She struggled to get out of bed without waking him. Picking up her clothes, she headed to the main bathroom and turned on the shower. It was nice to feel the heat on her body. Once she'd washed, she dried quickly, wrapping her hair in a towel, and dressed.

What are you doing?

"I haven't a clue," she whispered.

"Morning, gorgeous." Paul snaked his arms around her waist from behind and rested his chin on her shoulder. "I've missed this."

She smiled, unsure how to answer him. "I need to dry my hair, then get going. I wanna catch Rosie before she goes to work and let her know the plan."

Paul stiffened. "Is that the only reason you stayed, to help your mate?"

Yes.

"No. Don't be silly, stick the kettle on." She turned and pecked him on the lips.

Again I ask, what the fuck are you doing?

Millie headed to the bedroom. She hunted for her old hairdryer, but it wasn't there. In fact, a lot of her things weren't there. "Paul? Where's my hairdryer and perfumes? Have you thrown them out?"

Paul appeared in the doorway. "I haven't touched any of your things, they should all be where you left them."

His tart probably took them.

"Well, they've gone. I best get home and dry my hair." She threw the towel onto the bed and walked towards the door.

Paul still stood filling the doorway.

"This is your home… I'll buy you another hairdryer or you can go get one." He walked to the dressing table and pulled out a metal box. Inside there was a wad of notes. He took out a handful and passed it to her. "Buy whatever you need, you'll need it when you move back in, which will be…?"

"You said you wouldn't rush me… let me tidy up in here. Can you put the kettle on?" She began making the bed.

Paul's footsteps faded into the distance. She checked in her bedside cabinet. That appeared untouched. She had a quick peek in his. Her mouth dropped open. There were not one but three boxes of condoms, two of which were empty.

Christ, just how many women has he screwed?

"Too many."

She collected her coat and descended the stairs; she needed to get out of here. Paul was busying himself making the tea when she entered the kitchen.

"I can't wait for things to get back to normal. 'Course, need to sort Gran out and then we can concentrate on us." He placed the cup in front of Millie.

"Thanks." She sat at the kitchen table and glanced around the room. She had loved this place when they'd first moved in. The grandness of it. But now it had become alien to her. Was that because she knew she would never have another home like this, or was it because she was thankful for the love that filled the mobile walls? She couldn't answer that. She did, however, feel bitter that her home had been taken away from her, and although she was the one to walk out, it was Paul who'd made it impossible for her to return.

She finished the last of her tea. "I need to get back."

"I'll see you tonight," Paul said.

"What?"

"If I'm gonna help Rosie, don't you think I should get something in return, like my wife sleeping in my bed?"

***

Millie entered the mobile, still reeling from Paul's words. '...should I get something out of it, like my wife sleeping in my bed?'

"I am such an idiot."

"And why is that?" Duke said from behind her.

Spinning around, she stared at him. Christ, was he angry, too? "Dad."

"So you stayed with him after everything he's put you through. What exactly goes through your head that made you think that was a good idea?"

Silence.

Duke shook his head and sighed. "I can't look at you right now, I'm going to work."

Millie watched him leave, her heart sinking. She didn't answer because she couldn't. She didn't know why she did the things she did. All she knew was, she was weak when it came to Paul. The truth was, he was a game player who always won, and she'd kidded herself she could match him, when in reality she was still just a broken girl from a children's home and doubted she would ever be anything different.

Stop feeling sorry for yourself and do something about it.

"Like what, what can I do?" Millie walked to the bedroom. Sitting on the bed, she ran her brush through her hair. "I'm not cunning enough." She clicked the hairdryer on and began to dry her hair, but even that wouldn't drown out that annoying fucking inner voice.

For starters, keep away from him, until you're strong enough.

"I live at the end of his garden."

It's your garden, too. Your house, your businesses, and your money.

"Like I'll ever see a penny."

Stop being a quitter.

THE STEPNEY TAKEOVER

"Will you just shup up." Millie placed the hairdryer down. "I don't want his money or his fucking businesses, I just want happiness." She stared at herself in the mirror and smiled. She'd loved Paul once upon a time, but like all fairy tales, they come to an end.

See, it wasn't that hard, was it.

"Smart arse."

She reached into her bag and counted the money he had given her. One hundred and fifty quid. Why had he given her so much? Guilt? No. That was one emotion Paul didn't suffer. It was just another part of his sick game.

***

Connie dished the dinner up while Millie watched. The atmosphere left a bad taste in her mouth. Duke sat in the lounge drinking beer with Aron, and Rosie had gone out with Scott. Obviously she couldn't stand the atmosphere either. "Are you sure there's nothing I can do?"

"No, it's nearly done," Connie snapped.

Did she have the hump as well? She placed a plate down in front of Millie with a little too much force; clearly, the answer was yes. She then called Duke and Aron. They all sat around the table. The tension hanging in the air was as thick as the steam rising from the plates. Millie placed her hands in her lap, her stomach knotting with nerves.

"This looks lovely," Millie said to Connie. She was met with a curt nod.

"So you stayed with him last night," Connie eventually said. She didn't need to say Paul's name, the tautness in her voice made it clear who she meant.

"We just talked," Millie said.

"Just talked?" Duke's voice rumbled across the table, his eyes narrowed. "Really. So he's turned you into a liar as well?"

Millie swallowed, her throat dry. "I didn't plan it. Paul needed to talk, he'd just lost his gran."

"He always needs something, doesn't he?" Connie placed her cutlery down. "Why do you always go running, even after everything he's put you through?"

Millie's voice trembled. "I didn't mean to upset you both. I'm sorry."

Connie placed her hand on her shoulder. "But that's the problem, isn't it, Millie?" She sighed. "You keep letting him back in, and we all know where that leads. We watch him hurt you, and in turn, that hurts us."

"I'm sorry." Millie fought to hold back the tears.

Duke let out a heavy sigh, his frustration giving way to the love he felt for his daughter. "You haven't upset us, he has by manipulating you."

"I've already decided I can't see him again, at least until I'm stronger." Millie sniffed.

"Good, that's good. Now eat up before your dinner goes cold," Duke said.

Millie picked up her fork and stared at her dinner. The smell suddenly hit her nose. She jumped up and ran to the bathroom and, leaning over the toilet, she emptied the contents of her stomach.

"Are you okay?" Connie asked from the doorway.

Millie wiped her face on the towel. "Yeah, it's probably something I ate earlier." Or at least she hoped it was.

CHAPTER 20

Millie spent the next day in bed, refusing to eat and barely drinking. Duke and Connie were at their wits' end, helpless as they watched her withdraw. It was a couple of days later, at four-thirty a.m. that Connie had found Millie sitting at Micheal's monument. Her life was swiftly falling apart, and this was the only place she could think straight. And think she did. For the first time in the last few months, she could see what she had to do.

Paul had tried to drive a wedge between her and her family, she could see it now. The fact he hadn't bothered to contact her when she didn't show at his was all the proof she needed. Scott had kept her updated. Paul was living it up at the club with a different woman on his arm every night. No wonder he bought condoms in bulk, the dirty bastard. Today was the day she was going to make a life for herself. Today Paul Kelly would start to pay.

THE STEPNEY TAKEOVER

***

Millie paced the floor of the mobile, biting her nails. Rosie was at work, and Connie and Duke had gone visiting his brother. They wanted her to go, too, but she had other plans.

"Mil, you wanted to see me?" Scott asked from the door.

"Yes, I want you to drive me. I've stuff to sort out." She slipped on her shoes, grabbed her bag, and headed to the door. "Ready?"

Scott gave her the once-over and grinned. "Wow, you look hot."

Millie rolled her eyes, punched his arm playfully, and laughed. It eased the tension she felt, although her mind was already on the task ahead.

The first stop was the one she dreaded the most. The docks. She knew Paul's routine too well. This was where he would be first thing, before heading to the scrapyard.

Scott stopped the car and turned to her. "Are you sure about this, Mil? What if he's still angry?"

"I'm sure. You stay in the car, I won't be long." The sharp sting of salt air hit her immediately, reminding her of the seaside and happier times. Shaking off the nostalgia, she squared her shoulders and headed towards the office. Today was about taking back control of her life, and Paul Kelly was about to find out how serious she was.

She had made sure to dress for business. A dark-blue skirt and jacket hugged her figure, paired with a crisp white blouse, unbuttoned enough to show a little of her femininity without overdoing it. A dainty gold chain hung around her neck with a heart-shaped locket attached, bought for her by Paul. She thought it a nice addition as he would no doubt notice that when he was looking at her cleavage. Her hair was swept up into a messy bun, deliberately undone but striking and showing her slender neck. The outfit was finished off with a pair of towering six-inch stilettos. She was a sexy vision of power and control, exactly the image she needed to project.

As she opened the office door, she caught Paul's expression, the flash of surprise that flickered across his face before he quickly composed himself. Millie smiled knowing she had thrown him off balance, if only for a second.

"Leave us," she ordered, her voice sharp as she glanced at the men.

Paul, ever the one to assert his dominance, raised an eyebrow. "I give the orders around here," he shot back, quickly composing himself.

Millie didn't flinch, she held his gaze, tilted her head slightly, and frowned. "I'm not going to repeat myself." This time she wasn't about to let him gain the upper hand.

The men left after a nod from Paul.

He leant back in his chair and folded his arms, his expression hardening. "What do you want, Mil?"

"That's no way to greet your wife." Her voice was smooth but laced with sarcasm.

"Wife? That's a bit rich, isn't it?" Paul's lips twisted into a bitter smirk. "Where were you last week? I waited for you. We had a deal, remember? Well, that deal's now off. You're not a wife, you're a parasite."

"You didn't come looking for me, did you, you didn't bother to find out why I didn't turn up."

Paul's sneer deepened. "You would've been there if you wanted to; instead, you strung me along."

She held his gaze, her heart pounding, but her face calm. That was the look she was waiting for. The flicker of disdain, the coldness. It was all she needed. It showed her she meant nothing to him. She was just another of his possessions. "Whatever, Paul," she said, her tone dismissive. "I haven't come here for small talk."

"Then what have you come here for? Money, to beg for forgiveness? What?" Grabbing a bottle of scotch from the bottom drawer, he poured a large measure. "This is what you do to me, Mil, you turn me to drink."

"I'm sorry you feel like that, truly, but forgiveness is not on the table, not after what you've put me through." She took a step closer. "We need to sort this mess out. We either divorce, and I get the house and girls, or I continue to work in the business."

Paul downed the scotch and glared at her over the rim of the glass but said nothing.

"I'll leave you to think it over. Let me know what you decide."

She walked out without a second glance, and all he could do was sit there and watch. Even with everything, she still had a hold on him, an invisible grip that no other woman could ever match. She was the one who'd dumped him and yet still affected him, twisting his thoughts and stirring emotions he tried so hard to bury. He drained his glass in one go, feeling the burn, then quickly refilled it. Deep down, he knew it wouldn't help. No amount of whiskey or meaningless flings would ever let him forget her.

Millie headed back to the car. Scott was nowhere to be seen. Leaning back against the motor, she took a deep breath. She had found an inner strength she didn't know she had. It surprised her in a way because just looking at Paul made her knees go weak. Did she still love him? The question echoed in her mind, even after all that he had done? The betrayal, the lies. Her heart wavered, torn between the memories of who he once was and the harsh reality of who he had become.

He was always like this, you just never see it.

"No. He protected me."

"Hey, Mil, who ya talking to?" Scott appeared from the quayside.

"Myself."

"You know that's the first sign of madness." He laughed. "Get in, I have info."

She climbed in, glancing at Scott in the process. "Spill then."

"Paul's going to Ireland tomorrow, his gran's being taken back for burial."

"She won't be buried, she's Catholic." She wondered why Paul hadn't told her, but then why would he? It was none of her concern. "Did you find out how long he'll be gone for?"

"Two weeks, possibly four. Tony's in charge while he's gone." Scott started the motor and pulled away.

"Like fuck he is. My name is on every business. I'll be running things in my husband's absence, and you will be my right-hand man."

"Where to now, boss?" Scott laughed.

"Let's pay the girls a visit. It's about time I had a catch-up with Gladys."

***

Paul threw the last of his bits in the case and closed the lid. He was all set to leave in the morning. He sat on the edge of the bed and studied the room. This house was too big for him. Big and lonely. He now wished he hadn't sold his flat. That had been perfect. He turned his head towards the door, unsure if he'd heard a noise. He was getting jumpy.

Descending the stairs, he took a deep breath. He could smell perfume. Millie's perfume. Did he really miss her that much or was he going mad?

He continued into the lounge and towards the bar, ready to pour himself a drink. After the day he'd had, he needed one. A fucking big one.

"Hello, Paul."

He jumped, spilling half the scotch onto the carpet and the other half down himself. "Fucking hell, Millie, you can't sneak in like this."

"I'm not sneaking, you said this is my house, too, remember? I don't need an invite, just let myself in…"

"What do you want this time?" he said while mopping the scotch from his jacket.

"I've come to see what you've decided."

"I haven't decided anything, you need to give me a few days to think it over." Paul threw the cloth down and poured another drink. He then poured Millie a brandy. After passing it to her, he sat opposite on the sofa. "As I'm sure you can appreciate, I've got other stuff on my mind at the moment."

"I know you're off to Ireland tomorrow… I'm sorry about your gran, she was lovely, full of character."

He sighed. "It won't work. Us working together. I either want all of you or none of you."

"And you won't part with anything either. That puts us at a stalemate." She placed the brandy on the table, untouched. "I need money to live. Finn's offered me my old job and room back."

His stomach sank. The thought of her returning to the pub hurt him. It was yet another reminder of what a failure he was. "I'll give you an allowance."

"I'm not a fucking a child, Paul."

"No. You're my fucking wife," he snarled. "Look, so much has happened in such a short space of time, I think we need to slow down, not do anything hasty… You loved me once, we could get that back… With time." Paul stood and walked towards her. Kneeling in

THE STEPNEY TAKEOVER

front of her, he took her hand. "I fucked up, Mil, more than once, but I love you so fucking much. I would do anything to win you back."

"I don't know if it's possible," she whispered.

"Maybe it's not, but shouldn't we at least try, for our boy?"

Millie stared into his eyes. Was he trying to manipulate her, using their dead son? That was a low blow. "Micheal."

"What?"

"I named him Micheal." Millie pulled her hand away and stood. "I'll let you get on, you must have a lot to do before tomorrow."

"I'll let Tony know you'll be overseeing the businesses, and why don't you move back in here? I'll be gone two or three weeks."

"No. I'll stay where I am for now, we don't want to jinx anything," she replied.

"When I'm back we'll talk again. You know what they say, absence makes the heart grow fonder." He smiled, but it never quite reached his eyes.

CHAPTER 21

Paul had been gone two weeks. Millie hadn't heard from him but knew Tony had. Tony had also been watching her like a hawk. Every little thing she did, he was there, no doubt reporting back to Paul.

"I've got to go out in a bit. I'll be taking the accounts with me," she said.

"Paul doesn't like those leaving the premises," he said.

"But Paul's not here. I am. Now if you don't mind, get out of my way."

Tony didn't move, he stood blocking her path to the door.

"What's going on?" Duke asked. "Is there a problem, Mil?"

"No. No problem. Come on, Dad, I don't want to be late." She glared at Tony and then pulled the door shut.

Although the journey was short to the testing centre, her nerves still had time to kick in.

THE STEPNEY TAKEOVER

"You'll be fine. You've been driving long enough now to know what you're doing. Don't overthink, just let it come naturally," Duke advised her.

"Okay, duly noted. Now give me the keys."

***

Rosie sat on the sofa chewing her nails. She didn't want to put a downer on today, but after what she'd seen this morning, she couldn't let it go.

"They're back," Connie said over her shoulder while rushing outside.

Rosie joined her. "Well?"

"I passed." Millie beamed, waving the car keys in the air. "Hello, freedom."

"Not so fast." Duke snatched the keys from her hand. "I want you to go out with me a few times before you go on your own."

"But…"

"No buts, Millie, there's plenty of idiots on the road, I need to make sure you're safe." Duke plunged the keys into his pocket. "When I'm happy, I'll buy you a car."

"Actually, I've already ordered one from the garage up the road." She laughed nervously. "With Paul's money."

Rosie closed her eyes. This was not going to end well.

***

The weather had been beautiful today, and along with now being able to legally drive on the roads, unaccompanied, Millie's mood had lifted. That was until she received a phone call from Paul, congratulating her on passing. She knew Tony was watching her; she didn't realise, however, he was following her. Despite her shock, the phone call went well until she mentioned the new car. She had then been met with silence.

She wasn't stupid, she knew she was playing a dangerous game. Maybe Duke was right. Time to cut her losses and move on. The trouble was, every time she tried, she was drawn back to Paul. Did she still love him? She would have said no, but in reality, she didn't know.

"Mil?" Rosie's voice wafted through the door.
"Come in," she called back. "I'm nearly ready."
"It's been quite a day." Rosie perched on the end of the bed.
An awkward silence commenced.
"Is everything okay?" Millie asked suspiciously.
"I don't know, is it?" Rosie asked.
"If you've got something to say, Rose, then just say it."
"No. Scott's waiting outside, we need to go." She stood and walked to the door. "You know, Mil, there was a time when we didn't keep secrets from one another."

***

Duke lay his cards on the table and smiled. "Looks like I win again, boys." His smile soon fell when the pub door opened and Tommy Lee walked in.

Duke grabbed his winnings and wandered to the bar. "What brings you back here so soon? Thought you were working abroad."

"Nice to see you, too, Duke. Do you wanna drink?"

He shook his head. "I know about you and Millie. I want you to stay away from her."

Tommy Lee turned and stared him in the eye. "Doesn't she get a say in this?"

"She's a married woman."

"Separated."

Duke sighed. "Her old man won't take kindly to this, and I'll not have my daughter caught up in the middle."

"If Millie tells me to stay away, I will. As for her shit-cunt of a husband, I know all about him. If he wants to come for me, I'll kill him with my bare hands."

"But what happens if he comes for Millie?"

***

Millie sat in the VIP area watching the dance floor. Rosie sat to the right of her while Scott was down at the bar. The place was thriving. Millie's gaze wandered to the disco ball that hung from the ceiling. It spun, the light reflecting around the huge room. She remembered when Paul had first bought the old picture house and turned it into the club. The excitement they'd both felt at the prospect of being club owners. It had taken a lot of hard work to get it up and running. Did she really want to part with all this?

"Mrs Kelly, would you like any more drinks?" the bar manager asked as he stood over her.

"Rosie, do you want another drink?"

"I think Scott's getting me one," Rosie shouted back. "I see you're on the soft stuff again."

Millie waited for him to leave then moved closer to Rosie. "Are you going to tell me what's wrong?"

"Not here, it's too public."

Millie motioned for her to follow. "We can talk in the office, follow me."

They descended the stairs. She then led Rosie around the back and down a long hallway. It ran parallel to the length of the club.

She opened the office door and flicked on the light. "Take a seat." Checking the hallway to make sure it was clear, she then shut and locked the door. "Keep your voice down, the walls have ears."

"Then maybe we should have this conversation at home?" Rosie suggested.

A laugh escaped Millie's lips before she could answer. "You've got to be joking, it's worse there. I feel like I can't do or say anything. Anyway, you've got something to say, so say it." She leant against the desk and studied Rosie. She looked worried.

"You're wearing baggy clothes."

"I didn't realise that was a crime." Millie laughed.

"Millie, stop... When you were getting dressed this morning, I noticed your stomach. Are you pregnant?"

CHAPTER 22

Millie stood in front of the Range Rover and clapped her hands together like an excited little girl. "What do you think?"

"I think Paul's going to have a fit. Millie, did you really need this motor?" Duke asked.

"No, I didn't, but why shouldn't I have it? Why shouldn't I have something to show for my marriage?" She ran a hand over the bonnet. "It's so shiny."

Duke shook his head. "This isn't going to end well."

"Let me worry about Paul... I need to take the accounts back to the club, I'll only be an hour." She opened the door and climbed in. It was pure luxury.

Duke stood at the door. "Drive carefully." Pushing the door firmly shut, he waited for her to pull out of the lane before jumping into his

THE STEPNEY TAKEOVER

Transit. As he reached the end of the entrance to his ground, Tommy Lee drove in, in his Range Rover.

What is it with these fucking motors?

Tommy Lee wound his window down and popped his head out. "I'm here to see Millie."

"She's not here. Look, I'm in a bit of hurry, can you call back later?" Duke went to wind the window back up, but Tommy Lee stopped him.

"So you don't mind me calling in now? Why the change of heart?"

"Can you please move your motor? Like I said, I'm in a hurry," Duke spat.

***

Millie parked at the back of the club and quietly let herself in. The hallway was dimly lit, with shadows pooling in the corners. She used to be scared coming in here on her own. She found it creepy. With the accounts tucked under her arm, she unlocked the office door and then placed them on the desk before unlocking the safe.

The club was doing well. It was more than just a business, it was a steady cash flow. But the docks, that was the crown jewel. A lot of the big faces in London, Essex, and Kent, now relied on their services. It gave Millie a thrill knowing she had helped set it up by blackmailing the dock managers to get the spot.

She slumped back in the black leather chair behind the desk and smiled. Did she want to give all this up? No, but Paul had a point, they couldn't work together unless they were together.

And that was the question she couldn't shake. It wasn't necessarily about the businesses, although that was a small part. It wasn't even about the house. It was about how she felt for him.

A noise jolted her from her thoughts. Was that water? No. The sharp, unmistakable scent hit her. Petrol. It was coming from the other side of the door. Panic surged through her. She realised what was happening.

Taking a deep breath, she yanked the door open. Flames erupted in a violent roar. Heat seared her skin, and she slammed the door shut, stumbling back onto the desk. She grabbed the corner to keep herself upright.

"Hello? Hello! Is anyone out there? Help!" She screamed, her voice cracking in desperation. Was this where she was to die? In a fucking office? "Help!"

The roar of the flames echoed in the hallway, smoke billowing under the door.

Think, Millie, think.

She ran to the bathroom and wet the hand towel, then shoved it in the gap.

Why are you bothering?

"Because I don't want to die."

You'll be with Micheal.

The thought hit her harder than the flames ever could. She walked calmly to the desk and sat on the leather chair. For the first time in the three weeks that Paul had been gone, she noticed something — their wedding photo. It was gone.

How hadn't she noticed before?

The realisation washed over her, almost numbing her fear. As the smoke thickened and the heat seared, she found herself staring at the empty spot on the desk where the photo once proudly sat. It was just another cruel reminder of everything that had burned away long before today. She coughed violently and struggled for breath. Placing her hand on her stomach, she closed her eyes. Darkness soon followed.

Duke pulled a hose out and started to spray the hallway with water. "Tommy Lee, spray me as I go —"

Before Duke had finished, Tommy Lee had run into the hallway. He heard the crash of the door. Minutes later, he came out carrying Millie's limp body.

***

The noise in the hospital was doing Millie's head in, but that's what you get when half your family turn up to make sure you're okay. Everyone sat in the waiting room. Millie's grandparents, aunts, and uncles were all crammed in, keeping each other company. The gypsy/traveller community always supported each other in times of trouble.

THE STEPNEY TAKEOVER

The bloody noise of chatter wafting into her room had given her a full-blown headache. She felt sorry for the nursing staff, having to deal with them. Between the noise and the smell of disinfectant, she felt quite sick.

She had regained consciousness on the way to the hospital but couldn't remember the journey. She had then been examined by the doctor, concluding that she had passed out, therefore slowing her breathing, which most likely helped her survive. She did, however, have to stay in hospital for a couple of nights for observation. She did protest, but Duke and Connie had both put their foot down.

Connie sat holding her hand. Duke was outside speaking with the police officer who'd come to question her, although she couldn't tell them much. Paul had been notified, which worried her almost as much as the fire. She had been told he was flying straight back. Would he blame her?

"Do you want a drink of water?" Connie held the glass to her mouth. "The doctor said you need to keep sipping it to help your throat."

"That's enough, Mum. I need to speak with Dad, where is he?" Millie's voice was raspy, although it didn't hurt half as bad as it sounded.

"He's outside with Tommy Lee."

"Why's he here?" Millie asked.

"I don't know. Rosie is outside, too. Speak of the devil. I'll leave you two girls for a minute. Don't wear her out." Connie left the room.

Rosie sat the other side of the bed, her face tearstained. "I was so worried, Mil."

"I'm fine," she lied. "Do they know how it started?"

"I don't know. I heard your dad talking to some Irish bloke about petrol. Do you think it was deliberate?"

Millie closed her eyes. She didn't want to think about it. Had someone really tried to kill her, or was it about the club?

She couldn't help the tears. They ran down her cheeks, soaking the hospital gown. Her sobs brought Connie and Duke back into the room. When she opened her eyes, Tommy Lee was standing in the doorway.

***

Tommy Lee took his chance and sneaked out of the waiting room when no one was looking. He headed down the hall and opened Millie's door. Was she asleep? He couldn't tell. Slipping inside quietly, he closed it and sat next to her bed. She seemed peaceful.

"I'm not asleep," she said, opening her eyes. "And if you've come in here for a bit of the other, you're out of luck, I'm afraid. Doctor's orders."

He laughed softly. "That would have been nice, but I'm the patient type, I can wait... Mil, do you know who did this?"

"Do we have to talk about that now?" She sighed. "I—"

"I know, you want to forget it, but this is serious, so tell me what you can remember."

"I can remember everything. The sound of the petrol being tipped against the door. The roar of the flames..."

He held her hand and gave it a gentle squeeze. "Who did it?"

"I don't know..." A single tear ran down her face.

Tommy Lee wiped it away with his thumb. "They'll not get away with this. I promise. Now you get some rest, and I'll see you in the morning."

"No. Don't leave me, I don't want to be alone. Every time I close my eyes I'm back in that office surrounded by smoke, struggling to breathe, waiting to die..."

"Okay, I'll sit here while you sleep." He leant over and kissed her forehead. Then sat back deep in thought.

***

Paul pushed the hospital doors open then burst through, his chest heaving. He scanned the hallways. The sterile air and disinfectant hit him, but it barely registered. He hadn't breathed properly since hearing about the fire. All that mattered was finding Millie.

"Where is she?" he demanded, standing at the reception desk, his voice laced with panic.

"Room twelve, but—"

Paul didn't wait to hear the rest. He bolted down the corridor, his heart pounding as if it might burst through his chest any minute. He finally rounded the corner and spotted Duke standing outside the room with a face like thunder.

"How is she?" Paul asked breathlessly.

THE STEPNEY TAKEOVER

Duke's glare was icy. He stepped forward, squaring up to Paul, his hands clenched into fists. "You've got a fucking nerve showing up here. Haven't you done enough damage?" He growled.

Paul stopped dead, his gaze flicking over Duke's shoulder to the open door. "I need to see her."

"You think now's the right time, after everything you've put her through? She almost died, Paul. In your fucking club," he snapped. "You're toxic, I want you to stay away from my girl. I'll be the one to keep her safe. Me and her family."

Paul's face twisted in frustration. "I know I've messed up, but I love her. I have to see her, see that she's okay."

Duke shook his head and took a step closer. "You love her?" he asked in disdain. "You call this love? She's in that hospital bed because of all the crap you've done."

Connie came rushing out of the room, her eyes wide with worry. "Stop it, the pair of you, Millie can hear. This isn't the time or place," she whispered.

Paul took his chance and pushed past the pair of them. He stepped into the room, but the sight of Millie stopped him cold. She lay there, her face pale with an oxygen tube under her nose, her eyes half open. It broke him.

"Millie..." His voice cracked, and tears stung.

She opened her eyes and stared at him. "Paul, what are you doing here?" she asked with a raspy voice.

"I had to come, babe, I had to make sure you were okay." He moved to the side of the bed and grabbed her hand. "I'm so sorry. I'll get the bastard who did this."

"You should be in Ireland, with your family. Your gran..." She started coughing.

Connie rushed in and helped Millie up to a sitting position, rubbing her back. The coughing fit subsided. "I think you should go, Paul, Millie needs to rest."

Ignoring her, he bent towards Millie. "This has made me realise how much I love you. I want you back, and I promise I will never fuck up again." He kissed her gently on the lips, then left the room.

Walking out into the fresh air, he took a deep breath, inside his rage building. Was it because Millie nearly lost her life or was it because it was an attack on him? The latter, he decided.

CHAPTER 23

Paul's fists clenched, and the car rolled to a stop outside the club. His knuckles had turned white with the strain. The smell of smoke still hung in the air, a bitter reminder of how close he'd come to losing his business and reputation. His jaw tightened, and he glanced up at the building. The fire damage only extended to the hallway, which was a part relief, but the scars were still there to be seen.

He slammed the car door shut. Tony stepped beside him, lighting a cigarette.

"Put that fucking thing out, Tone," Paul demanded. There was enough smoke left in the air without that.

Behind them, two of his other men climbed out of the second car, both loyal and trustworthy.

Paul walked towards the door and inspected the fire damage. It was amateurish at best. "This wasn't a professional job. Looks more like some minor crank getting revenge."

Paul rubbed the back of his neck. "What did the Old Bill say, Tone, when they spoke to you?"

"Said it was arson, like we didn't already know that."

He kicked open the door, and the four of them entered the dark hallway that reeked of burnt wood and smoke.

"Could it have been kids?" one of the men asked.

"No. The light would have been on. Whoever did this knew someone was in here, and more than likely knew it was Millie," Paul said.

"One of the women you've been with maybe. You know what women are like for revenge."

"Let's not speculate, boys." Paul grunted. He didn't need reminding of his past fuck-ups.

The rest of the building was intact, but the hallway was a reminder of what happened when you let your guard down.

"Who have you pissed off, boss?" Tony asked, scanning the walls.

Paul scratched his head. "Millie."

He continued on through to the office, the room where she had nearly died. The walls were smoked-stained. Just the thought of what could have happened made him feel sick. "Tone, get all the men out on the street asking if anybody saw anything."

He waited for them to leave and then pulled open the top drawer. There, staring up at him, was the photo of him and Millie on their wedding day. He slammed the drawer shut. Would his life have been easier if Millie had perished in the fire? Probably. At least he wouldn't have had to worry about the blackmail letters.

Had it had been a shock seeing her like that, so weak? Yes, but he needed to remember she wanted to take what he'd grafted hard for. He couldn't control her anymore, not while Duke was around, and it pissed him off. He needed to separate them.

He would have to try harder.

***

Millie perched on the end of the hospital bed. She couldn't wait to get home. Three poxy nights she had spent here. Three full nights of thinking. The fire, the close call to death, and Paul, everything seemed to blur into a fog of confusion.

Not only that, though, she was sick of the noise and smell. It was either disinfectant or cabbage. Why did they feel the need to cook cabbage every other day? Couldn't they have mixed it up a bit? Carrots would have been her choice. Carrots with a nice bacon pudding and roast potatoes Connie had promised her tonight. It made her mouth water just thinking about it.

The door creaked open, and Rosie slipped inside. "Hey, how are you feeling?"

"I'm fine." Another lie. She was getting good at this pretending malarky. "Where's my dad?"

"Just parking. He dropped me off at the entrance. You all set to leave?"

Millie nodded, although her heart wasn't in it. "Yeah, just waiting for the paperwork."

She looked up when the bed moved. Rosie was sitting next to her, her leg bouncing nervously. A heaviness filled the air. Millie glanced at Rosie; she knew that look on Rosie's face, the look that said she knew she was holding something back, like she could sense the storm inside her that no one else could.

"How are you really, and be honest, this is me you're talking to, Mil?" Rosie asked, her voice soft like she was talking to a child.

Millie sighed, biting her lip. "Honestly, I don't even know anymore, everything's so messed up. I've messed up."

Rosie reached out and gave her hand a gentle squeeze. "You've been through hell these past few months, but you're stronger than all of this. You always have been."

Millie struggled to hold back her tears. She wasn't feeling strong, not with the secret she'd been carrying. She had tried to bury it, but now with the fire and nearly losing her life, it was too much. She couldn't hold it in any longer.

"Rose, I've got something to tell you, please don't be mad." Millie's voice trembled.

"Don't be daft, you can tell me anything. Who did ya murder? D'ya need help disposing of the body?" Rosie laughed.

Millie laughed, too. It broke the awkward tension she'd been feeling.

Deciding it was best just to say it, she blurted it out just as Duke entered the room. "I'm pregnant."

Millie turned to him, his face a mix of shock and disappointment. "I'll wait in the motor." He then left.

"Fuck." Millie placed her hands over her face and sobbed.

"Hey, come on, it's gonna be okay." Rosie wrapped her arms around her. "He was gonna find out sooner or later. It may as well be sooner."

"Stop being nice to me, I don't deserve it." Millie sniffed. "You asked me before if I was pregnant and I said no. I was scared, because of everything happening with Paul it…"

"Have you told him?" Rosie asked, dabbing at Millie's tears. "He has a right to know."

"No, that's just it, I don't know if he's the father."

Rosie's jaw dropped open. It took a minute to compose herself. "What do you mean?"

"Remember Tommy Lee, well…" Millie's throat tightened, but she forced herself to continue. "Theres a chance it could be his."

Rosie stared at her, stunned. She was obviously struggling with the news. "Does this Tommy Lee know?"

"No. No one knows other than you. Please don't say anything. I've been in denial, but since the fire, I now know I need to face up to it. Oh God, this is killing me. Maybe it would have been best for all if I'd died in the fire."

"Don't ever say that. Everyone would have been devastated. Now listen to me. We are gonna get you home and figure it out. Okay?" Rosie placed her hands on Millie's shoulders. "You didn't give up on me, and I am certainly not gonna give up on you. Capiche?"

"What the hell does that mean?" Millie asked.

"It's Italian for understand… Now grab your stuff, we need to go."

The door opened, and a young nurse handed Millie the paperwork. "Here you go, your discharge papers."

"Thank you." Millie took one last look at the room before leaving. She had a deep, nagging feeling that she was walking out of the frying pan and into the fire.

CHAPTER 24

Paul kept a close eye on the workmen as they repaired the fire damage to the hallway. He had another washing down the walls and ceiling, before painting in the office. In his mind, now that he had time to think about it, he was grateful that Duke had rescued Millie. Maybe this had taught her a lesson.

Tony appeared by his side. "How's Millie doing?"

"She's being released from hospital today. I'll go and see her later and make sure she's okay," Paul said. "I want the bastard who did this found by tonight." He growled.

Tony nodded, his face serious. "We've got a lead. A blonde woman was seen at the time, short, petite, and looking anxious. Remind you of anyone?"

"Nicky," Paul spat. His jaw tightened; another one of his fuck-ups. "I should have fucking known she wouldn't go quietly."

"What d'ya want us to do?" Tony asked.

THE STEPNEY TAKEOVER

Paul's eyes blazed with malice. "I'll sort the slag myself." He then turned to Tony. "One more thing, Millie mustn't find out about this."

***

The journey home had been filled with quiet moments, in between Rosie's excessive chatter about the Queen's silver jubilee, that she had missed because she was in hospital. Millie knew what she was doing, she was trying to take every one's mind off the pregnancy. It wasn't working, though. Duke had a face like thunder. She was in for it when she got home.

The pickup pulled up outside the mobile. Connie came rushing out before Millie had even opened the door.

"Quick, let's get you inside. It's not as warm today, and I don't want you catching a chill," Connie said.

She smiled, leaning into her mother as she helped her out of the pickup. She led her in and guided her to the sofa where blankets and a pillow were already waiting.

"Lie back. Do you want another pillow? Rosie, get another pillow off Millie's bed... The doctor said you need to rest. Are you comfortable?" Connie asked, throwing another blanket over her.

"Mum, please stop fussing, and take these blankets off. It's June, and I'm fine." Millie glanced up at Duke who stared back at her.

He lingered quietly by the doorway, his brow furrowed as he watched the scene unfold, his lips set in a tight line. Millie sensed something different in him, a different disappointment or maybe a deeper worry that he wasn't saying out loud.

"Put the kettle on, Con. Rosie, can you give us a minute?" That wasn't a question, it was a direct order from Duke.

Millie waited for them both to leave. "Dad, not now."

"Don't 'Dad, not now' me." Duke blew out slowly, trying to contain his temper. "Whose is it?"

"What?"

"Don't act stupid with me. This child is gonna tie you to either Paul, the man who's ruined your life, or Tommy Lee, the serial nutter who will no doubt ruin your life. Now which one is the father?"

She couldn't answer because she didn't know.

"Please don't tell me there's more than two choices?"

"No," she managed through the tears.

Duke's gaze softened, and for a brief moment she saw something shift in his expression.

"You know me and your mother will support you, you don't need either man."

"I know," she whispered, her throat constricting. "I bet you'd wish you'd never met me. I've brought nothing but trouble to your door."

"One of the greatest moments in my life was finding out you're my daughter, so don't think otherwise... Now get some rest. We'll talk about this later with your mother, when you're feeling stronger." He leant over and kissed her cheek.

Millie watched him leave the room, her mind turning to Paul and Tommy Lee. This was one mess that no one could fix but her.

***

Robbie McNamara pulled the last photo of Nicky off the wall. This time tomorrow he would be looking at the real thing, not just a picture. He placed it in the box and glanced around the cell.

Just one more night in this shithole, he thought, *and then I'll be in my own bed*. He couldn't wait to hold his Nicky in his arms.

"Hey, Robbie, you all set for tomorrow?" his mate asked. "I'll bet you'll be missing me and the boys by teatime."

"You're talking pish, man. I'll be glad to see the back of ya and that stinking arse of yours," he jovially replied.

This time he wasn't coming back, he was going to turn over a new leaf.

***

It was a little after midnight. Paul sat in a stolen motor up the road from Nicky's house. He planned to break in, murder her, and make it look like a suicide attempt. Once this was done, he could move on with his life and with Millie. There would be no loose ends to come back and bite him.

He could have got his boys to do this for him, but she'd made it personal. The audacity of some cheap tart damaging his club and attempting to hurt — no, kill — Millie was burning in his chest. No one touched what was his and lived. No one.

Pulling on his gloves, he left the motor and crept along in the shadows.

***

Millie's screams had Duke, Connie, and Rosie all rushing into her bedroom. She thrashed about in bed, sobbing while screaming for help.

Duke grabbed her and held her tightly to his chest. "Millie, it's just a bad dream. Wake up."

Her eyes opened, and she clung to him like a scared child. "Every time I close my eyes I'm back in that room." She sobbed.

"Shh, you're okay now, you're safe," he soothed. "Go back to bed, I'll stay with her," he told Connie and Rosie.

Millie sat up, wiping her eyes. "I could do with a cuppa and a chat."

Duke helped her up and into the front room. "Let me stick the kettle on." When he returned, Millie was lying on the sofa. He could see she had something on her mind. "Okay, what is it?" he asked, placing her tea on the side.

"I can't remember getting out of the office. I need to know what happened," she said. "It might help.

"I went to follow you, didn't like the thought of you driving that motor on your own, but Tommy Lee pulled in just as I was pulling out." Duke sighed. "If he hadn't stopped me, I would've been there to stop it."

"This isn't your fault, Dad, nor is it Tommy Lee's... What happened when you got there?"

"The flames hadn't taken proper hold. There was a hosepipe outside. I—"

"Paul had that put in for washing the motors," she vacantly added.

"Anyway, I rolled it out and started spraying the hall, asked Tommy Lee to spray me but he was already running in, then seconds later, he carried you out."

"So you both saved me... Why was he there?"

"Because I couldn't get rid of him, he had come to see you. I told him you weren't there, so he jumped in the motor." Duke shook his head. "I want you to forget about him, Millie, he's no good for you."

CAROL HELLIER

"But what if he's the baby's father?"

CHAPTER 25

Robbie stood at the entrance to the Scrubs and eyed the road for his lift. The toot-toot of a car horn had him smiling. There was his cousin, Colin, waving out of the window. He looked to the sky, the summer sun warming his face.

"Stick ya stuff in the back, and we'll go for a wee dram," Colin said.

"Just a quickie, I wanna see my Nicky. Has she been a good girl these last few months?" Robbie enquired, although did he really want to know?

"Haven't heard of or seen any more discrepancies... You need to remember, you've been banged up a fair while, Robbie. That poor wee girl has had to fend for herself."

"Aye, well, that's no excuse. Come on, put your foot down, man, me mouth is watering for that scotch."

THE STEPNEY TAKEOVER

***

Paul slammed the phone down. How dare Duke stop him from seeing Millie.

"That didn't sound like it went too well," Tony said without looking up.

"She's my wife. If he thinks he can stop me seeing her, he's in for a shock. A fucking big one."

"Calm down, Paul, she's just come out of hospital. He's doing what any father would do. Protecting his daughter until she's well enough to make her own decisions."

Paul chose to ignore that comment. Instead, he stared out of the window. It was a nice day, just a pity he sat in the Portakabin at the scrapyard.

"You haven't told me how last night went?" Tony added.

"The less you know the better. Let's just say the problem has been dealt with." Paul grinned. She wouldn't be causing anyone else shit. It had given him a thrill when he'd pushed her down the stairs. It made him feel powerful. Invincible. The crack of her neck was like music to his ears.

"What time's the other business getting here?" Tony checked his watch then glanced at Paul.

"Later this afternoon. Make sure the smelter's fired up." Paul sighed. He loved work, loved being the boss, the one who told every other fucker what to do. Everyone apart from Millie; she was still being a problem. He sighed louder. Duke was another problem that needed disposing of. He knew Millie would never speak to him again if she found out he'd topped her old man, but if there was a way of getting rid of him, that would be all his problems over and then he could control her again. He grinned.

"What you smiling at?" Tony asked.

"Ya know Duke's the only fly in the ointment, and he needs scooping out and squashing. Once and for all."

"Even you can't be that daft to take on the gypsies. Paul, Mil won't forgive you for that."

"Yeah, well, she won't know... where there's a will, there's a way." Paul tapped the side of his nose. He had formed a plan.

***

Millie sat at the kitchen table while Connie prepared the dinner. Her chest still felt tight after the fire, but it had only been a few days. Neither of her parents would let her do anything other than sit, not that she felt like going out dancing, but Christ almighty, she was bored.

Duke was outside with her brother, Aron, tinkering with the pickup truck. She couldn't understand why he didn't cut his losses, scrap it and buy a new one.

'That's the trouble with you young folk, everything's disposable,' he had said. 'We were brought up to look after our things, doesn't matter how much money you have.'

She guessed he had a point.

"Are you okay?" Connie asked. "You look a bit peaky."

"I'm fine, Mum, just bored. When's Dad gonna let me out of this prison?" she asked.

"Don't let your father hear you say that, and you'll go out when you're better." Connie placed a pan on the lit stove. "Did you see on the news Charlie Chaplin's coffin was found ten miles from where he'd been buried? People have no respect for the dead these days."

"You sound like Gran," Millie grunted in reply.

"I do not." Connie swung around, her face a picture of shock.

Before Millie could reply, Duke and Aron walked in. He glanced between Millie and Connie. "What 'ave I missed?"

"Your daughter thinks I'm turning into your mother." Connie huffed.

Duke laughed. "You know you've upset her when she calls you my daughter." He slipped his arms around Connie's waist and planted his lips on hers.

Millie smiled. It was good to see them still close after all they'd been through. Her thoughts turned to Paul. Why hadn't he been to see her? Was it all lies he'd told her at the hospital? A tiny flutter beat in her tummy, and she instinctively placed her hand over it. This was the first time she'd felt it. Her baby.

***

Robbie staggered up the path towards the front door. The house looked exactly the same as the last time he'd been here, all those years

THE STEPNEY TAKEOVER

ago. The red brick and gleaming white woodwork. The small patch of shrubs underneath the front room window as neat as the day he'd got nicked, although a lot bigger. It was a vision of happier days.

He knew he was in for a bollocking from Nicky. It was now six twenty-five p.m. She was not going to be happy. He knocked loudly and leant against the wall for fear of falling over. When she didn't answer, he knelt and called through the letter box, "Nicky, open the damn door."

He sat back on his haunches. Had she gone out? He pushed himself up, while swallowing his irritation, and stumbled to the side of the house. He'd let himself in round the back. When he managed to get through the gate, he glanced around for the pot that always had a spare key under it. "Ah, there you are, ya bugger." He kicked the pot over and stared at the empty ground underneath.

Robbie turned to the kitchen window. He doubted she'd had it fixed. It had always been an easy way in when he'd forgotten his keys.

Placing an old garden chair underneath, he began to climb up, giving the window a swift push. He smiled. Some things had remained unchanged. He climbed through, falling onto the sink. A cup fell to the floor and smashed.

"Fucking hell, woman." He mumbled. Once he was in and upright, he studied the room. It was exactly the same. The familiarity gave him a warm feeling. Something from the past unchanged. The area was different, the boozers seemed different, but his home was still the home he remembered.

"*Nicky... Nicky, where are ya?*" He continued through the hall and into the front room. He scanned it, which was also unchanged. He plonked himself in his chair and flopped back. This was more like it, this was where he belonged. His eyes grew heavy, and within the minute he was soundo.

***

Paul stood outside the mobile and knocked. The door opened, and Duke appeared.

"What the fuck do you want?" he asked.

"I've come to see my wife, to make sure she's okay. *Millie?*" Paul called.

"I told you, she needs to rest, she can't have no more dramas—"

"Dad, it's fine. A little walk will do me good," Millie said. "I'll just get my coat." She disappeared inside and returned minutes later.

Paul could hear Duke telling her she had thirty minutes before he'd come and get her. Fucking cheek, who did he think he was?

Paul smiled when she reappeared. "I've missed you. I did phone earlier, but Duke wouldn't let me speak to you." He helped her down the step.

"He's protective." Millie smiled.

He gritted his teeth; she was defending him. "What does he think I'm gonna do to you over the phone?"

"We're not here to talk about my dad, Paul, so can you get to the point?" She held her stomach as she stumbled over a rock.

Paul grabbed her and held her upright. "I'm protective, too." He pulled her round to face him. "I want you to move back in, start again fresh. You call the shots."

"I can't move in until I'm better. I need my mum to care for me. I know I seem okay, but my chest still hurts, and the doctor said I have to rest for a week or so."

"I can hire a nurse for you," he quickly replied. "Whatever you need, I'll take care of it."

"What I need right now is to be with my mum, not a stranger, and if you love me, you'll understand."

"So you don't love me then, Mil?" he asked.

"Of course I love you. I've always loved you. That's what's made this all so difficult." She sighed. "I'm still hurting from Rita and losing the baby…"

"Micheal." Paul whispered. "I'm hurting, too, and as for the other stuff, I can promise nothing like that will ever happen again."

"Will you let me stay with my parents till I get the all-clear from the doctor?"

"If that's what you want," Paul agreed.

"And one more thing, I—"

"Anything," he countered before she'd finished her sentence.

"I want a new bed."

"I'll order a new bed in the morning." He leant into her and brushed his lips against hers before poking his tongue in her mouth. He kissed her passionately, pleased she responded.

Pulling back, Millie smiled. "I tell my parents, not you."

THE STEPNEY TAKEOVER

"Of course… I'd best get you back before Duke puts a price on my head." He smiled. A smile that said he had won.

CHAPTER 26

Robbie rubbed his head before he opened his eyes. His mouth tasted like the bottom of a bird cage, and he guessed it would pretty much smell like one, too. He glanced at the clock on the mantelpiece: seven-thirty a.m. How the fuck had he slept all that time, and more to the point, where was Nicky?

He stood and stretched his arms over his head. He had to admit, that was the best night's sleep he'd had in years. With a smile on his face, he made his way to the stairs, stopping dead as he reached them. Nicky was lying at the bottom, crumpled in a heap. He knelt and rolled her over.

"Nicky," he whispered softly, giving her a gentle shake. "Nicky, wake up."

Her skin was cold to touch, and her beautiful supple lips had a blue tinge. He pulled her to him and cried out. "No, please God, no."

THE STEPNEY TAKEOVER

Rocking backwards and forwards with her in his arms, he cried like a baby.

***

Rosie helped Millie out of the bath. "Girl, your stomach is getting bigger. What happens when you can no longer hide it?"

"Shh, keep your voice down. I can only be three and a half, maybe four months pregnant. I was never this big with Micheal. Why's it showing already?"

Rosie shrugged. "Dunno. I'm no expert, but maybe it's a big baby? Anyway, answer the question."

"I've thought about nothing else for the last few days." Millie wrapped the towel around herself while Rosie rubbed her hair to dry it.

"You haven't told me what happened with Paul either."

"He wants us to get back together."

Rosie stopped. "I hope you told him where to go."

Millie sighed. She knew her friend meant well, but what was she supposed to do? "No, I said I would, when I'm better. I still love him, not like before, but there is something there."

"The Paul Kelly who I know won't want another man's baby, so what are you gonna do, pretend it's his even if it's Tommy Lee's?"

"No. You know me better than that, Rose."

"I thought I did, but your decisions these last few months have left me wondering." Rosie sighed. "What happens if it's not his? What are you gonna do then?"

"Then I'll raise it on my own."

"And what about the actual father, Mil, doesn't he get a say in it?"

"I'm not trapping Tommy Lee. Of course I'll tell him, but that's as far as me and him go." Millie grabbed her clothes and walked through to her bedroom with Rosie hot on her tail.

"Don't you think you should tell your mum and dad what you're planning?"

"Rose, please, just give it a rest. I'm waiting until I'm better before anything happens. We all know everything could change in that time."

***

Duke sat at the bar in the Old Artichoke.

Finn placed a beer in front of him. "So how's Millie doing?"

Duke frowned. "To be honest I'm not sure. She seems different since the fire."

"Well, I guess a near-death experience will do that to you. She's lucky to have you and Connie," Finn said.

Duke sighed. "I'm trying to keep her away from Paul. I think he's manipulating her."

Finn frowned. "In what way?"

"In the way that he's meeting me here in an hour to discuss her with me... Like my daughter has anything to do with him." Duke took a large gulp of his pint, then stared at the glass. "I wanted to ask you, man to man, if she were your daughter, would you be happy her going back to him?"

Finn shook his head slowly. "In all honesty, when I first met Millie, that very first time she knocked on this door and asked for a job, she was a sweet, innocent girl. Her life growing up and her first marriage had hardened her to certain things. She had the appearance of a survivor, you could see it in her eyes. But she shouldn't have to survive. She deserved better, and to be honest, I thought Paul would give her that. But now..."

"But now you don't?" Duke asked.

"But now I think you and Connie are what she needs," Finn said. "After seeing her the other day, she was like a scared little girl, and we all know little girls need their mummies and daddies."

Duke drained the beer from his glass. "That's how I feel. I'm gonna tell him to stay away from her."

***

Millie sat biting her nails. Her brain wouldn't give her a minute's peace. The thought of telling her parents she was thinking of getting back with Paul left her feeling nervous. Would they disown her? "Where's Dad?"

"Went to the pub for a bit, he shouldn't be long... Is everything okay, Mil? I noticed you picked at your dinner." Connie perched on the edge of the sofa. "You know you can tell me anything."

THE STEPNEY TAKEOVER

Millie opened her mouth to speak, but the sound of the door slamming stopped her.

Duke walked in, his eyes blazing. "When were you gonna tell me?"

Connie jumped up, shocked. "Tell you what?"

"Millie, would you like to tell your mother, or shall I?"

Connie turned to Millie. "Tell me what?"

"She's decided to go back to him," Duke said before Millie had the chance.

Connie's eyes watered up.

Duke pointed at her. "See what you've done? You know the thing that hurts the most is Kelly took great pleasure in telling me because my daughter was too gutless to." He turned and marched out.

"Mum."

"Not now, Millie, I need to go after your father, he's hurting."

Millie sat there staring at the door as Connie walked out. What had she done? More to the point, what had Paul done?

"Mil, is it safe to come in?" Rosie asked, poking her head around the door.

"You should run as far away from me as possible, I'm a disaster."

"Well, on the bright side, you don't have to tell them now." Rosie smiled.

"I was supposed to tell them, I told Paul that, it was one of the conditions. He's let me down again… Paul Kelly wants, so Paul Kelly takes, and fuck what anyone else wants."

"And this is the man you want to spend the rest of your life with?" Rosie grabbed her hand and squeezed it. "He's still manipulating you, the situation, for the outcome he wants."

"He loves me."

"He does, Mil, but in the way of loving a possession. He thinks he owns you, and the man I know will go all out to get his property back. I thought you would have realised that after what you told me about Rita."

***

Duke pulled up outside the mobile. "I think she's still up."

"I don't want her upset. You need to reason with her, and if you can't change her mind, we need to be there when it all goes wrong." Connie climbed out of the Transit without waiting for a reply.

Duke grabbed her arm. "I can't watch her make mistake after mistake, Con, she needs to be accountable for her actions."

"I know, but at the moment she's carrying her child, our grandchild, so that's our priority, because if she loses this baby, I don't think she'll survive it."

"Fine." Duke pulled open the door and marched to the front room.

"Dad." Millie's eyes were red from crying. "I'm sorry."

"You seem to be sorry a lot lately."

"Duke," Connie reminded him.

He sighed. "Do you know how I felt when he told me, the fucking gloating that radiated off him? I wanted to knock that smirk off his face."

"He had no right telling."

"No, he didn't, it should have come from you… Am I that much of a monster that you can't tell me things?"

"No." She stared down at her hands. They shook.

He knelt in front of her. "Just have a dick at what he's doing, Mil, he's driving a wedge between us. He's gonna make sure you have no one. Is that what you want?"

"Of course it isn't. I love you and Mum. You're both important to me."

"Well, in Paul's world there's no room for us." He stood. "I'm going to bed, I'll see you in the morning."

"Get yourself to bed, you're supposed to be resting. All this drama isn't good for your recovery or the baby." Connie helped her up and into the bedroom, while Duke stood back, his anger for Paul growing.

Millie settled into bed. She doubted she'd sleep. Just what was Paul playing at? He never used to be like this. Was it because she now had family?

"Mil. Can I come in?"

"Yes, but be quiet, Rose."

"I heard all that. Your dad's got a point. What are you going to do?"

"I'm staying here until Paul sorts himself out." Millie explained.

THE STEPNEY TAKEOVER

"And what if he doesn't?" Rosie asked in a hushed voice. "Because from where I'm standing, Paul's goading your dad into a fight. And I don't think he intends to fight fair."

Millie sank back onto the bed. Paul never fought fairly, the deck was always stacked in his favour. "Well, if Paul's gonna fight dirty, then so will I."

"You're no match for him, girl."

"Yeah, that's what I thought, too, Rose, but I need you to trust me."

CHAPTER 27

Millie watched Duke hitch up the trailer. They were off to Kent as Jasper and Sherry's baby was due any day. It had been three days since the argument, and four days since she'd seen Paul. He'd phoned to tell her he had a new bed coming. When she asked about him seeing Duke, he'd said he bumped into him in a boozer.

"Are you sure you're going to be okay?" Connie asked, worry etched across her face.

"I'll be fine, Rosie's here with me." Millie smiled. "You need to be there with Jasper."

"I really think you should come with us," Duke added.

"I'm not gonna do anything stupid." She glanced towards the house. Something was bothering her. "Dad, where did you see Paul, when he told you we were getting back together?"

"Where he told me to meet him. In the Artichoke."

THE STEPNEY TAKEOVER

"So he arranged to meet you, this wasn't a chance meeting?" Her mind spun. Paul had lied again.

"No, Mil, he set it up. We gotta get going. I'm sure your mother will phone to check up on you."

Duke climbed into the Transit and glanced at Connie. "You okay, Con?"

"We shouldn't be leaving her."

"She'll be fine. There's no way she'll leave Rosie on her own here. Let's just hope in the next two or three days she comes to her senses." He started the motor and pulled away.

Millie waved them off, her heart sinking. She missed them already, and they weren't even at the end of the lane, but she was also glad that they were out of the way. Connie's non-stop fussing was driving her mad, and they deserved to be there when their first grandchild arrived.

She made her way back into the mobile. Rosie was at work, Aron was God knows where, and she was all alone, until lunch time when she was meeting Rosie in the Wimpy. Deciding to drive down to the high street early, she grabbed her bag and locked up the mobile. This would be the first time she'd gone out since the fire. Her hands shook when she unlocked her motor. Sweat gathered on her forehead. She wiped it away on the back of her coat sleeve.

"You can do this," she whispered.

It was only a five-minute drive. She passed Kelly's nightclub on her right and shuddered. Her mind alight with the fire, taking a deep breath to steady herself, she gripped the steering wheel to stop the shaking. She pulled in near the Wimpy and squeezed her eyes shut, her breathing erratic. She could taste the smoke as if she was back in that office, waiting to die.

A loud tap came from the closed window. "You all right, miss?" the man called through.

She glanced at him, nodding while wiping at her tears. "I'm fine, thank you."

No you're not.

She rested her head back on the seat after he'd walked away. She needed a distraction. Keep busy and not think. Climbing out, she locked her motor and walked to the newsagent's.

Smiling at the woman behind the counter, she had a quick look for a magazine. Her eyes were drawn to the local paper. On the front was an article about the fire. She took a copy and paid.

Heading towards the Wimpy with the paper gripped tightly in her hand, she entered, found a table, then started reading the article. It made it sound so matter-of-fact. Arson attack on Kelly's. All about Paul. It even had him quoted. Was that it? Millie sighed. It was always about him. She turned the page. The picture of a woman who had died in a tragic accident caught her attention. She was sure she'd seen her before. She studied the woman's face.

"Shit."

"Is everything okay? Would you like to order?" the waitress asked.

"Just a cup of tea, please. I'm waiting for my friend to get here, then we'll order." She waited for the waitress to leave before refocussing on the picture. It was the woman Paul was seeing, the same woman he'd taken to the house. Tragic accident?

"Hey, Mil." Rosie headed over to her. "You okay, you look a bit pale?"

"I'm fine, let's order." Her appetite had gone, but she needed to act normal. She sat and listened to Rosie's chatter, nodding and smiling in all the right places, or so she thought.

"Okay, let's hear it," Rosie demanded. "And don't tell me it's nothing, you've spent the last half hour pushing your food around the plate and not hearing a word I've said."

Millie sighed and grabbed the paper. She turned to the article about the woman's tragic accident. "Look at that. That woman is the one Paul was with."

Rosie studied the picture. "So? You know he's had other women. It couldn't have bothered you as you've agreed to go back with him."

"I think she was murdered," Millie whispered.

"What!" Rosie's eyes widened. "Oh my God, you think Paul did this?"

Millie nodded. "It's his style, tying up loose ends."

"Mil, if that's what you think, whether it's true or not, you can't go back to him. What happens when *you're* a loose end?"

***

Paul stood at the front of the club staring at Millie's motor. Would she come over and see him? If she loved him she would, and more to the point, if she was well enough to go out, she was well enough to move back home.

***

Millie sat and read the article in depth. The woman, Nicky, had a husband who had been released on the day after her accident, but didn't find her until the following morning. The coroner stated that she had been dead at least forty-eight hours, before being discovered. There was no way the husband could have done it, he was still banged up.

A loud knock came from the door, and Millie jumped. She stuffed the newspaper behind the sofa and went to answer the door.

"Hello, Millie," Paul said.

"Paul. What are you doing here?"

He'd caught her off-guard, but she composed herself quickly.

"Ain't you pleased to see me?"

"Of course I am, but I wasn't expecting you. Come in." She stood back.

He climbed in and grabbed her around the waist. "I saw your motor parked up the road from the club."

"I met Rosie for lunch, just to get me out for a bit."

"Why didn't you come over and say hello?" Was he angry?

"I'm not ready to go back to the club, Paul. Not yet."

"And are you ready to move back to the house? You're obviously well enough if you can go out on your own." Paul's eyes were unblinking, like he was trying to catch her out.

"I can't move back until my parents return home. I'm not leaving Rosie here on her own."

Paul laughed. "Always thinking about everyone else. Isn't it time you put me first?"

"What, like you put me first? I told you I wanted to tell my parents, but oh no. The great Paul Kelly arranged to meet my dad, behind my back, and tell him."

"I didn't want you to change your mind." His eyes blazed with anger. "Your so-called father, you know, the one who let you grow up in a children's home, warned me off ya. I don't take orders from no one, least of all a dirty fucking pikey."

"Firstly, he didn't know I existed, as you well know, and Connie thought I was dead. And secondly, if he's a dirty fucking pikey, then so am I."

"Stop making fucking excuses for them. You are nothing like them. You don't belong here, this isn't your life." He let go of her. "I have business to attend tonight, so I'll give you until tomorrow evening to move your stuff back." He turned and walked away.

Millie closed the door and locked it. Was she afraid? Yes. He was out of control. She stood there, unable to move for what seemed like ages. Her mind was replaying the events of the past few months.

The door handle twisted. She grabbed her chest. Had he come back?

"Mil, the door's stuck."

She relaxed at the sound of Rosie's voice. "Hang on." She undid the lock, and when the door opened she ushered her through, relocking it after. "I'm gonna let the dogs off later, so stay inside."

"What's going on? Why are we living in Fort Knox?"

"It's just a precaution." Millie grabbed the kettle and started to fill it. "There's food in the fridge, help yourself."

"Stop." Rosie grabbed the kettle and set it down. "Just stop… What's he done now?"

"It doesn't matter what he's done, this is all my fault and I'm gonna fix it."

CHAPTER 28

Connie held the baby in her arms, her face a picture of happiness. "Just look at her curls, Duke, she gorgeous."

Duke smiled, although his mind was on Millie. She hadn't sounded right on the phone last night. Like she was up to something. As proud as he was of Jasper and Sherry for giving him a grandchild, he couldn't shake the thought that he should be at home with his own child.

"It's so good to have you both here." Sherry beamed. "I'm gonna need all the help I can get raising this one."

"Just as well you have your family around you then, cos we will be going back in a day or so," Duke informed her.

He noticed the look from Connie, which said she wasn't going anywhere just yet.

"Right, I think we need to go and wet the baby's head, Jasper." Duke needed to get out of the hospital. He hated these places. All disinfectant and sick people.

"I can't go yet, Dad, Sherry's just given birth. I'll meet you later after visiting time," Jasper said.

Duke turned and left without another word. He didn't even say goodbye to Connie. Jasper would make sure she got back to the trailer safe. He stopped at the first pub he found and ordered a pint before using the phone. It was now eight-thirty p.m. He dialled the number and spoke to Millie. He didn't bother telling her about her new niece, she wouldn't be interested. The conversation lasted all of three minutes before she said she had to go. That was all he needed to know — she was up to something, he could hear it in her voice. She sounded nervous. He downed his pint and left to make his way back to Stepney.

***

Millie let herself in through the kitchen door. She continued to the lounge. Paul stared at her over the top of his glass when she entered the room.

"About time, I thought I was gonna have to come and get you."

"You always were impatient."

He looked at her coldly. "It's good to have my wife back, where she belongs."

"It's good to be back." She smiled. "Let's get Chinese to celebrate, I'm starving."

"I'd rather go straight to bed." Paul placed his glass down and grabbed her hand.

He held it firmly; she couldn't pull away.

Her heart pounded. "No. Not yet, I've something to tell you." She glanced at the clock. It was nearly nine-thirty p.m.

"You can tell me on the way up to bed."

"Paul, I'm pregnant."

A glimmer of surprise crossed his face. "You sure?"

She lifted her top up and showed him the bump. "I'm only about four months, but yes, I'm sure... Well, say something!"

"That's good news." He picked her up and spun her around. "This is a new beginning."

Millie laughed as he placed her down. "Chinese?" she reminded him. "I am eating for two."

"Anything for you. I'll go get it." He planted a kiss on her forehead.

"I want to come." She laced her hands around his neck. "Please."

"Okay, if you can't bear to be away from me, you can come." He grabbed his keys from the side and opened the door for her. "After you."

Millie walked to the motor, her heart thumping. She climbed in, placing her hands in her lap.

"Aren't you forgetting something?" he asked. He tapped his seat belt. "You're carrying a precious life. We want to keep this one safe."

That was a dig about Micheal. It hit her right in the centre of her heart. "Oh, of course." She smiled. "Can I have a chicken curry, please?"

"I don't think you should have anything spicy. How about sweet and sour chicken and boiled rice?" he said.

Was this how he thought it was going to be? A dictatorship? "Okay." There was no point arguing now.

Thank God the journey was short. Millie felt stifled sitting next to him, the air in the motor toxic from each word he spoke.

"I'll wait here while you run in and get it," she said, unable to stand another second in his company.

"I'll take the keys, Mil, just in case you decide to leave me here."

"Am I your wife or a prisoner?"

"I haven't decided yet." He laughed then slammed the door and crossed the road.

***

Duke looked at Rosie. "What?"

"Please don't shoot the messenger. She said she is sorting the mess out that she's made and she will be back later."

"Didn't you try and stop her?" he asked.

"This is your daughter we are talking about, she's not called Millie the Stubborn for nothing." Rosie stood and walked to the window. She pointed at the house. "She's in there with him, and I don't like it any more than you do."

THE STEPNEY TAKEOVER

Duke didn't reply. He grabbed a knife, stuck it in his pocket, and left. Paul Kelly was not going to ruin her life.

***

Millie sat chewing her fingernails. It was strange, she hadn't bitten them since she'd been with Levi, and then all this trouble with Paul it had started again. Stress, worry, anguish, and fear. All caused by men.

She watched the door open. Paul appeared with their food. He began to cross the road. All Millie could remember were the blinding headlights, Paul's body flying up into the air and landing with a thud.

She jumped from the motor and ran towards him. Screams, she could hear screams. Were they hers? She knelt. "Paul."

He was lying in a pool of blood. His eyes, once sharp and alive, now stared blankly.

"Paul!" Sirens. "Paul!"

He never replied. He was gone.

CHAPTER 29

July 1977

The funeral was a blur, just like the houses passing the window of the car. The wake, however, was still fresh in her mind. The hatred on Paul's mother's face, there for all to see, was directed at Millie. Even now she could remember her telling Paul he couldn't marry her. That he needed to find himself a good Catholic girl. Maybe she'd had a point. It would have saved all this heartache.

***

Connie dabbed at her eyes. She wasn't sorry to see the back of Paul, but just seeing Millie in such a state pained her.

She glanced at Duke. "We should be in the car with her."

"She's with Rosie and Scott, she may open up to them," he said.

She knew what he meant. Millie had shut down since Paul's death. She had hardly spoken, eaten, or slept. It worried them all.

"I hate him, for what he's done to her," she whispered.

"So do I, Con, but she loved him; we can't say anything bad about him, we need to support her."

***

Millie threw her keys on the side and headed to the lounge. She flopped down onto the sofa and sighed.

Rosie sat next to her. "Can I get you anything?"

"No."

"I'm gonna put the kettle on. Your mum and dad will be here soon. They were in the car after us."

"I don't want any more tea, Rose." She sighed.

Rosie nodded and made her way to the kitchen.

Today had been the hardest so far. Standing looking at Paul's coffin. It had been worse watching it lower into the ground. He was gone, and she was here, left on her own. A widow for the second time. The vision of his mother flashed through her mind. The woman was broken.

The church had been packed. A lot of big faces had been there to pay their respects. That was a fucking joke, they were more than likely there to pick over the bones, see what they could take. Tony had already warned her these same people would come for the businesses, especially the docks and scrapyard. She had to now be ruthless, just like Paul had been. That's why she'd put on a show, for their benefit. Duke, his brothers, and cousins had walked in with her. To show she was protected.

"Mil, are you okay, darling?" Connie sat and threw her arms around her.

Did it bring comfort? No.

It was two weeks since the hit-and-run. The memory of Paul's lifeless face was there every time she closed her eyes. Whoever was responsible hadn't been caught. The police assumed it was a business deal gone wrong. Gangsters killing gangsters. They would never put themselves out to catch the culprit. She knew that.

"Mum, I can't breathe." Millie pushed her away. "I'm gonna go and get changed." She spotted Duke coming in the door just when she reached the stairs. "Dad. Can I speak with you later, when everyone's gone?"

Duke nodded. "How are you feeling?"

"You know, numb, sad, angry, frightened, lonely. The list goes on." What she didn't tell him was that she felt confused.

"Don't ever feel lonely, Millie, I'll be right here whenever you need me, and you've nothing to be frightened about. I'll get you through this. You've got good people around you."

"I know." She continued up the stairs and opened the door to her bedroom.

She had slept in here since the accident. Rosie had moved in with her and now had her own bedroom. Connie had stayed the first few nights, but Millie had sent her home. She plonked herself down onto the bed. The new bed that Paul had bought for her. Paul Kelly, the love of her life, the man who had also ruined it. It was almost laughable.

She undid her dress and let it fall to the floor. Her swollen tummy was well hidden by her jacket. No one else knew she was pregnant, and that's how she wanted it kept. Opening the wardrobe, she stared at the row of neatly pressed suits. Another reminder. They had to go. In fact, everything had to go. She wanted to start afresh.

***

Duke poured himself a scotch and stood at the window. He was worried about Millie. She had been behaving erratically since the accident. One minute sad, the next behaving like nothing had happened. Was she in denial? Probably. But the thing he found the strangest was the fact she hadn't cried. Not one tear.

He turned when Millie entered the room. "How are you feeling?"

"I wish people would stop asking me that," she snapped.

"It's because people care," he countered. "Why don't you move back in with your mother and me? This place is too big."

"This is my home, Dad… it's the last place I was happy."

"Happy! When was that exactly?" He swallowed his temper, reminding himself to support her. "You weren't happy here, Millie, you left him. Remember?"

THE STEPNEY TAKEOVER

"I remember when he bought this place, when he carried me over the threshold." Her mind drifted off to a happier time.

It was Saturday the fifth of June. Paul stood in front of the house with his hands covering Millie's eyes. "Ready?" he asked her. This was one surprise he had struggled to keep quiet. Although he had told her about the house, he wouldn't let her see it. Not until today. The day they moved in.

"Yes." *She squirmed.* "Hurry up."

He took his hands away and waited for her reaction. She didn't disappoint him. He watched her mouth drop open and her eyes light up.

"Oh, Paul." *She laughed.* "It's beautiful."

Paul turned his attention to the large four-bedroom house. It had a double garage and spacious driveway. The tall iron gates at the front would give maximum security, and the trees would give privacy. "You like it then?"

"I love it," *Millie gasped.*

He opened the door to their new home and picked Millie up then carried her over the threshold. "Some traditions need upholding, although my back probably wouldn't agree. Christ, what did you have for breakfast?"

"Cheeky sod, I had bubble and squeak the same as you, only I had about a third of the amount you had." *Millie punched Paul's chest playfully.* "Put me down, I don't need you ending up in traction."

"Not a chance, Mrs Kelly." *He carried her up the stairs.* "We, my darling wife, need to consummate the bedroom."

She smiled. "He'd hurt his back, but he still insisted on carrying me in. I remember the nights we spent snuggled up on the sofa. I remember... I can't breathe."

Duke held his arms out, pleased that she ran into them. "Everything's gonna be okay. It just takes time."

"And do you think with time his mum will forgive me for not having Paul cremated?"

"It doesn't matter if she does or doesn't, you were his wife. It was your decision." He stroked her hair. "The only thing that matters now is you and the baby."

Millie pulled away, looked up at him, and smiled. "Thanks, Dad."

"What for?"

"For being here. I know I don't always show it, but I do appreciate you and Mum."

"We both love you and always will. Now let's go and see what your mother is up to. It smells like she's cooking."

"You go. I need a minute." She waited for Duke to leave then grabbed her bag and silently let herself out.

***

Millie entered the office of the club. Tony was there with all the men. They fell silent when they spotted her.

"Mil, you shouldn't be here." Tony's voice was sympathetic and annoying both at the same time.

"Shouldn't I?" she snapped while perching on the desk. "We have unfinished business. I want the bastard responsible for Paul's death, and I'm sure you do, too, so have you any leads?"

Tony shook his head.

"Do you think I'm stupid?" She glanced around the room, all faces on her. "I know he was seeing a woman. Nicky, was it?" She stared at Tony. "Her old man was released at the same time; my money's on him."

"What do you want us to do?" Tony asked.

"I want you to fucking kill him… and make sure it's painful." She stood and took a seat behind the desk. "One of you go and get a bottle of whiskey and glasses, I think we should toast my husband's memory."

When the drinks were poured, she handed each man a glass, her own filled with water. "To Paul," she announced.

"To Paul," they replied in unison.

"Now go and get the bastard."

Paul always tied up loose ends, and now she was in charge, she would do the same.

CHAPTER 30

It had been three weeks since Paul had been buried. Robbie McNamara had been dealt with, and his remains had been stuck in the smelter. Millie had got them to cut his tongue out first; she couldn't handle the screaming or cursing, and she certainly didn't want him talking. Then she had let Tony have his way.

It was now the end of July. Her clothes were too tight on her body; she had bought some larger sizes but tried to avoid maternity wear. Did anyone know she was pregnant, other than her parents, Rosie, and Scott? She had planned on keeping it a secret for as long as she could, but there was no denying the bulge of her belly.

She sat in the Portakabin at the scrapyard, the smell of engine oil making her queasy.

Tony entered and took a seat on the couch. "You wanted to see me?"

"I wanted to speak about all the businesses. I don't know how Paul did it, juggling all this and a life at home."

"I did tell you it would be hard." He pointed to the half-empty bottle of scotch on the filing cabinet. "May I?"

"Help yaself." She watched him closely. She liked Tony, he had been loyal to Paul, but would he be loyal to her?

He poured the drink and sat back. "The girls run themselves, all that's needed is a bit of muscle to keep the punters in line. The club again is easy when you've got staff you can rely on. That was the one thing Paul was good at, sniffing out good staff. The scrapyard and docks are a whole different ballgame. Paul's name kept any wannabes away, but Paul's gone, and you aren't…"

"Paul," she finished.

"Sorry, Mil, but that's the truth. They are gonna come for you."

"And what about your name?" She noticed the surprise in his eyes. Did he not think his name was enough?

"I'm just the hired help." He laughed.

"But what if you weren't?"

He stared back at her blankly. She would have to spell it out for him.

"What if I gave you a twenty percent share of the docks?"

Tony laughed. "You'd be willing to just sign over twenty percent?"

She stood and walked around the desk, leaning back on it so she was looking down on him. "I think you've earnt it. Your loyalty to Paul deserves to be rewarded." Millie could almost see Tony's brain cells whirring. "There's only one condition. You have my back if anyone comes for the scrapyard… What do you say?"

"You have an army of gypsies behind you, you don't need me."

"I might have muscle, but this is a different game, you know that. This is Paul's legacy. It's important to me, so…?" She raised a questioning eyebrow.

Tony grinned. "Deal."

"Good. I've had the paperwork drawn up. If anything happens to you, your share will pass back to me. If anything happens to me, however, my share will be put in trust for my child."

"Your child?" Tony's gaze dropped to her stomach. "To be honest, I did wonder."

"I would rather this stays between us, not many people know yet." Millie handed the paperwork to him. "Read it through, and if you're happy, sign on the dotted line. Right, I need to make tracks."

"Hang on, what about this place?" he asked. "I can be here if you need help, but to be honest, you need to put someone here full time."

"I've got this covered." She smiled and let herself out.

The dust caught in her throat when she marched to the motor. She wished she didn't have to come here, but now her days would consist of the same routine Paul once had. She climbed into her Range Rover and stared at the grab. It swung, clutching a car. The noise of crunching metal echoed around the place. Did she really want to keep this place? No. It was, after all, the place that had ended her marriage.

This place didn't end your marriage. Paul's greed did.

She wiped a tear from her cheek. The truth often hurt.

***

Millie sat at the kitchen table opposite Rosie, Scott to the side of her. "I think it's time we sorted out the missing patients, don't you?" She didn't have to look up to know they were both staring at her. "What?"

"Don't you think you're doing too much at the moment, running the business, keeping house, and now you want to go after the dodgy doctor. Mil, you've just buried your husband," Rosie said.

"That was twenty-one days, four hours…" She checked her watch. "And sixteen minutes ago."

"And the fact you know that shows you should slow down, Mil." Rosie looked at Scott for support.

"Why are you staring at each other? You should have eyes on me." Millie glared at Rosie. "The fact that I know how long it's been means I need to keep busier, maybe then I'd actually sleep at night."

"I think you're suffering from PTSD," Scott added.

Millie sighed. The world and its dog had an opinion on her wellbeing. "I appreciate you both care for me, but I need to get through this in my own way."

The door opened, and Duke came in followed by Connie.

"I thought you were going down to Kent to see baby Sherry?" The words almost caught in her throat. Fancy naming your child after yourself, vain cow.

"No, that's what you wanted us to do, Mil. We ain't leaving you until we know you're okay," Duke said. "Or unless you come with us. It's about time you met your little niece."

"I've got businesses to run, I can't just pack up and leave."

"D'ya know who you sound like? Paul Kelly. Putting business above family," Duke spat.

Millie took a sharp intake of breath. He may as well have punched her in the gut. "Thanks for that, Dad, you've made me feel so much better."

"Don't you think we've all had enough of watching you on your way to self-destruct?"

"Duke. Calm down, please." Connie grabbed his arm. "What your father means is you have a baby to consider. That should be your first priority."

Millie stood. "My first priority is making it through each day, and just so we are all clear, this baby is the only reason I'm keeping going." She turned and left the room. Stomping up the stairs, she climbed onto the bed. She was tired of trying to cope when in reality she knew she couldn't. It was always the same. What was the saying, one step forward, two steps back? She rolled over at the sound of approaching footsteps.

"Not now, Dad," she said.

"Yes, now." He drew the pillow away from her as she tried to bury her face. "You've shut us all out."

"You don't want to be in my head, trust me, it's a train wreck."

"Do you think any of us are coping any better?" He sighed. "Come back downstairs and let us help you."

"Fine." She rolled off the bed and followed him down. "I'm sorry, everyone. I just…"

Connie pointed to a chair and motioned for her to sit. "We know. I'll put the kettle on."

"I don't want any more tea, thanks. At this rate I'll end up looking like a teapot." Millie said.

"We'll need to go food shopping tomorrow, there's hardly anything to eat," Connie said to no one in particular.

Duke sat next to Millie. "So what have you been up to these last few weeks?"

Millie grimaced. Would he like to hear the gory details of what she'd had Tony do to Paul's murderer? How she'd watched while he had his tongue cut out, all his fingernails yanked, and then had a red-hot poker shoved in his left eye. And let's not forget the grand finale of tipping battery acid down his throat.

"Not a lot, just sorting work. Actually, I wanted to talk to you, Scott, about an exciting opportunity." She laughed. "I need you to be my eyes and ears when I'm not around. You'll obviously get a pay rise and a motor; actually, you can have mine, I'm gonna get a new one."

"What about Paul's motor?" Scott asked. "Surely you're not gonna leave that just sitting there, it's a waste."

"I want it scrapped."

"What!" Duke choked, his tea spraying the table.

"It's another reminder... I don't want anyone else to have it."

"See what I mean, you're not thinking straight." Duke stood. "I need a drink."

"So do I. In fact, there's nothing I'd like more that to get shit-faced right now, but I can't, can I?" Millie took a deep breath. "I'm trying to deal with everything in my own way."

"I know, but you may regret it further down the line. I don't want you to make any rash decisions," Duke said. "Act in haste, repent at leisure."

Jesus Christ, now he was giving her a sermon. "Okay, I'll move it into the garage for now." She had already tried, but when she'd climbed in, the smell of his aftershave was ingrained into every inch of it. When she closed her eyes it was like he was still there. But he wasn't, he was gone, and there was no point pretending otherwise.

It went quiet, the silence deafening. No one had anything else to say, obviously. These were the times she hated the most. Being stuck in a room full of people and feeling lonelier than she ever had in her life.

CHAPTER 31

Millie was up and out early the next morning. She had a full day planned. Check on all the businesses and then go and order a new motor. She stood on the quayside breathing in the salt air. It was a great day, she just wished she felt great, too. She turned and made her way to the office. Tony was already there, going through paperwork.

"Morning, Mil," he called as she walked through the door.

"Morning. How's things?"

"Things are bloody amazing. Work's coming in left, right, and centre. Never known it to be so busy."

She glanced at Paul's desk that was now hers. Taking a seat, she opened the top drawer and rummaged through.

"Are you looking for anything in particular, I might be able to help?" Tony asked.

"No, just looking. Why's this bottom drawer locked?" she asked.

Tony shrugged. "Fucked if I know."

She removed Paul's keys from her bag and fiddled around until she found a small key. She twisted it, and the lock clicked open. She took out the mountain of paperwork and started to read through. An envelope caught her attention. It had Paul's name scribbled on the front. Taking the letter out, she scanned the page. Her head spun. This couldn't be right. Who the fuck was Lily, and more to the point, why was she telling Paul she was expecting his baby? Millie checked the date of the letter. It was dated last year. Which meant he was screwing another woman while they were still together.

"Everything all right?" Tony asked, his eyes narrowing.

"Tell me everything you know about Lily." She sat back and stared at him.

"Lily?"

"Don't play dumb, Tone, it doesn't suit you."

Tony blew out slowly. "She was some woman Paul had taken a shine to."

"Where did he meet her?"

"I don't know. He kept her a secret as such. I only found out when I saw him coming out of a hotel with her... He loved you, Millie, she was just a bit of fun."

"He was supposed to have fun with me, not some tart." She shoved the letter into her handbag. "So she was pregnant?"

"Paul paid for her to get rid of it. She already had a couple of nippers and didn't want any more."

"And what about him, did he want it?" She swallowed down her nerves. Did she really want to know?

"No. He told her from the beginning that he was happily married. He paid for the abortion and bunged her some extra. As far as I know that was the end of it."

"Considering he kept her a secret, you seem to know a lot about the situation."

"He came to me for advice. I asked him what the most important thing was in his life. He said you. That was why he got rid of her."

"Got rid of her, do you mean like he did Nicky?" It pleased her to see the shock on his face. "That's right, Tone, I'm not stupid." She picked up her bag and stuffed the rest of the papers into it. "I know the lengths Paul will go to... I'll read this lot at home in case there's any more surprises."

***

Millie sat waiting for Scott. She had phoned him as soon as she'd returned home. When the door opened and Duke walked in, she couldn't help but show her disappointment.

"Well, that's a great welcome." He sighed. "Shall I go and come back again? You can pretend to be pleased to see me then."

"Sorry, Dad. I'm always pleased to see you, even if I don't seem it."

"So what's going on now?"

Millie handed him the letter she had placed on the table. "Read that."

After a few minutes, Duke's face hardened. "The no-good dirty bastard. It's lucky he's dead cos I would fucking kill him with my bare hands."

"You'd have to get in the queue. Cos I'd be first." She pushed her hair away from her face. "I keep thinking how could he, but then he's done a lot of things, hasn't he. This." She pointed to the letter. "Is just another to add to the list... you know, I think I hate him."

A knock came from the kitchen door. Scott stuck his head in. "All right, Mil, you wanted to see me?"

"Come in and take a seat." She beckoned.

"Did you know?" Duke rounded on Scott.

"Dad, no... Scott, read that letter and tell me what you know." She watched his eyes move as he read it line by line.

"Shit," was all he could manage to say.

"Did you know?" She glared.

"Don't be silly, Mil, I would've told you, you know that."

"Do you know anyone called Lily?" Duke asked.

"The only Lily I know works at the house for Gladys, I mean, for you, Mil." Scott glanced at her. "But wouldn't that be a bit close to home?"

"Mr fucking Invincible, Paul Kelly, wouldn't give a shit how close it was. What he wants, he takes. You can drive me there, come on." Millie stood, grabbing her bag and the letter.

***

Millie sat in the back as Duke insisted on coming. The journey was done in silence, and when they pulled up, Millie was the first to jump out. "I will do all the talking, you two keep out of this."

She unlocked the door and marched straight to the office. Gladys sat behind the desk scribbling on a piece of paper.

"Millie, what a lovely surprise. How are you doing, sweetheart?"

"Is Lily here?"

"She's in the kitchen waiting to start work, why?"

"My husband was having an affair with her... Did you know?"

Gladys shook her head. "Not for sure, which is why I never said anything."

"Go and get her." Millie waited for Gladys to leave, then she sat behind the desk. When Lily walked in she felt like crying. Paul had been shagging some brass. What did that say about her?

"You wanted to see me, Mrs Kelly?" Even her fucking voice was sickly sweet.

"It's been brought to my attention you've been shagging my husband." Millie watched her face turn red. That was all she needed. "You won't be working here anymore, get your stuff and fuck off. Oh, and if you're thinking of grassing the place, just remember, we know where you live. I wouldn't want anything to happen to your kids, funerals aren't cheap these days."

Lily paled, her eyes going wide. Was she going to faint?

"I told you to fuck off," Millie reminded her, satisfied when she walked out without a glance back.

"Really?" Duke stared at Millie. "You threatened to kill her kids?"

Millie stood and leaned towards him. "That wasn't a threat."

***

Duke slammed the mobile door. He kicked his dealer boots off and stormed to the front room. "Connie."

"Whatever's the matter?" she asked, jumping up.

"Our daughter, that's what's the matter. She's turning into Paul fucking Kelly," he fumed.

She handed him a beer. "Slow down and start from the beginning."

"She threatened to kill some tart's kids, all because Paul had an affair with her... You don't threaten kids, Con, it's an unwritten rule." He took a long gulp of his beer.

"Paul had an affair... Poor Millie, she must be devastated." Connie slipped her shoes on.

"What are you doing?" he asked in amazement.

"I'm going to see if she's all right." She headed towards the door and paused. "I can't believe he's gone and still causing her heartache."

Duke scratched his head. What was wrong with the fucking women in his life?

CHAPTER 32

It was the sixteenth of August 1977. The days all seemed to roll into one. Millie sat in the Portakabin reading the newspaper. She was waiting for Duke to turn up with Paul's motor. After finding out about his affair, she wanted rid of it. Rid of anything and everything that reminded her of him. Duke now agreed with her. Connie and Rosie had emptied the bedroom of Paul's clothes and personal belongings. Paul's jewellery had been given to his mother. She deserved to have something, even though she had birthed an arsehole. The decorators had made a start on her bedroom, and in the meantime, she was sleeping in another room.

The sound of Paul's car caught her attention, so she stood and walked to the door. As much as she fought it, the memory of his betrayal still hurt. The thought of him sleeping with another woman and then coming home and sleeping with her made her feel physically sick. He was still hurting her, even from the grave.

"Were shall I leave it?" Duke asked.

"Leave it there, one of the men will come and get it." She returned to her seat.

"Still seems a waste," Duke mumbled while stepping into the Portakabin.

"I heard that… It's gonna be stripped down and the parts sold. I told the men they can take what they want."

He nodded. "Are you ready to drop me back?"

"It's only four p.m. Why the hurry?"

"I don't like it here, too many memories."

She looked at Duke, surprised. "Really?"

"Why don't you sell it. This isn't a place for a woman, Mil. Look at it. It's dirty, it stinks. How can you enjoy being here?"

"I don't, but like you said before, I don't want to make any hasty decisions… turn the radio up." Millie stopped and listened. "Did they just say Elvis is dead?"

***

Rosie poured herself a glass of wine and sank back on to the sofa. The radio was on low, but she could still hear the Elvis song, 'Heartbreak Hotel'. That was a joke in itself. Her own relationship had gone tits up, and then Millie's, only Millie's had ended differently, and she was now in denial.

The noise of the door slamming made Rosie jump. "Mil, is that you?"

She came storming in and grabbed the wine bottle. "A small one won't hurt."

"It might." Rosie snatched it away from her. "What's happened now?"

Millie slumped onto the sofa next to her. "I thought I'd feel better once all his stuff had gone but I don't. If anything, I feel bitter."

"Because of his affair?"

"Affairs, plural." She turned to Rosie. "I found receipts in amongst that paperwork. Receipts for hotels, one of which was dated the week after we got married… How could he?"

"You need to stop thinking about it. He's gone and can't hurt you anymore."

"I thought that, too, and then I find out he's a serial cheat. Rose, we were at it like rabbits. Wasn't I enough for him?"

"You're wasting your time trying to work him out. What's done is done. You need to concentrate on you and the baby. Have you seen a doctor yet?"

"No." Millie kicked her shoes off and rested her feet on the coffee table.

"Don't you think you should?" Rosie asked. "You must be five or six months pregnant, and I know you think you're hiding it well, but even a blind man can see you're expecting."

"I'll phone tomorrow and make an appointment. Anyway, how was work?"

"Boring, I'm gonna look for another job." Rosie drained her glass. "Shall I put the kettle on?"

"Okay, I've only had fifty cups today, another one won't hurt." Millie paused. "Wait. Why don't you come and work for me?"

"I'm not a gangster, Mil, nor am I a prostitute."

"I've got enough of those already, I was thinking more like my assistant." Millie grinned. "Money's good, and there's plenty of perks."

Rosie laughed. "Like what?"

"Well, for one you get to spend more time with me, but seriously, I need people I can trust around me. When this baby arrives, I'll be out of the game for a few weeks. You and Scott are the only people I really trust, other than Duke and Connie."

"What would I have to do?"

"Come to work with me and I'll show you, you'll pick it up in no time... I've also roped Aron into joining the firm."

"Hello," Connie called from the kitchen.

"In here, Mum."

The clatter of bags followed. What had she bought now? The cupboard doors opened and shut. She'd obviously been food shopping.

Connie poked her head through the door a few moments later. "I've got a bacon pudding on the stove, I expect you both for dinner in an hour." She turned and left.

***

THE STEPNEY TAKEOVER

Millie sat at the table, the smell making her mouth water. Since finding out about Paul's infidelity she had lost her appetite, but now she was ravenous. "Can I do anything to help?"

"No. It's nearly done." Connie placed the cutlery on the table. "Your father wants a word, he's in the other room."

Millie sighed. She knew another lecture was coming. She smiled at Rosie. "Won't be long."

Duke was sitting on the edge of the armchair. His elbows rested on his knees, with hands clasped underneath his chin. He was deep in thought.

"You wanted to see me?"

His eyes flicked towards her. "Sit down, Millie."

"What's wrong?"

"I want to talk about the scrapyard."

"Not this again. I've already told you I don't want to do anything hasty." She sighed.

"Just hear me out." He held his hand up to silence her. "I know you're stubborn, but I think I've come up with a solution."

"I'm not selling," she said. "And the more you go on, the more I will dig my heels in."

"I know, that's why I've thought long and hard to find an answer. You won't be able to manage all these businesses with a baby. So why not take on a partner?"

"Sell half, you mean. I don't think I trust anyone enough to give up half the business. I like being the boss, and I know what you're gonna say, I'm just like Paul, well, maybe so. After all, they say you learn what you live."

Duke shook his head. "Do me a favour and think about it. If you take on the right partner, you won't have to worry about anyone trying to muscle in on the business."

She stared at Duke. She knew he was trying to help. More to the point, she knew she was a nightmare daughter and he worried about her. "Okay. I'll think about it. But I'm not making any promises."

***

The harsh ring of the phone jarred Mille awake. Switching on the bedside lamp, she glanced at the clock beside her. It was three-fourteen a.m. She grabbed the phone, a sinking feeling settling in the pit of her stomach.

"Millie, it's Andy from the yard." His voice was low, almost a whisper, but she still picked up on the urgency through the crackled phone line. "Someone's broken into the yard, poisoned me dog, the Portakabin's busted open. Whoever it was, they meant business."

"I'm on my way," she said, then slammed down the phone.

"Mil, what's going on?" Rosie asked as she entered the bedroom.

"Go back to bed, Rose, it's nothing for you to worry about." Millie threw the bed covers back and jumped out.

"Being woken at this ungodly hour is cause for concern. Where are you going?"

"Someone's broken into the scrapyard, I need to get over there." Millie picked up the phone and dialled Tony's number. He would have to meet her there as well.

She grabbed her clothes and started getting dressed. She needed a gun. Reaching under the bed, she took out a box. There, nestled inside, was Paul's gun.

"I'm coming, too." Rosie's eyes flicked to the gun, her expression one of horror. "Don't you think we should let your dad know?"

"No. He already wants me to sell the place, I'm not giving him any more ammunition." Millie continued to get dressed and slipped on her shoes.

"Why would someone break into the yard? Maybe it was just kids messing about, Mil."

"Kids don't poison dogs. If you're coming, you stay in the motor, understand?"

Rosie nodded. "Pretty low move, poisoning a dog," she mumbled.

Millie started the car while Rosie climbed in. She glanced at her before pulling out of the drive. "Are you sure you want to come? I don't know what I'm walking into."

"Which is why I'm not letting you go on your own."

They drove in silence through the empty streets. When they reached the scrapyard, the main gate was open ready for them.

Millie stopped the car and ran towards Andrew. "Are you okay? Did they hurt you?"

"I'm fine. I was in the hut when I heard a noise. By the time I found the dog they'd already broken in to the cabin. I'm sorry, Mrs Kelly."

"As long as you're okay, that's fine." She scanned the area. The tall piles of cars cast jagged shadows over the ground. It was eerie knowing someone could be hiding there, watching them.

Millie turned at the glare of headlights; it was Tony.

He drew up and ran towards them. "Have you checked inside, Andrew?"

"No, I didn't want to disturb anything in case you wanted to check first."

"Wait here, Mil, I'll have a look and check it out." Tony disappeared inside the Portakabin.

The door was splintered, the lock completely busted. They certainly wanted something from inside. Millie walked to the door and put her head in. Papers were scattered across the floor.

"This doesn't make any sense. I had gone through everything here, there was nothing of any value, written or otherwise."

"Well, they obviously wanted something." Tony's gaze fell on Rosie. They had briefly met at the funeral, but it wasn't the time or place to chat her up.

"I think whoever came here wanted to make their presence known, it's a scare tactic," Millie finally said.

"I think you're right. I did warn you about this. Maybe it's time you think about selling, before whoever did this…" He pointed around the room. "Ups their game."

"No. I won't be threatened. Whoever this is, I will find them and then they'll pay in blood." She turned to Andrew. "Tony will get a few of the boys here tonight to make this place secure. Rose, you ready?" Millie marched back to her motor.

"Are you okay, Mil?" Rosie asked, concern dripping from each word.

"Ya know, it's funny how this has happened right after Duke's asked me to sell the place. Maybe he was right." She glanced at Rosie. "But on a happier note, I noticed you and Tony giving each other the eye."

CHAPTER 33

It was packed in the doctor's. Millie sat there with Connie by her side, watching people saunter in and out. "I don't know why I'm here. The doctor didn't do any good last time."

"Things happen—"

"For a reason. I know." Millie rolled her eyes then glanced at her watch. She was meeting Tony later at the scrapyard. He had suggested beefing up security. Rosie had been keen when she'd told her. There was definitely a spark between those two, and Rosie would be seeing a lot more of him once she started working for her.

"Mrs Kelly."

Millie entered the doctor's room and took a seat.

"And what can I do for you, Mrs Kelly?"

"I'm pregnant."

"Have you done a test?"

It was at that point Millie stood and undid her coat. She pointed to her ever-growing bump. "Do I need to?"

The doctor's eyes bulged. "You look almost full term. Have you registered the pregnancy?"

"No, that's why I'm here. I'm about six months, give or take a week."

"Can you lie on the couch, I'll have a feel." The doctor pulled Millie's blouse up and after rubbing his hands together, to warm them, he held them to her stomach, moving them around and pressing firmly in places.

Millie noticed the frown spread across his face. "What's wrong?" She swallowed down her fear. "Is something wrong? Tell me."

"No, nothing's wrong. I'd like you to go to the hospital for an ultrasound. As you haven't been seen by a doctor, I think it will be good to see how many weeks along you are."

"Do I need to book?"

"I'll phone, they will see you today." He washed his hands and scribbled on her notes.

"And you're sure there's nothing wrong with the baby?" she asked hesitantly.

"I'm quite sure. I will get all the relevant paperwork done this afternoon." He looked up briefly. "Now off you go."

***

Tommy Lee sat on a bar stool next to his brothers, John Jo and Sean Paul, in a little boozer in Romford. "What did you want to see me about?"

"We've got a job lined up. Pay's good. Thought you might be interested," John Jo replied.

"Doing what?"

"Security for a scrapyard." Sean Paul added.

"Now why did yous think I'd be interested in a fecking job like that?" Tommy Lee shook his head.

"Because of who it's for, brother." John Jo grinned. "You remember Millie; wasn't you sweet on her, despite me warning you off?"

Tommy Lee's heart rate increased. "I'm all ears."

"Turns out her old man was killed in a hit-and-run, so she's left running his kingdom. Now some arsehole is playing games with her. That's where we come in. She needs us to run the place and guard it."

"She contacted you?"

"No, a man called Tony did, that was Paul's right-hand man... So what do ya say, you in?" John Jo raised a questioning eyebrow.

Tommy Lee rubbed his chin. This wasn't his normal line of work, but maybe it could be fun. "Count me in, boys."

***

Millie lay on the couch, dazed. This could not be happening.

"Here, drink this." Connie placed a cup on the coffee table.

"Oh great, another cup of tea. Just what the doctor ordered." Millie pulled herself up and placed her legs on the floor. "I don't understand how this has happened."

"I'm sure you know about the birds and the bees. Think I'll make an Irish stew for dinner, you'll definitely need to keep your strength up now." Connie fluffed up a pillow and shoved it behind Millie's back.

"How am I gonna cope?" The click of the door drew her attention. "Is that you, Rosie?"

"Yes," she called. "I've officially left Woolworths." Popping her head into the room, she smiled. "I'm just gonna get changed."

"I'll make you a cuppa," Connie said.

"Aww, lovely, thanks, Connie."

Millie watched the pair of them, almost smiling. Connie with her fucking 'tea solves everything' attitude and Rosie with her new lease of life. It was refreshing. Millie turned her attention back to her own problems. Tony had new men coming in, who she didn't know but she would make it her priority to meet them tomorrow. Tony said Paul had used them before and they were trustworthy, but she would decide if they were or weren't. After all, she was the one paying them.

Rosie came in and sat on the armchair. "So what's happened in my absence?"

"China has declared a tea emergency because my mother is using up all their stocks, and I have not one but two buns in the oven."

Rosie sat with her mouth open.

"I heard that." Connie placed the newly made cup of tea on the table. "I'm going to go get dinner started. I'll let you know when it's ready."

"Thanks, Mum."

"Yeah, thanks, Connie." Rosie refocused on Millie. "Two?"

"That's what the scan showed. Two heartbeats... I don't understand, though. I've got twin brothers. It normally skips a generation, so my child would be more likely to have twins, and I don't think there's twins in Paul's family... How the fuck am I going to manage two babies?"

"What about Tommy Lee's family?"

"I don't know anything about him, Rose. It was a bit of fun, nothing more."

"But you liked him?" Rosie continued.

"Look, he's gone, probably still abroad. It was a fun couple of dates, that's all. I'm not interested in men, I haven't got the time or energy to waste."

"Okay, okay, what will be will be. Now what's our first job tomorrow?"

"Meeting Mr Lover-Lover at the scrapyard." Millie smiled.

"Who?"

"Tony." She winked.

CHAPTER 34

Millie pulled into the scrapyard and stopped the motor outside the Portakabin. "You all right, Rosie? Not nervous?"

"Will you stop going on, and do not embarrass me in front of him," she said.

"You took ages doing your makeup this morning. I guess you want to leave a good impression." Millie laughed.

Rosie rolled her eyes. "I mean it."

"Fine, come on, let's get this over with." She climbed out of the motor and waited for Rosie to join her. "Ready?"

"As I'll ever be… bloody hell it stinks here. How do you cope with the smell?"

"You get used to it after a while." Millie stepped up into the Portakabin and froze.

Tommy Lee was perched on the edge of her desk. He smiled at her before his attention dropped to her bump.

Shit.

"Sorry I'm a bit late," she told them before sitting at the desk. "I take it Tony has filled you in?" She kept her eyes on the paperwork in front of her, until she heard him speak.

His Irish accent was soft. "We know what we need to do."

She glanced up at him. "Good." He had caught her totally off-guard. So much so she felt vulnerable. "Tone, can you show them around, please. Rose, perhaps you should go, too, so you know what happens here." She refocused on the papers and didn't look up until the door closed. She let out a long, slow sigh.

"Is there anything you want to tell me?" Tommy Lee hadn't left. Instead, he stood by the door.

Oh fuck.

"About?"

"Don't play games, Millie, you're having a baby. Am I the father?"

"That's no concern of yours, but if you must know, it's Paul's. Now you're here to do a job, so if you don't mind..." She pointed to the door.

He lingered for a minute but eventually left. Her heart thumped. She fanned her face, the heat radiating from it like volcanic lava. She had just lied. Truth was, she still didn't know who the father was. Shouldn't she have been honest?

Every child deserves to know where it came from.

"I know."

Shit.

Walking to the window, she watched them chatting. Rosie was fixated on Tony. When Millie allowed herself to look at Tommy Lee, he was staring straight back at her.

Holy shit.

He was heading back towards the Portakabin. She calmly took a seat behind the desk when the door reopened. He stood there, with his hands in his pockets.

"We've got the measure of the job. I think it's best if you stay away. A woman in your condition shouldn't be around a place like this." His voice had turned cold.

***

Rosie was in the bathroom getting tarted up for her first date with Tony. Millie had teased her all the way home.

"Make sure you take some protection, Rose, you don't want to end up like me." Millie laughed, but she didn't really find it funny.

She had bare-face lied to Tommy Lee. Didn't he deserve to know the truth? Didn't he deserve the choice? But they might not be his, then what? Get accused of playing him along? No, this was best for everyone, at least until she was sure.

The only thing she could wish for, which would make her life easier, was that he finished the job and then buggered off abroad again.

Coward!

She did wonder if the little voice in her head was right. Was she being a coward? Shouldn't she at least have explained her situation? No. Now wasn't the time. With everything else going on, she could only contend with one problem at a time.

But what about the twins?

"They ain't a problem," she mumbled. "They're a blessing."

Rosie walked into the bedroom, dressed up to the nines. "What d'ya think?"

"I think Tony is a very lucky man. Where's he taking you?"

"I have no idea. Knowing my luck it will be the Wimpy."

Millie laughed. "Lucky the Wimpy's closed then."

"Will you be okay on your own?" Rosie asked. "I can always cancel."

"Oh no you don't, you are not using me as an excuse. Come on, let's go downstairs, he should be here soon." Millie waddled down the stairs and flopped back on the sofa. "I think a car's just pulled up. Now go and have fun."

Once Rosie was gone, Millie was left with the blissful sound of silence. "Perfect."

"What is?"

"Dad, I didn't hear you come in." Was it too much to ask for five minutes? "Did you want something?"

"No. I came to see my daughter, is that a crime?" He had that look in his eye, one that meant she was in for a bollocking.

***

Tommy Lee sat in the Portakabin with his feet up on the desk and his hands behind his head. John Jo had poured them all a drink of the scotch Millie had kindly left them.

Millie? She had played on his mind all day. He could have sworn she was lying when she'd said the baby was Paul's. Had he been wrong about her? Was she just another tart looking for a bit of rough? Why did it bother him, though?

A loud crash had him jumping up and running out of the door before John Jo had even put his glass down. He snuck around the edge of the yard, listening for any telltale signs of intruders. He wanted to find out how they had got in.

"Anything?" John Jo whispered.

"Shh." Tommy Lee held a finger to his lips.

The squeaking of a door caught his attention. He slowly moved towards it. Yanking it open, he stared down at two eyes that caught the faintest glow of moonlight. He smiled when the fox shot off between his legs.

He marched back towards the Portakabin with his brother in tow. "That crash wasn't caused by the fox."

Sean Paul stood outside, scratching his head. "Whoever that was then, they've gone."

"I'm more interested in how they got in here. Go grab me a torch, I'm gonna check the walls," Tommy Lee ordered.

"Don't you think it would be better to check in the morning?" Sean Paul asked.

"I want to look now. They may not have had time to cover their tracks properly, and anyhow, I doubt I'll be sleeping now." Tommy Lee made his way back to the shed. He shone the torch up the wall, looking for a light switch. He flipped it, and the place lit up.

John Jo stood beside him.

"You take that side, I'll meet you the other end." It was a large shed, full of copper wire that had been stripped. There were old oil drums full of the stuff.

"Over here," John Jo said.

"What is it?" Tommy Lee asked, crouching next to his brother.

"These boards are loose." John Jo pulled one away. "You can get straight out into the street."

Tommy Lee took a closer gander. "The screws have been undone from the inside... It's got to be someone who works here." He stared around the shed. "We need to fix these back up, then put something in front of it that can't be moved."

"Where are you going now?"

"I'm going round the other side, I want to know why there's no fence." Tommy Lee opened the small gate that was inside the entrance gate. He marched along the road until he came to a gap. He studied it; the wire had been cut away. Whoever had broken in hadn't had the time to roll it back into place. There was an old cable tie hanging from the top.

He now had the how, he just had to figure out the who and why.

***

Millie lay on the sofa waiting for Rosie to return home. She glanced at the clock. Well, there was no way she'd be coming home now. It was gone two-thirty a.m. At least one of them was having fun. She hoisted herself up and turned the light off then climbed the stairs.

Duke's words still smarted. She could understand his anger at her not telling him about the break-in at the scrapyard. She should have, but Tommy Lee shouldn't have taken it upon himself to grass her up. What sort of a man did that?

One who maybe cares about a pregnant woman being put in danger.

"No. One who wanted to get his own back. Fucking arsehole." She pulled the covers back and slid between the sheets. As she closed her eyes and drifted off, it was at that particular moment the twins decided to have a game of football.

CHAPTER 35

Millie sat at the table sipping her tea, the bags under her eyes testament to the sleepless night she'd just had. Connie walked in just as Millie yawned.

"You shouldn't be having late nights, you need your rest."

"Try telling your grandchildren that." Millie huffed. "How come you're round so early?"

"Me and your father are driving down to Kent to see Jasper and the baby. I just wanted to check it's okay with you."

"You don't need to ask permission, Mum, go, I'll be fine. Rose should be back soon, then I'll be off to work," Millie informed her.

"Didn't she come home last night?" Connie asked, concern written all over her face.

"No, Mum, Rosie now has a life. Anyway, send Jasper my love and give the baby a kiss from me. Oh, hang on a minute, I've got something for her." Millie went upstairs and brought down the giant teddy that Paul had bought. "Here you go."

"You do know they live in a tourer. Where on earth are they supposed to put that?"

"I don't care, Mum, just take it." She waved her off then searched for her shoes. She wasn't going to wait any longer for Rosie, she wanted to get cracking so she could spend the afternoon relaxing.

First stop would be the docks, then she'd nip over to the scrapyard. She wouldn't have anyone telling her to stay away, least of all Tommy fucking Lee.

***

The docks were a hub of activity when she arrived. Her men were unloading a small boat, the cargo piled on the quayside. She stumbled around it, her belly getting in the way.

"Sorry, Mrs Kelly, I'll get that moved," one of the men said while grabbing her arm to keep her upright.

She nodded but didn't answer. Her mind was still on the scrapyard. When she entered the office, Tony was sitting there with Rosie on his lap.

"Not interrupting, am I?"

"Mil—"

"Mil what?" she snapped while taking a seat behind her desk. "I was waiting for you this morning. You could have had the decency to let me know you wouldn't be coming to work today."

"I'm sorry." Rosie stood.

"Don't blame her, I was the one who dragged her here. What's with the moody attitude?" Tony asked.

"As I understand it, I still employ both of you, so a little common courtesy wouldn't go amiss."

"Duly noted," Tony agreed.

Millie glared at him. People were taking the piss. Paul was gone, and so was the respect she'd once had from the men. Rosie she could forgive, her life had been shit up until now, but everyone else needed to know she was now the boss, and as such, show her the respect she deserved.

"There are a couple of cheques that need signing while you're here," Tony began. "One for the skipper and one for the cargo."

She reached into her bag and pulled out the cheque book. Paul had always made it look legal. That way there were never any comebacks from the taxman.

"Where's the invoice?"

Tony handed it to Rosie so she could pass it over.

"Thanks." Millie studied it. "This is more than last time."

"Now Paul's gone they've changed their terms."

"Oh, have they now." Millie stood and made her way out. She motioned to the skipper. "You can take this lot back. Boys, reload it."

The skipper's face hardened. "Mrs Kelly, we had a deal."

"That's right, we did, but seeing as you've taken it upon yourself to change the terms, deal's off. Now load your shit up and fuck off."

She stormed back to the office, slamming the door behind her.

"What the fuck are you doing?" Tony yelled. "Paul built this business, and you've come in and ruined it within the space of five minutes."

Before she replied, the door opened, and the skipper stepped in.

"Mrs Kelly, you can't—"

"Oh, but I can, and I just did. You all think because I'm a woman you can walk all over me and take the piss, well, let me remind you I was Paul Kelly's wife, I know how he worked, what he would do, and more to the point, how he would do it. So like I said, take your cargo and do one... and as for you, Tony, don't you ever fucking shout at me again, cos it won't end well."

***

Millie smiled as she pulled into the scrapyard, content that she'd got the upper hand on Tony and the skipper. This was what she needed to do, assert her dominance.

She parked up next to the office. When she entered, Tommy Lee was sitting in her chair at the desk, his face glaring up at her.

"You're in my chair." She frowned.

"I thought I told you not to come back here," he said through gritted teeth.

"I wanted to see if you've made any progress." She threw her bag down onto the desk. "So have you?"

"It's only been twenty-four hours."

THE STEPNEY TAKEOVER

"So nothing's happened. Great." She sauntered to the window and stared out. The men were all busy working. The presence of these three Irishmen had them nervous, she knew that. That was part of the plan. "I don't expect anyone will try anything now they know you're here."

"Someone did—" he began.

"So something has happened. Why didn't you say?"

He sighed. "I think it's someone who works here, trying their luck."

"What do you mean, trying their luck?"

"From what I can make out, someone's been sneaking in and taking the copper wire from the shed. I found a length of it on the path outside when we disturbed them last night."

"Oh great, my own employees stealing from me." She threw her hands up in the air. For every victory she achieved, she was met with another problem. "Do you think you can find out who?"

"And what do you want me to do if I find them?" he asked.

She thought for a moment. What *did* she want him to do? "I don't know, what would you do?"

"Find out why he was stealing from you. There may be a good reason for it."

"A good reason for it? I want my employees to respect me, not think they can get one over on me just because I'm a woman."

"That's not respect you want, Millie, you want them to fear you. Is that what you learnt from your husband?"

"Maybe." She walked to the sofa and sat. "You're being paid to do a job, not to question me."

"Well, I think it's time for you to stick your job, I'm done."

"What are you doing?" Her gaze followed him as he grabbed his belongings.

"I told you, I'm done." He pushed the door open then turned to her. His eyes narrowed. "If you want respect, sometimes leniency is better than punishment."

***

It was late when Duke and Connie arrived home. Connie had the best time having cuddles with baby Sherry. Duke, on the other hand, had spent the entire time worrying about Millie.

"Millie's light's on, I'm just gonna check on her," Duke said to Connie. She was getting ready for bed.

"Shall I come?" she asked.

"No, I'll only be five minutes." He trudged over to the house. The kitchen door was unlocked. He would warn her about that. Two women living in a house with no men should keep the doors locked at night.

"Mil?"

"I'm in here." She sat on the floor surrounded by baby clothes. "I was just sorting this lot out." She smiled.

"You seem in a better mood."

"I'm trying to keep busy, and I don't know how much longer I've got, so…"

"Where's Rosie?"

"Out with Tony, she should be back soon." Millie glanced up at him. "I'm sure you haven't come over here to make small talk. Say whatever it is that you've got on your mind."

"Have you thought any more about the scrapyard?"

"No." She frowned. "I've got enough on my plate at the moment."

"You're not gonna be able to pay the Ward brothers indefinitely. What happens then when somebody else comes for it?"

"Why are you so worried about the scrapyard, shouldn't that be my job?" Millie shoved the clothes back into the bag. "I know you care about me, and I appreciate it, but please let me sort this and stop worrying." She stood. "I think Rosie is back. I'll come over and see you in the morning, when we've both had a good night's sleep."

Duke wrapped his arms around her. "Okay, I'll see you in the morning and, Mil, don't ever tell me to stop worrying about you. When the chavvies are here, you'll realise that you never stop."

She waved Duke off then stood in the doorway and waited for Rosie. She burst through the door with a big smile on her face.

"I needn't ask how tonight went, judging by your smile," she said.

"It was great. I'm gonna go up and shower. I'll see you in the morning and tell you all about it." Rosie turned and swiftly ran up the stairs.

Millie picked the bag of clothes up, then went and checked the doors were locked before taking herself up to bed. She had been hoping for a distraction. Hearing about Rosie's fun would've taken away her own miserable problems, but that wasn't to be.

After cleaning her teeth, she climbed into bed. Tommy Lee seemed to be her brain's choice of torture tonight. The not-so-pleasant conversation they'd had just before he'd grabbed his stuff and told her to stick her job.

Had she really turned into a female version of Paul?

CHAPTER 36

It was now October, and with only a month to go until the twins were due, Millie was finally beginning to take things a bit easier. Mainly on account of the overwhelming tiredness. Duke and Aron now ran the scrapyard for her with a couple of other family members. That kept all the men in line. Duke said he'd give her six months to either sell or find a partner. Nothing made you feel better than being put under pressure.

Today Scott had taken Rosie to check on all the businesses; she was becoming a pro.

Millie didn't feel great on account of looking like a big fat blob and finding herself tiring quickly. She didn't tell them that, though, it was bad enough Connie fussing around her.

She lowered herself into the bath, the warm water covering her body. She felt relaxed, maybe a little too relaxed, when she sank deeper. She swirled her fingers through it, making small ripples on the surface.

Then it happened.

Her belly tightened, the pain commenced. This pain was different and not like the Braxton Hicks she had been experiencing; they had been mild in comparison. She sat up straight when the pain subsided, the sudden movement sloshing the water out of the bath.

"Fuck."

She reached for the towel, pulling herself up to stand. Another pain hit, and she stood leaning against the wall. Climbing out of the bath, she stumbled towards her bedroom and reached for the phone, then, dialling the number, she waited for Connie to answer.

"Mum, it's happening. Call a—" But the phone had gone dead before she'd finished the sentence. She stared blankly at the receiver then placed it down.

"Millie!" Connie called.

"I'm in here," she answered while drying her whale-like body. "Quick, I need to get dressed and get to the hospital, something's wrong."

"I'll call an ambulance," Connie said calmly. "And nothing's wrong, you're in labour."

"But it's too early."

"Twins normally come early, now stop worrying." Connie picked up the phone and began to dial.

Millie continued dressing while her mum was on the phone. She had no sooner put her shoes on than the sound of a siren caught her ear. "That was quick."

"Come on, time is of the essence," Connie warned. Helping Millie downstairs, she threw open the front door just as the ambulance pulled in.

The journey was a blur. The contractions were coming every four or five minutes, and although the ambulance man assured her there was plenty of time to get to the hospital, Millie doubted him.

"Oh my God, this fucking hurts," she blurted out.

"Millie, stop swearing," Connie chastised.

"This really isn't the time to tell me off, Mother, oh fuck." Millie screamed. "Why's it hurt so fucking much?"

She flopped back in between the contractions and glanced at Connie who was sitting opposite her. "I can't do this."

"Yes you can. We're here, Mil." Connie stood back while they wheeled her out.

She felt every fucking bump on the path while they took her into the hospital, then along to the delivery room.

"Let's get—" the midwife started, but Millie was out of the wheelchair and on the bed like she was on speed.

"I need to push," she yelled.

"I can see the head. You made it here just in time," the midwife announced.

Another contraction hit. Millie pushed, then, breathing heavy, she closed her eyes. "I'm tired."

"Millie, I want you to pant. Short, sharp breaths," the midwife told her.

"I'm not a fucking dog."

"Millie!" Connie gasped.

"Mum, if you're gonna keep moaning you can go and wait outside." Millie grunted. "Oh God, I need to push again."

"Millie, do not push, you need to pant, like they showed you in your antenatal classes."

Millie looked at her blankly. "What antenatal classes?"

"Oh God," Connie whispered.

"I need to pushhhhhhhh." And push she did. She felt the gush of the baby leaving her body. She lifted her head at the sound of a gentle cry.

"You have a son, Millie." The midwife beamed. Then she took him away.

"Where are you going with my baby?"

"It's okay, we need to clean him up. The nurse is going to weigh him and make sure he's healthy, and now we get to do that all over again."

"It's coming." Millie groaned; the next contraction hit. "I need to push."

"That's it, you're doing well, here comes the baby's head."

"Oh God, why does it hurt so fucking much?" She flopped back. "I need to push."

"Pant, Millie, please."

"This is fucking ridiculous, can't you give me something for the pain?"

"It's a bit late now, young lady, in a couple of minutes your second baby will be here. Now when the contrac—"

The second baby slid from her body, and she relaxed. "Oh, thank fuck."

"Another boy," the midwife joyously called. "Twin boys. Have you got names for them?"

"No, wait, I've got another contraction, oh shit, not another baby, what's going on?" she cried.

"It's the afterbirth. Once that's all out, you're done." The midwife examined her belly, squeezing it to help it come away. "There now, how would you like a cuddle with your babies?"

Once she was propped up, Millie's gaze fell on the two tiny bundles the nurse and midwife were holding.

"This is your firstborn, five pounds twelve ounces, that's a very good size, and this pickle is five pounds eight ounces."

Millie held them, one in each arm, studying them closely. Both blue-eyed with a few wispy curls of dark-blond hair. She knew parents were biased, but they were the most beautiful babies she had ever seen. Now she finally knew what love at first sight meant.

CHAPTER 37

Millie returned home three weeks later. The first thing she did was soak in a nice hot bath. She scrubbed the hospital smell off her body until it was raw. After her bath, she wrapped her robe around her and descended the stairs. Connie fussed over the twins like an old mother hen. Duke sat watching the horse racing on television. It was like she hadn't been away.

"You really need to name the boys, Mil, you can't call them One and Two forever," Connie complained.

"I will, Mum, when I decide what to call them. It's harder than I thought."

"Are they gonna be Kellys or Wards?" Duke added.

"Don't start, Dad… Mum, can you watch the twins tomorrow for a couple of hours? I want to show my face at work." Millie waited for the bollocking from Duke to follow.

"You've just got out of hospital, and may I remind you, these boys are your responsibility not your mother's."

"Fine, I'll get Rosie to babysit." She walked over to Number One and swooped him up in her arms. "You don't mind Mummy popping out, do you?" She stared at his button nose. "You are just the cutest twins ever." She kissed his soft cheek and placed him back down. She then moved on to Number Two and did the same to him.

"I'll look after them if your dad goes with you," Connie replied.

"Don't I get a say in this?" He groaned.

"No," Connie said. "You know what our daughter is like, she'd probably take them with her."

"Fine, I'm going back to the trailer so I can watch me racing in peace." He stood, bent over the cot, and kissed both babies and then left.

"Thanks, Mum."

"Don't thank me. Your father's right, Millie, they are your responsibility. Now what do you fancy for dinner later?"

***

Finn sat at the bar. He had a new barmaid working. Sharron, his main barmaid, was teaching her the ropes, but he wanted to keep an eye on her. The men loved this new one, on account of the massive pair of knockers she had, but she seemed a bit slow to him. Always getting the change wrong. If she didn't start to improve he would have to give her the old heave ho. He thought back to when Millie had started. She'd taken to it like a duck to water.

The knock came earlier than he'd expected. He had to give her ten out of ten for eagerness.

"You're early," he moaned; he didn't want to look pleased.

"Better to be early than late," she said. "My name's Millie by the way."

"You'd better come in then, Millie." He stepped back and ushered her in. She looked so young. "Go and put the kettle on, you may as well make yourself useful. It's just through there."

She emerged twenty minutes later with the cups and handed one to him.

"You're gonna have to speed up a bit if you want to work here. That should have only taken you five minutes." He took a sip. "At least you make a good cuppa."

"I couldn't help but notice the washing up needed doing, so I did it, I thought it would save you the job as I'm working here," Millie said.

"And that's another thing, you do the jobs I tell you to do. Understand?"

"Yes, sir, sorry." She turned away, her eyes watering. "So where shall I start?"

"That box of mixers need to go in that fridge there, and make sure you keep them in straight lines. I'll open up." Finn sauntered to the door and unlocked it. Next, he moved to the fire and placed another log on it. He knew she was sizing him up.

"What should I call you? Boss?"

"My name's Finn. If you've finished putting the mixers away, you can wipe the optics over. Now it won't be busy this lunch time, so you can manage on your own."

"What?"

"Millie, you have worked in a pub before?"

"Not exactly." Her face reddened.

"Jesus fecking Christ... Have you any experience at all? With anything?" he asked her.

"Not pub wise, no." Her face reddened even more.

"How do you expect to work in a pub if you don't know how? What happens if there's trouble, can you even defend yourself?"

"I don't need to defend myself. I can take a good hiding, better than anyone. Look, I'm sorry I've wasted your time." Millie grabbed her bag and coat then headed towards the door.

"So you're a quitter, too," he called after her.

"I'd rather walk out now than listen to another person telling me how useless I am."

Finn felt like he'd been punched in the gut. "Whoa, kid. Where did all that come from?"

"It's come from the way I've been treated most of my life."

"Stop, Millie. Come back." He motioned. "Do you know why you're here?" he asked her.

"Because I asked for a job."

"Yes, and I told you to get lost, but you didn't. You persevered. That's why you're here. You wouldn't take no for an answer. That's a good attitude to have, child, it will see you through life. If you want experience, you'd best get back behind the bar."

THE STEPNEY TAKEOVER

And the rest, as they say, was history.

He smiled at the memory. Just look at her now, two little nippers and running Paul Kelly's kingdom. How times had changed. His smile dropped. He'd heard through the grapevine someone was going to muscle in on her businesses. He didn't know who, and it could just be idle chitchat, but he'd best warn her. He necked the last of his pint and trudged out to his motor.

***

Millie settled the twins down after bathing and feeding them. Now she was going to sneak a crafty wine, just the one. She couldn't get pissed now she was a mother. She descended the stairs quickly and made her way to the fridge. There was a half-empty bottle that Rosie had opened. Grabbing it, Millie poured herself a large glassful. The first sip was heaven.

"Mmmm, now that is good." After shoving the bottle back into the fridge, she flopped down onto the sofa. "This is the life." Then her peace was shattered when a knock came from the door.

Shit.

She opened the door and smiled. "Finn, what a lovely surprise, it's good to see you, come in." She motioned. "What can I get you to drink?"

"I'll have a small scotch, thanks," he replied. "This isn't a social call, Mil, and I know you've just come out of hospital, but…"

"But what?" she asked. "You're starting to scare me."

"Maybe Duke should be here."

"No, you've come here to tell me something, so tell me," she demanded.

Finn scratched his head. "I've heard through the grapevine, and please bear in mind people talk shit when they're on the sauce, but just in case there is something to it, I thought I'd better tell you."

"Finn, just spit it out."

"There's whispers of some big shot going after your businesses. Now Paul's dead, they think you're an easy target." He sighed. "Sorry, Mil, I know it's bad timing and not the type of surprise you were expecting."

"The only thing that surprises me is that they've left it so long, but it makes sense. There's been trouble at the club every weekend, to the point where I could lose my licence, and someone's tried it on at the scrapyard."

Finn rubbed the back of his neck. "Jaysus, Millie, you need to tell Duke, he'll know what to do." He drank his scotch in one. "I'm sorry, but I need to get back. I've got a new barmaid, and I'm scared she'll bankrupt me if I'm not back soon." He moved towards the door then stopped. "It goes without saying, I'll keep my ear to the ground, but if you need me in the meantime, just give me a shout."

"Thanks, Finn, I appreciate it. I'll pop in soon to see you." She waved him off then returned to her wine.

She remembered Tony's words: *They'll come for you, Mil.* Well, they'd taken their sodding time. She knew she should tell her dad, but it would only give him more ammunition to insist she sold up. She had three more months of him running the yard, that meant three months to sort this out.

Shit.

CHAPTER 38

Kelly's nightclub was an oasis of life, buzzing with music and laughter. Rosie stood by the bar, fixated on the crowd. Tony was in there somewhere, looking for some toerag who'd got into an altercation with one of Millie's bar staff.

The last few weeks' hassle seemed to spring up from nowhere. Tony had told Rosie to keep it to herself and not worry Millie, and although Tony was more than capable of taking care of himself, she worried about him. The rough characters who had been showing up lately were from out of the area. They were intent on causing problems for the club. She could see it worried him. Glancing across the dance floor, she spotted him. He stared at a tall, rough-looking man who stared back.

She pushed her way through the crowd to try and stop the fight that was brewing. However, before she reached them, the man shoved Tony in the chest, almost knocking him off his feet. With a speed that surprised her, Tony had the man by the collar and frogmarched him out. The crowded dance floor parted as the people nervously backed away.

It had never been like that in here. Rosie had always felt safe, but now, she wasn't sure. She followed Tony to the back of the club where he pushed the man to the floor.

"You're gonna regret this." The man grinned.

"Then I'd better do something worth regretting," Tony said.

"Tony, stop," Rosie shouted.

But Tony seemed focused on one thing and one thing only.

Lifting his foot, he stomped on the man's hand hard enough to hear the bones break.

Rosie's hand flew to her mouth.

The man, clutching his broken fingers, let out a gasp of agony. "Is that the best you can do?" he spat.

"Tony, no," she continued. "He's goading you."

Before Tony could reply, two police officers rounded the corner. "Rose, call Millie."

***

Millie rolled her eyes when the phone rang. She had just put the twins down and was looking forward to an early night herself.

"Hello."

From the other end of the phone came Rosie's panicked voice.

Millie listened, taking it all in. "I'll be there shortly."

She then phoned her solicitor for Tony, then her mum to babysit, and finally dressed, ready to leave as soon as her parents arrived.

"What's happening?" Duke grunted while running in.

"Tony's been arrested. I need to get to the club." She turned to her mum. "The twins have just been fed, they shouldn't wake until roughly midnight." She grabbed her bag and left with Duke following.

"Are you going to tell me what's going on?" he asked indignantly.

"Get in, Dad, please." Pulling open the door, she climbed in. "Tony broke some arsehole's fingers, that's as much as I know. I need to speak to Rosie and find out what's going on." She had a nervous knot in the pit of her stomach. What with Finn's warning, the attack on the scrapyard, and now this, things weren't looking as good as she thought.

They drove the rest of the way in silence, her thoughts on Tony. If he went down, the docks would be easy pickings, too. Could she tell Duke? She glanced at him. His face was set like stone. She knew she had to, but he was going to go ballistic.

She parked at the back of the club, almost holding her breath as she let herself in.

"Rosie," she called, while heading to the office.

Rosie sat on the sofa, her eyes red, her cheeks tearstained. "Mil, they've taken him."

She sat next to her and took her hand. "You need to tell me what happened."

Duke perched on the edge of the desk. "And don't leave anything out."

Rosie nodded. "For the last three or four weeks we've had trouble here. It's not the same people, but they do the same stuff, cause shit. Pick fights. They don't come from around here, Mil."

"How do you know that?" Duke asked.

"I've lived here all my life. With each group of people who come in here you recognise one or two. Someone you went to school with, or it could be their little brother or sister. Sometimes someone you worked with. There's normally someone you would know or a face you would recognise. These arseholes I'd never seen before. Tony said they'd never been in the club either. They started causing grief from day one, they—"

"Why wasn't I told about this before?" Millie asked. "This is my fucking livelihood."

"I told you to sell," Duke interrupted.

"Not now, Dad." Millie tutted. "Go on, Rose, what else?"

"Tony didn't want to worry you, you were about to give birth, Mil. He wanted to wait until you'd had it, and then you did, but it was twins, so he thought he could deal with it on his own… He was thinking of you."

"Thinking of me. How can I protect myself if I don't know what's going on?"

"You need to sell up," Duke mumbled.

"Dad, please, I am not selling anything. Jesus Christ, give me strength." Millie rolled her eyes. This was more serious than she had first realised.

"The solicitor's gonna phone once he knows what's happening with Tony. In the meantime, I need more muscle." Rosie stood. "I'm gonna get a taxi to the Old Bill station."

"No, Rose, they'll keep him locked up until trial." Millie patted the sofa next to her.

"Why will they?" Rosie asked, before sitting again.

"What do you think GBH stands for? Grievous bodily harm. He broke the bloke's fingers... he's got the best brief, so let's wait and see what happens. Now I'm going out there to have a nose around. Dad, do you wanna take Rosie home?"

"No. I'm not leaving you here on your own, Mil. Have you listened to anything she just said? There's been trouble here for weeks now, and it's for your benefit. Someone is coming for Paul Kelly's kingdom, and I'm not letting you get taken with it."

Millie stood and faced Duke. "This isn't Paul Kelly's kingdom, it's mine, and as such I will fight for it. Now take Rosie home. I'll get one of the boys to drop me back when I'm done." With that, she stormed out of the office.

She entered the main part of the club, scanning the room.

"Evening, Mrs Kelly," Jason, one of the doormen, said.

She nodded in reply then headed up to the VIP area. This was the best vantage point in the club. She glanced around, trying to spot anyone, or should that be group, who looked out of place. The dance floor was so tightly packed, it was hard to spot anybody.

An ice bucket with a bottle of champagne was placed on the table behind her. "I didn't ask for that."

"A gentleman bought it for you, Mrs Kelly," the bar manager said.

"What gentleman? Show me." She spun back towards the bar.

"He paid and left—"

"What did he look like?" She sighed.

"About six feet tall, broad shoulders, dark hair. Extremely well groomed. He reminded me a bit of Mr Kelly." He smiled vacantly. "Real handsome man, and those brown eyes..." It was as clear as day he fancied him.

"Can we focus here, please? Did he have an accent, walk funny, anything?" she asked, picking up the bottle. It was the best champagne they sold, and more importantly, it was her favourite. Did he know that? She shoved it back in the ice bucket. "Well?"

"No, but he did ask me to give you a message." His face paled.

"Spit it out then," she demanded.

He swallowed loudly. "He said… he'll be in touch soon."

CHAPTER 39

Twice in the night Millie had been awakened by the shrill noise of the twins crying. She wouldn't have minded, but each time her mind had gone into overdrive about the mysterious man.

Would he come to the house? This was supposed to be her sanctuary. The place she was safe, with her boys. She looked down at the two sleeping faces, One and Two. Two squirmed and opened his eyes—his blue eyes were more piercing by the day. She reached in and grabbed him, pulling him close to her chest. Breathing in his baby scent.

"You're not going to wake your brother," she murmured into his soft wavy hair. She walked to the window and glanced out. It would be Christmas in a few weeks. She'd need to buy presents and decorate the house, but she wanted to skip it this year. The boys were too young to know what was going on, but she knew her mother wouldn't let her. She also knew she had to name the boys. The nagging from her mother had been constant.

Now Two had quieted, she lay him back in his crib, his little face staring up at her. "You're handsome," she whispered. "Just like your dad."

What?

***

"Morning, Mil." Rosie yawned. "Have you heard anything this morning?"

"Solicitor phoned. Tony's been charged with GBH. He's more than likely gonna get a custodial sentence, Rose."

She watched the emotions change on her face, first denial, then sadness, then anger. "Do you want a cuppa?"

"What I want is my boyfriend," Rosie snapped.

"I know, but at least he's still alive." Millie marched out into the kitchen. Had that comment had been a bit harsh? Maybe. But it was true, Tony was only banged up, and to be perfectly honest, he was probably in the safest place.

"Sorry, Mil," Rosie said from behind her. "I know it's not your fault."

"It's fine, I know you were talking about moving in together. If it's any consolation, the brief reckons he'll only get six months. It was self-defence."

"It wasn't self-defence, Tony deliberately stepped on his hand." Rosie gasped.

"Yes, but you're not going to say that, are you?" Millie sighed. "Perhaps you should keep away from him until he's sentenced."

Rosie took her tea and sat at the table. "Of course I won't say anything… What happened last night after I left?"

"Whoever was there had gone." Not wanting to divulge any information until she knew what or who she was dealing with, Millie changed the subject. "I need to name the twins."

"About time. Connie will be pleased." Rosie laughed.

"My mother will no doubt find something else to nag about." Millie smiled. "Anyway, I was thinking Tommy for Number One and Duke for Number Two."

"So Duke after your dad and Tommy after theirs?" Rose asked in shock. "Shit, Mil, don't you think you should tell him?"

"I only realised this morning, Rose. How can you drop a bombshell like that on someone... I told him Paul was the father... and what about the surname, I can't call them Kelly, it's a lie." Millie sipped her tea thoughtfully. "Everyone believes they were mine and Paul's. I never corrected them... everyone's gonna hate me."

"Who's important in all this?" Rosie finally asked.

"What?"

"Who matters the most to you?" she continued.

"My boys, Duke, Connie, Finn, you, and Scott, why?"

Rosie smiled. "And do you think we could ever hate you? You've never worried about what other people think so don't start now."

**

Duke didn't know whether to laugh or cry. On the one hand he was happy as Larry — after all, who wouldn't be, having a grandson named after him — but finding out Tommy Lee was the boys' father had floored him. He would much rather they had been Paul's, especially now he was dead.

"Well, are you going to say something?" Connie asked. She had a tight grip on Tommy boy, while Duke held baby Duke.

"I'm happy, Millie, and pleased you've named them, but what happens now?" He stared down at his namesake. "You can't keep a man's children away from him. It's not fair."

"Look, he could be anywhere in the world right now, I'm not going to fret over telling him." Millie finished rinsing the babies' bottles and turned to her parents. "I've got work this afternoon, I need to concentrate on that first."

"This isn't something you can hide from, Mil. The longer you leave it, the harder it will be," Duke warned her. If Tommy Lee found out before she told him, World War Three would break out.

**

Millie pondered her life while sitting at the desk in the Portakabin. She had decided to visit Gypsy and find out where Tommy Lee was residing at this time. Surely he wouldn't be away working for Christmas.

Christmas shopping.

"I know." She rolled her eyes. The sound of a motor outside had her tipping the chair back so she could look out of the window. Was that a Rolls-Royce? The chair tipped back further, and she lost her balance. The sound of the crash had the driver running in.

"You all right down there?" he asked, standing over her.

Millie stood, tugging her skirt down. Her face had flushed, and her head hurt where she'd banged it on the floor. "I'm perfectly fine, thank you. She lifted the chair back up and slumped into it. "And you are?"

"I am here to see if you enjoyed the champagne I left for you," he said smugly.

His eyes twinkled with... Millie couldn't decide if it was mischief or malice. Maybe a bit of both. She reached into her bag and took out the unopened bottle.

"Here, my dad told me never to except gifts from strangers."

He looked surprised. Good.

"Tell me what you want, Mr...?"

"You can call me Sid." He held out his hand. "You don't mind if I call you Millie, do you?"

"Yes, I do, it's Mrs Kelly to you. Only my family and friends get to call me Millie."

"But you're not Mrs Kelly, are you? He no longer exists. You, my dear, are in a man's world with no one to protect you."

"Maybe I don't need protecting. Now this is the last time I'm gonna ask. What do you want?"

"I thought I'd made myself perfectly clear: the poisoned dog, your right-hand man out of the picture, stock from the docks going missing."

Millie silently cursed. She knew nothing about goods from the docks being stolen.

"I can see you look surprised... The goods from the docks went this morning, I expect you'll get a phone call any minute." Smugness and sarcasm dripped from his voice.

The phone rang just as he'd finished speaking.

Millie snatched it up. After listening, she slammed it down. "I think it's time for you to go, Mr Sid."

"I take it that was your man from the docks. I hope he wasn't injured too badly. I did tell my men to take it easy with him, but they get a bit carried away." He placed the champagne on the desk. "Can you see how easily it would be for me to take everything from you? You're unprotected, Millie, Paul's dead, Tony's banged up. At the very least you need a new partner."

"And I guess you're offering," she said sharply. "But what happens if I don't want a new partner?"

"This was just a courtesy call to let you know what's happening. Comply, don't comply, I'm taking all the businesses, one way or another."

Millie jumped as he slammed the door shut behind him. Her hands shook, her heart thumping. How the hell was she supposed to take this prick on?

***

Millie entered the Artichoke. Finn was busy serving a customer. He spotted her and smiled. Taking a seat on a stool at the bar, she waited for him to finish.

"Lovely to see you, Mil, but I suspect this isn't a social visit by the look on your face."

"I didn't know who else to go to." She glanced behind her. "Do you know a villain called Sid? He's about six foot, dark hair and eyes, well-spoken and well dressed. Drives a Roller?"

Finn shook his head. "No, but I can ask around. What's going on?"

"He's the one going after my businesses... I can't fight if I don't know who I'm fighting." She sighed. "He scares me."

"You should be telling Duke this, he's the one who can protect you," Finn advised.

"I can't. He wants me to sell up, this will just give him more ammunition."

"Would that be such a bad thing? You're a mum now, you need to put your babies first." Finn poured a glass of wine and handed it to her. "Surely you'd be set for life with the money they're worth?"

"Something tells me this Sid won't part with any money." She took a large gulp of her wine. "I'm so angry... Tommy Lee told me it was someone who worked at the scrapyard, and I believed him. Maybe he's in on it."

THE STEPNEY TAKEOVER

"I wouldn't speculate, Mil, you need to get all the facts first."

Downing her drink, she grabbed her bag and nodded. "You're right, it's time I pay Tommy fucking Lee a visit."

She ignored Finn's protests and left the pub. First she would drive to Wickford. If anyone knew where Tommy Lee was it would be Gypsy and John Jo.

CHAPTER 40

Millie pulled up outside the gate. She had the twins in the car, because she didn't want to explain what was going on to her parents. Duke was already giving her grief about the scrapyard. This would've given him all the ammo he'd need to force the issue.

She scanned the area, amazed how beautiful the site looked. There were two mobiles about halfway down and a few trailers tucked behind them, she couldn't see how many.

They had certainly gone all out to make this their home. The lights were on in the mobiles and some of the tourers. She was unsure whether to drive in or just honk the horn. Deciding that was a bit rude, she unlatched the gate, then drove through. Dogs barked, and she hoped they'd be tied up. She certainly didn't need a trip to the hospital and a tetanus shot or stitches. After she shut the gate, she drove down towards the mobiles. Uncertain which one to knock at, she parked in the middle of the two.

THE STEPNEY TAKEOVER

Before she got out, John Jo came striding towards her. "What do you want?"

Nice greeting.

"I need to speak with your brother."

"Which one?"

Was he being an arsehole on purpose, or was this what the Ward brothers were like? "Tommy Lee. It's urgent."

"He's not here."

Gypsy came out of the mobile and made her way towards her. She smiled. "Hello, Millie."

"Hello." Millie scribbled down her phone number and handed it to Gypsy. "Can you get Tommy Lee to phone me? Please."

When baby Duke started to cry, Gypsy turned her attention to the twins in the back. Bending down, she appeared to be studying them.

"Look, I really need to get home, before they both wake for feeding. Please pass that to Tommy Lee."

She restarted the motor just as Tommy boy woke and screamed along with his twin.

Shit.

"You can come in and feed them," Gypsy said. "It won't be much fun driving with that racket."

This cannot be happening.

"I don't want to put you out, they should fall back to sleep once I'm driving," Millie replied loudly over the noise of her twins.

"And what if they don't? Anyway, it will be nice to have a chat." Gypsy whispered something to John Jo; he then disappeared around the back.

Millie grabbed the baby bag and slipped it over her shoulder then unclipped baby Duke from his car seat.

"Shall I take him?" Gypsy asked while holding her arms out.

"Thanks." Millie then unclipped Tommy boy, lifted him out, and followed Gypsy into the mobile.

It was a typical traveller home. All Crown Derby and cut glass. In the front room stood a cabinet with figurines in.

"Take a seat. Here, hold your baby, I'll just boil the kettle." Gypsy disappeared into the kitchen.

Well, this isn't uncomfortable!

"How old are your twins?" she asked from the kitchen.

"Nearly five weeks, they were a few weeks early, they shouldn't have been here until November... The midwife said twins always come early." Millie glanced down at her boys. They had now decided to go back to sleep. "Maybe I should go now they're sleeping, I don't want to be a nuisance."

The feeling of being watched had Millie looking up.

Oh fuck.

Tommy Lee stood in the doorway staring at the babies. He stepped closer. John Jo had said they looked like him. He couldn't see it. Babies all looked the same. "You wanted to see me."

She didn't answer, she just sat there, her face red. He could see she felt awkward.

"I haven't got all day, Millie."

"It was about the scrapyard... You told me it was one of my men nicking a bit of scrap on the side. I just came to tell you, you were wrong, but you probably already know that. How much did he pay you?"

"You're not making any sense, woman." What the feck was she talking about? "And who's he?"

"The man who's now come to take everything I own. He calls himself Sid, ring any bells?"

"I think you should start at the beginning." Tommy Lee took a seat opposite her. His gaze rested on the twins when they squirmed. "Here, give me one. What's his name?"

"Duke, after my dad. I call him baby Duke." She gazed at Tommy Lee as he stood and rocked baby Duke back to sleep. "You're a natural."

"Sean Paul has three chavvies and John Jo has one, so I've had plenty of practice." He glanced down at Millie. "So what's the other boy called?"

***

Millie arrived home late afternoon to find Duke sitting in the lounge waiting for her.

"Where have you been, Millie? Me and your mother have been worried sick. Please don't tell me you took the chavvies to work with you." He shook his head in despair.

"Of course I didn't," she said indignantly. "And I wasn't aware I needed permission to take my own children anywhere."

"You don't need permission, but you could have let us know where you were going. You know your mother worries, and when she worries, I get it in the neck."

She didn't want to quarrel. The day had already been a total disaster without adding any more arguing. "Fine, next time I will give you my itinerary. Now if you don't mind, Dad, I need to sort the twins."

"I'll let your mother know you're back."

"Dad. I just need an hour on my own, tell her to pop in later." Millie lay Tommy boy down in the crib and then did the same for baby Duke.

Her father left the house.

Glancing out of the window, she spotted Rosie walking up the driveway. She ran to the door, opening it. She was eager to hear how Tony was and more so to know if he knew who this Sid was.

"Oh, I hate busses, they are never on flipping time." Rosie stepped in. "I've spent twenty-five minutes sat at the bus stop freezing me arse off."

Millie shut the door and followed her into the lounge. "How's Tony holding up?"

"He's okay, it's not like it's the first time he's been inside. He reckons he's a pro." Rosie laughed, but Millie could see right through it.

"He'll be okay, Rose," she assured her. "And what does he know about this Sid prick?"

"Nothing, it's like he's appeared from thin air. He did warn me for you to be careful, though, cos if he's driving around in a Roller he must be doing something right." Rosie nodded to the kitchen. "Wine?"

Millie nodded, although she could have done with something much stronger. "What if this Sid isn't his real name?"

"Oh, come on, Mil, if you're gonna use a fake name why would you pick Sid?"

Good question.

"How did it go with Tommy Lee, was he in on it?" Rosie shoved the bottle back into the fridge. "Cheers." She clonked her glass against Millie's.

She grimaced just at the thought of their conversation. "I asked, he didn't have a clue what I was talking about... I don't think he's in on it."

"I didn't think he would be... did you tell him he's a dad?" Rosie pulled out a chair and sat. "I bet that was a shock for him."

Millie thought back to the moment he'd asked Tommy boy's name. She could feel her palms sweating just thinking about it.

"Well, Mil?"

"He knew before I saw him. Gypsy had seen the twins and put two and two together because they look like him. They've got the same eyes and nose. She told John Jo to go fetch him without me knowing. The thing is, he didn't say anything, he just asked their names."

All she could see was that strange look on his face. She couldn't place it. It wasn't surprise, or delight, it wasn't even anger. She sighed. "I won't be seeing him again."

"So what are we going to do about this Sid?" Rosie grabbed the wine from the fridge and refilled her glass. "D'ya wanna top-up, Mil?"

Shaking her head, Millie thought back to the stolen goods. "He's stolen from me, Rose, he's played games with me, but the one thing I can't forgive him for is the dog. He shouldn't have poisoned the dog... I want you to take two weeks' holiday, on full pay."

"What? I'm not leaving you at a time like this, not when some creep is trying to take over all the businesses."

"And I'm not letting you get mixed up in this, Rose. I'm on my own and I'm gonna have to play dirty," she warned.

"This isn't the time to be a martyr, you have the twins to consider now, so whatever you're planning, I'm in."

CHAPTER 41

December 1977

The weather had been reasonably mild so far this winter, but today Tommy Lee was freezing. He blew into his cupped hands, trying to bring the feeling back into his fingers, while he stood behind the Transit.

"You need to reverse a bit more," he said to John Jo. "Whoa, that'll do." He then began unloading the logs.

His brother appeared at his side and picked up a couple. "It's been two weeks since Millie was here."

Tommy Lee nodded but didn't reply.

"Don't you wonder what those chavvies are like now?" John Jo continued.

THE STEPNEY TAKEOVER

"Listen, I know you mean well, but I'm not interested in her or the chavvies." He threw the logs into the shed. "She had the chance to tell me." He snatched two more. "I even asked her outright." He stopped and looked at John Jo. "She bare-face lied to me. Now just drop it."

"Okay." John Jo held his hands up in surrender. "I just don't want you regretting your decision."

Throwing the wood down, Tommy Lee marched to his trailer, cursing under his breath. He'd always prided himself on knowing everything that happened in his life. He was in control. There were no secrets in his world, at least none that could stay hidden for long. He was angry, angry at the situation and angry with himself. He'd had a nagging suspicion he was the father, but he'd taken her word for it, the word of a fecking liar.

When he stepped inside the trailer, he slumped down onto the bunk. He'd had many a sleepless night, thinking about the twins. Thinking about her. How could she? And then there was this Sid she'd accused him of working with. The woman was mentally unstable and a fecking liability. But what worried him the most was what if the chavvies weren't safe with her? He picked up his keys and left.

***

The scrapyard buzzed with life. Millie watched from the window of the Portakabin, as the men completed their day's tasks. Duke walked with Aron towards the smelter, Aron carrying a large item over his shoulder. She had been paid handsomely to destroy that.

She turned to Rosie. "It's been a couple of weeks since that Sid made himself known. It's making me nervous, this silence."

"I still think you should tell Duke what's going on. Just in case this bloke tries anything."

"I'm trying to piece everything together... Don't you find it funny that this Sid turns up on the only day Aron and Duke aren't here?"

"So you think they're watching the place?" Rosie asked nervously.

"No, I think Tommy Lee was half right, there is an inside man, who's acting as Sid's eyes and ears." She rubbed her forehead. "We need to find out who it is... Phone Scott and get him here."

"That's another thing, Mil, I don't like my brother working at the brothel."

"Okay, Rose, would you prefer it if I put Tony there when he gets out?" Millie glanced at her; she looked suitably horrified. "I can tell from your face what the answer will be."

The door creaked open, and Duke popped his head in. "Stick the kettle on, Mil, we've nearly finished."

"Dad," she called before he closed the door. "Have any of the men asked what days you're working or if you're not coming in?"

"Why?" He glanced at Millie. "What's going on?"

Shit, he looks suspicious.

"Just wondered, you know what they're like. If no one's here to keep an eye on them they take the piss." She smiled. "Just need to keep on top of things."

"When you sell up, that'll no longer be a problem." Duke closed the door.

She may have got away with that one, but it was crystal clear he wouldn't back down over the yard.

"How are you gonna find out, Mil, it's not as if they're gonna own up?" Rosie asked.

"That's why I asked my dad; if someone had, it would have made it so much easier, but it looks like we're gonna have to do it the old-fashioned way."

"And what's the old-fashioned way?"

"Threats. Torture."

Scott would know what to do.

***

Duke arrived home just after seven p.m. The lights in the mobile were all off, which could only mean one thing. Connie was still looking after the twins. Duke stormed through the gate and up the path, cursing under his breath. They were Millie's responsibility, and he was going to tell her exactly that when he saw her. Opening the kitchen door, he said, "Connie."

"In here," she said back.

"*Where's that daughter of mine?*" he bellowed.

"Duke, keep your voice down, you'll wake the twins."

THE STEPNEY TAKEOVER

When he walked into the lounge he spotted Tommy Lee, sitting in the armchair with Tommy boy nestled in his arms. "Where's Millie?"

"Good question," Tommy Lee replied. "Does she leave my boys every day, cos if she ain't capable of looking after them, they should come and live with me."

"These babies ain't going nowhere with you. They belong with their mother," Duke said.

"Then where is she?" He stood and passed Tommy boy to Connie, readying himself to square up to Duke. "Maybe we should take this outside."

"No one's taking anything outside," Millie said as she stormed into the room. "What are you doing here?" she barked at Tommy Lee.

"I've come to see my sons, or are you going to stop me from seeing them?"

"I think you should leave," Duke intervened.

"If I leave, I'll be taking my chavvies with me."

"*Enough!*" Millie screamed. "No one will ever take my children away from me, no one." She picked baby Duke up as the shouting had woken both babies. "Mum, thank you for watching them for me. Pass Tommy boy to his father. Dad, take Mum home."

"I'm not leaving you alone with him." Duke stabbed a finger at Tommy Lee.

"I'll be fine, now please, I'll phone you later." Millie walked to the kitchen with her parents.

"If he hurts you in any way," Duke warned.

"Dad, he won't hurt me." Millie closed the door and joined Tommy Lee on the sofa. "Why did you really come here?"

"To talk."

"About?" she asked, surprised.

"Firstly, why didn't you tell me about the twins?" He appeared visibly hurt. "I asked you if I was the father."

"I wasn't sure they were yours, I didn't want to mislead you... I only realised a few weeks ago when I looked into their eyes and saw you staring back." Millie stood and lay Duke back into his crib. She then took Tommy boy and lay him in his. "I didn't mean to hurt you. I'm sorry."

He gave a nod.

"You can see them whenever you want, I would never stop you," she added. "But they live here with me... What else did you want to know?"

"The scrapyard, whatever's going on there I don't want you involved." He sighed.

"You are aware that I own it... Christ, you sound like my dad. He hasn't put you up to this, has he?" she asked.

Tommy Lee shook his head. "No, but if that's what he thinks, I agree. Have you even thought about the twins in all this? What happens if this Sid bloke decides to come after them?"

"I asked you for help, you weren't interested," she reminded him.

"Surely Duke will help you."

She didn't know whether to laugh or cry at that statement. "Nope, he wants me to sell up or take on a partner." Avoiding his stare, she walked to the fridge and poured a glass of wine. "Can I get you a drink?"

He followed her into the kitchen. "Tea, please."

That surprised her, she was expecting him to ask for a scotch. "I have beer."

"I'm not a big drinker, tea will be just fine." He turned and headed back to the lounge. "They're handsome boys."

Millie laughed. "Is that because they're like you?"

"I can see you in them as well, they both have your lips... I want you to keep away from that man."

Millie passed him his tea. "I'm not letting him swoop in and take everything, this is my livelihood, and the twins' inheritance."

"They need their mother, Millie, not some dead gangster's legacy."

His words stung. Another one who thought she was living off the back of Kelly's empire. She had to concede it was partly true, but she'd been a helping hand when Paul needed it. She'd kept him alive when Ronnie Taylor had his sights set on doing away with him. Only Duke, her brothers, and Paul knew that story, it wasn't for anyone else's ears.

"It's all under control," she lied. "Drink your tea while it's hot."

So this was it. No help would come from Duke or Tommy Lee. It was time to use her loaf. She'd killed before, she could kill again. She just needed to find the right partner in crime.

CHAPTER 42

Millie had six weeks left until Duke quit the scrapyard. Six weeks to find out who Sid was, where he came from, and more importantly, what game he was playing. She needed a day without Duke and Aron there, then maybe he would show his face again.

Millie walked around the yard, nodding to the men as they greeted her with a smile or a simple good morning. They seemed like a cheerful bunch, which made it harder to spot Sid's snitch.

"What are you doing out here?" Duke shouted from the grab. He turned off the machine and then climbed down. "Get inside, you'll catch a chill." Taking her by the arm, he marched her back to the Portakabin.

"I'll put the kettle on," she shouted over the racket of the machinery, whilst slipping away from his grasp. She stepped up into the Portakabin and rubbed her hands together. "I wonder if its gonna snow for Christmas?"

THE STEPNEY TAKEOVER

Rosie glanced at her. "That would be nice, a white Christmas. Of course, it would be nicer if Tony was here."

"The time will soon go, Rose." Millie laughed. "Then you'll be back in his arms doing the kissy-kissy thing."

"The kissy-kissy thing. Really, remind me how old you are again." Rosie rolled her eyes, but they twinkled with amusement.

"Come to think of it, you haven't told me about the sex. How big, length, girth," Millie teased.

"A lady never asks or tells, Mil."

"And yet you asked me when I got with Paul…" Millie put her head down. She hardly thought about Paul now and mentioned him even less. When he did slip into her mind, though, it gave her mixed emotions. The love they'd once had burned in her heart until it had been extinguished by his infidelity.

"Okay. He must be a good seven inches, and when I say thick, I mean thick." Rose held her hands up. "It's a two hander."

Millie smiled. Rosie obviously noticed her sadness. "Well, I'm glad you both get on so well. Are you seeing him Saturday?"

"Yes, I've got my VO. What are you doing?"

"Going to the market with Connie. I need to get the rest of the Christmas presents."

That was, in fact, a lie. Saturday she was setting a trap for Sid, if that was his real name. Millie had spent all week rearranging her men to make sure all the businesses were covered, in case there were any more attempts to undermine her. She had coerced her parents into going and seeing Jasper and baby Sherry in Kent. Gladys and Maggie were babysitting the twins, leaving her free to hopefully corner Sid.

"If I'm back in time I'll meet you there," Rosie said. "I need a few more bits, too."

"Okay, but remember I won't be out all day cos I'll have the twins." Millie didn't like lying to her family or friends, but needs must, as they say. "Rose, have you thought any more about the missing patients?"

"Funny you mentioning them, I told Tony on my last visit. He said he'll help me find out what's happening."

"I reckon we should stake the place out, see if any ambulances are spotted." Millie stood and walked to the window. "Once we see what's going on, all we need to do is stop an ambulance and rescue them. Then we could go to the police... Oh shit, Duke's coming. Bung the kettle on, Rose."

***

Tommy Lee sat holding his cards close to his chest. He wasn't expecting to win, he was only playing as a distraction. He needed distracting from the guilt he felt. Had he put Millie in danger by not doing the job she'd paid him for and then losing his temper? He'd never lost his temper with a woman, least of all a woman who was paying him to do a job. This was different, though, she'd got under his skin. He could kick himself because he'd allowed himself to break his own number one rule. Never mix business with pleasure. Now, here he sat, wondering if her and the chavvies were safe.

"Tommy Lee," John Jo shouted. "Are you in or not?"

He threw in his cards. "I've got a bit of business to take care of. I'll see you in the morning."

***

Millie sat back on the sofa and popped her feet up. This was pure heaven. The twins were settled in their cribs.

"Here," Rosie said while handing her a glass of wine.

"You excited about tomorrow, Rose?" Millie asked after taking a sip of the wine.

Before Rosie could answer, they were both disturbed by a loud knock. "I'll get it, as you've got your feet up." She returned a minute later. "You've got a visitor, Mil."

She looked over Rosie's shoulder, surprised to see Tommy Lee.

"Hello." He smiled.

"Hello. What brings you here so late?" she asked. Had he come to see the twins or had he had a change of heart and was willing to help her?

"We need to talk... In private," he said.

"I'll be in my bedroom." Rosie stood and stared at Tommy Lee. "If I hear screaming I'll be straight back down."

"I'm not gonna hurt the mother of my chavvies," he snapped.

"Not her screams, yours. She's the one likely to inflict pain these days." Rosie pushed past him and ran up the stairs.

"How is it I'm the bad man when I haven't done anything wrong?" he asked, sitting next to Millie.

"She's protective. Anyway, you wanted to talk, so talk." She turned towards him.

He glanced around the room while finding the right words. "I know you well enough to know you're not gonna back down from this man, so I've got a solution." He could see he had her interested.

"And that is?" she asked eagerly

"I take over the fight. I'll watch the scrapyard and deal with him. In return, you look after our boys."

"You're banning me from my businesses?" She laughed.

"No. When you need to go there, either I take you or Duke does, but your first priority is the twins… I'll leave you to think it over." He stood, having laid his cards out for her. He wasn't sure what he would do if she said no. Take the chavvies to keep them safe? He looked down at her. "You've got until tomorrow night to give me your answer."

CHAPTER 43

Millie was up early, the twins were sorted, she was showered and dressed and now sat in the kitchen waiting for Rosie to leave. The Transit had gone, meaning Duke and Connie were on their way to Kent, blissfully unaware of the day's events she had planned.

"I hope the bleedin' busses are on time, I don't fancy being stuck in the freezing cold, Mil," Rosie said.

"I don't know why you don't get a taxi, it's not like you're skint anymore."

"Old habits die hard. I remember the times we had nothing growing up, it's made me frugal." Rosie searched her bag for the visiting order, then waved it in the air. "This is all I need. I'll see you later."

Millie waved her off then waited for Gladys and Maggie. It had gone ten a.m. by the time they arrived.

"Oh, look how big they've grown," Maggie gushed.

THE STEPNEY TAKEOVER

She was a close friend and ally to Millie. She'd worked in the brothel for years, a real hard-faced woman who'd helped Millie when she was most in need and formed a real bond. She often thought about that day at the docks. The day she realised she was stronger than she thought.

Millie stood behind the head office of the docks. She could smell the salt air. It reminded her of a trip they'd had at the children's home. Every year they'd go on a train to Southend-on-Sea. It was magical as a child. Millie smiled; those were her happy memories. She turned her attention to the river, it was the Thames estuary, wider here than in town. The waves lapped gently at the quayside; Millie found it mesmerising.

"Can you see any movement?" Maggie asked.

"All four men are in there, seated at their desks. Where's the camera?" Millie whispered.

"It's here," Gladys said.

Millie studied the large professional camera as Gladys waved it in the air. "Where did you get that from? It looks professional."

"I borrowed it from one of the brothel's clients. He didn't want to lend it, but after a bit of blackmail he had no choice. After all, he didn't think it would do his marriage or career any good if it came out he likes bondage." Gladys grinned.

"Good. Wait for the girls to go in. I'll check through the window. When they all have their pants down, you run in, get the pictures, and leave. Do not stay, the photos are the most important thing. Is everyone ready?"

The four girls nodded in unison.

"I've got this." Millie held up Finn's shotgun. "So any trouble, and I'll be in there. Do not let them hurt you."

"Fucking hell, Mil, you can't use that." Maggie gasped.

"I don't plan to use it. I don't even think it's loaded. But if they start it should deter them. Okay, let's go."

Millie keep her eyes on the four women as they entered the office. They were wearing very little and had all their goods on show. After waiting ten minutes, Millie peered through the window and smiled. The four pathetic men, who had their pants down, so to speak, were partaking in sexual activities with the girls. Waving to Gladys, Millie quietly followed her in and snapped away while the men were oblivious.

"Smile for the camera, gentlemen." Millie laughed.

The men turned towards her, and the realisation of their situation hit them.

"Gladys, go and get three copies of each."

The men scrambled for their clothes. Millie ushered the girls out, while Maggie stood beside her.

"I'm not leaving you on your own with them," Maggie said.

"I'm not on my own. I've got this." Millie held up the shotgun and smiled. "Right, gentlemen. This is what's going to happen. You are going to sign the lease contract for Mr Kelly and Mr Taylor. Or... Your wives will be getting some beautiful colour photos of your exploits. As you are aware, we know where you all live. Any questions?"

They all shook their heads. She then passed Maggie the paperwork so she could hand it to the men. After they had signed, Millie checked the signatures and nodded.

"Thank you. It's been a pleasure doing business with you." Millie turned and left the office with Maggie following. The two women walked back to Maggie's car. Millie burst out laughing. "That was fun!"

"You looked happy doing it," Maggie smiled.

"I'm not gonna lie, it was exciting. It's made me feel different."

Maggie looked at Millie and laughed. "You are different. You, my love, are now a gangster."

Millie sighed. If she could sort the docks, then she could sort Sid. "They've not long been fed," she said to her friends while grabbing her bag. "I'll be as quick as I can, and if anyone turns up here, tell them I had to pop out and that I won't be long."

"I guess I shouldn't ask where you're going," Gladys said while peeking at baby Duke.

"Ask no questions and I'll tell no lies. See yous later." Millie rushed out of the house and jumped into her Range Rover. Her nerves were kicking in. Should she have taken Tommy Lee up on his offer? Probably, however, it was too late now.

The journey was a nightmare. If she caught one red light she caught them all. It was nearly eleven a.m. by the time she arrived. She climbed out of her motor; the smell of old engine oil and burnt rubber hit her nose, while the noise of the grab and crunching metal echoed in her ears. The first time she'd come here she'd hated it. That was the time she'd realised Paul was being blackmailed. Soon, she'd quickly realised the blackmailer was Rita, Ronnie Taylor's widow. Her silence for sex, and Paul had agreed. If only Millie had known the extent of Paul's betrayal back then. She wouldn't have been forced into hiding, thinking she was the target. That seemed a lifetime ago, and now he was gone, and this place had grown on her, even the dirt, the smell, and the noise.

She unlocked the Portakabin and stepped in. It felt colder in here than it did outside. She blew out, watching her breath turn white. Her first job was switching the little electric heater on. She held her hands out to warm them, then rubbed them together. She hated the cold. Her second job was making a cuppa. Then she sat back and waited.

Just after twelve-thirty p.m., the sound of a motor coasting in caught her attention. Shoving the paperwork into the drawer, she peeked out of the window. Sid stood with three of his men, no doubt giving them their orders.

When the door opened, she remained calm. With her head down, she mumbled, "Good afternoon, what can I do for you?"

"No need for rudeness, Millie," Sid said.

With a loud sigh, she stared him straight in the eye. "You're standing in my office, acting like you own the place, when in fact, I do, so I'll ask once more. What can I do for you?"

He walked towards the desk and leant against it. "I've brought the contract for you to sign. Now, as you can see, everything is signed over to me forthwith. I will, however, give you time to clear your belongings out."

She grabbed the contract and scanned the first page. "So I just sign everything over for free?" She laughed.

"It's not for free, I'm allowing you to walk away with your life. Now hurry up and sign, there's a good girl."

The click of a gun being cocked had her glancing over to the bruiser standing at the side of Sid. "If you kill me you still won't own this place, or the docks, so I'm guessing this is a scare tactic."

"We are capable of forging a signature." Sid laughed. "Now last chance, what's it to be?"

She realised she had fucked up. In her attempt to play the boss she was about to lose everything. Why hadn't she told Duke or even let Tommy Lee know what she had planned? He had given her a way out of this shit, but she was too proud. What about Tommy boy and baby Duke? How could she have put herself in danger when they relied on her?

She stared at the contract, knowing full well if she signed they'd kill her anyway. It was easy enough to make a death look like an accident. She picked up the pen and hovered it above the paper.

A dark shadow covered the Portakabin. Millie glanced out of the window. A loud crash followed.

Sid's men ran out. There was screaming and shouting. Sid stood at the door, his face pale.

"What's going on?" she asked, running over to the doorway.

There, on top of Sid's Rolls-Royce, was an old scrap car. It had been dropped from a height that had smashed the roof completely. Millie turned towards the grab; whoever had done that was a dead man. She gulped down her fear when she spotted Duke. He came marching towards her. Flicking her attention to the man with the gun, she scowled; he was pointing it towards him. The gunshot made her recoil in terror, but Duke was still striding towards the man but now held a pickaxe. She turned. Blood pooled around a man; he lay on the ground, unmoving.

Tommy Lee came closer, holding a shotgun. He pointed it towards Sid. "Get away from her." He grabbed the man's arm and yanked him outside, then turned to Millie. "Stay in there and lock the door, I'll deal with you later."

He waited for her to lock the door and only then dragged Sid towards the rest of his men. "Men like you make me sick," he whispered to him, "picking on a fecking woman." He shoved him to the ground and waited for Duke to join him.

Duke looked like a madman, his eyes blazing with vengeance. "She," he said, pointing towards the Portakabin, "is my fucking daughter." He swung the pickaxe at the first man, the chunky blade cracking through the man's skull.

Tommy Lee watched as he dropped to the ground. "Duke. Not in front of Millie." He'd spotted her staring from the window. "Boys, take them into shed where the smelter is." He grabbed the pickaxe from Duke. "Go and see Millie. I'll wait in the shed for you."

Millie walked to the fridge. Without thinking, she poured herself a glass of wine; she didn't think tea would quite cut it today. She turned at the noise of the door creaking open.

Duke stepped in. "Why didn't you tell me what was going on?"

He looked hurt.

"I didn't want you to worry."

"Worry?" Duke pushed his hand through his hair. "You told Tommy Lee about Sid. Does this mean you trust him more than me?"

"I told him about Sid, I didn't tell him what I had planned. You'd already made it clear you wanted the business gone. I didn't know what to do." Millie jumped when Duke smashed his fist into the desk, her wine spilling.

"You're a mother of two beautiful baby boys — they should come first, not some dirty fucking scrapyard. I'm telling you now, you either sell or take a partner, because this is just the beginning. They're gonna keep coming after you, Mil, and what happens next time if you're on your own?"

She remained silent. She didn't know what to say.

"I'll let you think about it while I go and finish this." He turned and left.

Tommy Lee stood over Sid, who was now tied to a chair. The two dead men were already being loaded into the smelter. The other man sat tied and gagged. His gaze darted around the shed; was he looking for a way out? Duke entered, pulling the door shut behind him.

"Is she okay?" Tommy Lee asked.

"Who knows. I think she was with Kelly too long, she seems oblivious to death." Duke sighed.

Tommy Lee felt for him, having a daughter who so freely diced with death. "I think we should start with the hired help." He turned when the door opened. His eyes met Millie's as she headed towards him.

"You can't be in here, Millie." Duke's voice was low and angry.

"Not now, Dad. I need to speak to Sid, if that's his real name," she demanded. "Take his gag off."

Tommy Lee glanced at Duke, who gave him a simple nod.

Millie bent down so her eyes were level with Sid's. "Something doesn't add up... D'ya know what I think? This whole shitshow was a test."

"A test for what?" Tommy Lee asked.

"A test to see what defences I have, how many men, who would come to my assistance." She straightened herself. "But why?"

"You're nowhere near close." Sid laughed. "You may as well get this over with cos I won't tell you anything."

"Put his gag back on." Millie smiled at him. "I know you won't, but what about your friend here. Take his off." She pointed to the other man.

Sid began shouting, but the noise was muffled.

"Oh, do shut up," Millie said. "You had your chance, now it's only fair we give your mate one. What's your name?" she asked him.

"Barry. Barry Greaves," he said, a slight tremble in his voice.

"You don't need to be afraid, just answer truthfully. How well do you know this man?"

He glanced at Sid, then back to Millie. "Not that well, this is my first job."

"Is this your normal line of work, you know, threatening women?" Tommy Lee spat.

Millie placed her hand on his arm. "I would say not, look at him." She sighed. "He's a nervous wreck."

"Who do you work for?" Duke added. "Is it him or someone else?"

"I take my orders from him, but I don't think he's in charge. Whenever something doesn't go to plan, he runs off to the phone. It's like he's asking what to do next," Barry said.

Millie shrugged. "I dunno. I think yous need to torture Sid here and find out as much as you can, and if he won't talk, there's a container the other side of the yard. Stick him in there and set fire to him."

"And what about this one?" Tommy Lee motioned with his head towards Barry.

"He's seen you both kill two men. I would say he's seen too much, but as you've both pointed out, I'm just a woman playing in a man's world, so who am I to decide?"

CHAPTER 44

Millie said goodbye to Gladys and Maggie at the door. "And thanks again for watching the babies for me."

"It was our pleasure." Gladys beamed. She walked towards her motor while Maggie lingered in the doorway.

"Mil, I don't know what you're up to, but be careful. Paul had his reputation to fall back on, you don't have that luxury." Maggie then turned and left.

Millie closed the front door and leant back against it, squeezing her eyes tightly shut. Today had been tough. The thought of what could have happened if Duke and Tommy Lee hadn't turned up and rescued her sent a chill down her spine.

What were you thinking?

"I don't know." She headed into the lounge to see her boys.

What good is having a conscience if you don't listen to it?

"Give it a fucking rest."

They both slept soundly, oblivious to their mother's monumental cock-up. She turned around at the sound of footsteps. Duke then Tommy Lee walked into the room.

"Did you find out anything from him?" she asked.

"We're not here to talk about the scrapyard," Duke said.

"We're here to talk about you and my chavvies," Tommy Lee added.

"I think we've done enough talking. I know what you both think, but I still have businesses to run. Besides, whoever's behind this won't try anything so soon, at least not now they've seen what you're both capable of. What did you do with Barry and Sid?"

"Duke, can you leave me and your daughter alone for five minutes?" Tommy Lee asked.

Millie swallowed down her nerves. Would her dad leave her alone with this man?

"I'll go and see if Connie's back." Duke left without looking back.

"Dad, you can't leave me alone with him," she called after him, but he had already gone.

Shit.

"Millie, sit back down," Tommy Lee said, his voice gentle.

"Stop telling me what to do." She sighed.

"I gave you the perfect scenario last night, and what do you go and do? Ignore it."

She could see he was desperately trying to hold his temper together. "It wasn't like that, I'd already set today up. It was too late to change it."

"So why not tell me, let me deal with it?"

"Because if you were there, he would never have turned up… I'm sorry, okay? I appreciate everything you and Duke did today."

"I don't seem to be getting anywhere with you, so let me make it simple. If you continue to work, I'm taking my boys. They may as well get used to not having a mother as she's so set on getting herself killed."

That comment hit Millie like a punch in the gut. "Don't say that. The boys mean more to me that anything."

"So prove it, take me up on my offer," he demanded.

"What happens when there's no more attacks, cos I can't see anyone taking me on now after this?" She stopped and studied him for a minute. "You've found out something else, haven't you...? You managed to get Sid to talk."

"Do we have a deal, or shall I take the chavvies now?"

He wasn't backing down. The sheer determination in his voice made her question what he'd found out.

"We have a deal, as long as you tell me everything." She held out her hand, ready to shake.

Why isn't he shaking on it?

After a second or two, he spoke. "Okay, but also I will be spending Christmas Day here with you and my boys, then Boxing Day you'll be spending it with my family."

Millie's jaw almost hit the floor. "What?"

***

Rosie climbed onto Millie's bed. She'd brought the wine up and placed it on the side. "It's not a bad thing that he's protecting you, surely?"

Millie didn't agree. Between Duke and Tommy Lee, she had been backed into a corner. "I don't like being told what I can and cannot do, and as for him thinking he can take the twins away from me, that will never happen." She took the glass Rosie handed her. "Anyway, enough about my shitshow of a life. How's Tony?"

"He seems happy for someone who's banged up. Maybe he was just putting on a happy face so I don't worry... We did talk about when he gets out, though. He wants me to move in with him straight away."

"What, already?"

Rosie's smile dropped.

Shit, Millie, be supportive. "If that's what you want then I'm happy for you. Tony has always been loyal to Paul, and I trust him. You both deserve some happiness."

"And what about you, Mil, don't you deserve happiness, too?"

"I am happy," she said, a little too quickly.

"Then why do you always look so miserable?" Rosie grabbed the wine and refilled both their glasses. "You always come across like you've got the weight of the world on your shoulders."

Millie sighed. "Heavy is the head that wears the crown... I don't know how Paul made running the businesses seem so easy, maybe

Tony was right. Paul had his reputation, not many men would cross him."

"Well, you've got Duke and Tommy Lee behind you. With them two, God help anyone who tries to cross you, cos I don't think they'll live to tell the tale."

Millie smiled and drained her glass. "I'd better get my head down while the twins are asleep. I've got the great Tommy Lee coming over tomorrow to tell me what happened after I left today." She placed her glass on the side. "Take the wine, Rose, I'm sure you'll have no trouble finishing the bottle."

"Why didn't he tell you earlier?" She quizzed.

"I think he needed to calm down. I could see he was struggling to keep his temper in check… Anyway, night Rose."

She checked on the twins, who were both sleeping soundly, before climbing into bed. If only she could sleep as well. Her mind turned to the day's events. How did Duke and Tommy Lee know she was up to something? That was what she really wanted to know. Had she slipped up?

CHAPTER 45

Connie stood at the sink peeling potatoes, while Millie sat at the table feeding baby Duke. Tommy boy was fed, changed, and now sleeping. "Mum, how did you manage with twins?"

"What do you mean, manage?" Connie asked. She turned to face her daughter. "Are you struggling?"

"No, not really, but when they're both hungry, I have to lay them down and hold both bottles at the same time. It's not often they wake separately, especially at night."

"You're doing a good job, Millie, stop worrying, and besides, they should start sleeping through soon," Connie said. "I'd best get the beef in the oven. Your father will be starving when he gets back."

"I am grateful, for all the help you've both given me." Millie placed the empty bottle down and sat baby Duke up. A loud burp followed. "Pardon you, little man." She laughed.

"We know you are. I know Duke's worried about you. When Tommy Lee came round the other night, they —"

"He came round to see Dad?" Millie shook her head. "And what exactly did he see him about?"

"I don't know, I went to bed and left them to it." Connie placed the potatoes on to boil. "I've got cabbage, carrots, and peas. Do you think that will be enough?"

"Don't change the subject. Was it about me?"

Connie sighed. "Yes, but I don't know what was said. Now you sort your son out, a nasty smell is coming from him."

Millie took him through to the lounge, ready to change his nappy. A loud knock came from the front door. "Never get a minute's peace in this place." She tutted.

"I'll get it," Rosie shouted while running down the stairs.

Millie lay baby Duke on a towel, kneeling beside him, when Tommy Lee walked in.

"Morning, Millie, I hope you're in a better mood today."

"My mood is just fine, thank you."

"That's a no then," he muttered.

"I heard that," she said.

"Kettle's on," Connie called from the doorway.

Tommy Lee smiled at her.

Millie rolled her eyes. "So what happened with Sid?"

"We will talk about that in private," he said, kneeling next to her. "Jaysus, the boy stinks." He promptly stood.

"If we're talking in private, why are you here?"

"I was invited to dinner by your mum, didn't she tell you?"

"No. She didn't." She picked the baby up. "Here, hold your son while I dispose of this." She then marched out to the kitchen.

Connie was just stirring the tea. Millie stormed past her, opened the door, and threw the soiled nappy into the bin. Slamming the lid down for good measure, she closed the door and glared at her mother. "What are you playing at, inviting him for dinner?"

"He is the twins' father, Millie. You need to get on, for their sakes."

Millie knew she had a point, but this was too much, too soon. "I know you mean well, but please ask me first next time. He makes me feel uncomfortable."

"Well, he didn't make you feel uncomfortable when you were in bed with him conceiving the twins," Connie whispered. "Next time, maybe you'll think twice before whipping your knickers off."

"Mum!"

"Is everything all right out here?" Tommy Lee asked as he entered the kitchen. "Food smells cushty, Connie."

Millie took baby Duke from him and headed back into the lounge, placing him in his crib.

"You okay, Mil? Your face is ever so red," Rosie asked, grinning.

"You won't believe what my mum just said." Millie stopped when Tommy Lee walked back in holding two cups of tea.

He passed one to Millie. "Do you want to go somewhere private and we can have that chat. Your mood might improve then."

"Sarcasm, great… Follow me." Millie led him into the study and closed the door. "Take a seat." She sat behind the desk and sipped her tea. She rarely came in here these days. It was a reminder of Paul. Everything from the leather sofa he had bought, for when he had business acquaintances round, to the paintings that hung on the wall. Another fully stocked bar stood in the corner. His expensive scotch and cut-crystal glasses out on display. He liked the finer things in life; unfortunately, now so did she. Glancing around, she realised it was a waste of a room.

Maybe I could turn it into a playroom.

A subtle cough from Tommy Lee brought her attention back to him.

"So what did you find out?"

He placed his cup down. "This is a big house." His gaze darted around the room. "I'd prefer something smaller, like a trailer."

She stared at him blankly. Was he taking the piss? "Can we keep to subject, please?"

"Why are you so abrupt all the time? You weren't like that when we first met."

"I didn't have all this responsibility then." She sighed. "And the twins. I wake up every day ready to fight."

"You shouldn't have to, the boys should be your only worry. Making sure they're safe and happy. Duke reckons you should sell up."

"I work for them so they'll have everything they need. I am not selling anything."

"That's my job, not yours," he said. "I'm the man, their dad. It's my responsibility to provide for them... Look, I'm not best pleased with the situation either, we're now tied together whether we like it or not."

She eyed him. His body language had become defensive. She needed to change the direction of the conversation. "Yes, you are their dad, and you can buy them whatever you want, I'll not stop you. Now can we get back to the reason we are sitting in here?"

"These businesses are draining the life out of you, Millie, you need to think long and hard if this..." he pointed around the room, "and the scrapyard are really worth it."

Silence followed. Millie was becoming more anxious. Was he going to tell her what had happened or was he here to bully her into selling everything?

"Sid was just a front man," he continued. "The real threat is from a group of men from up north. I think Paul may have had dealings with them as Sid thought they knew him."

"So Sid was testing the waters... Makes sense."

"Millie, you need to sell the scrapyard, cos if they come for you, you won't be able to stop them."

"But you will, or are you cutting and running?"

"I never cut and run, and neither does Duke, but even if we sort this lot out, someone else will be waiting for their chance." Tommy Lee sat forward. "I know it's a profitable business, but your life is worth more than that."

"What if I took on a partner?"

She glanced at Tommy Lee. He looked deep in thought. What was he planning now?

***

After an excruciatingly painful dinner, Millie and Rosie cleared everything away. Millie ordered Connie out of the kitchen, as she had cooked the meal, and she also wanted to chat with Rosie alone.

"So what were you gonna tell me earlier before we were disturbed? It must have been bad cos your face was the colour of a tomato." Rosie giggled.

"Remind me how old you are." Millie laughed. "I asked my mum why she'd invited Tommy Lee for dinner, as he makes me feel uncomfortable. She said…" She looked at the closed kitchen door and in hushed tones she continued. "…he didn't make you feel uncomfortable when you were in bed with him conceiving the twins."

"Blimey, that was a bit harsh."

"Hang on, there's more: next time maybe I'll think twice before taking my knickers off."

Rosie burst out laughing. "Well, she didn't hold back."

"Connie's never spoken to me like that before. I didn't realise how badly she thought of me."

"She doesn't think badly of you, and she dotes on the twins. She was probably defensive cos you made her feel bad for inviting him."

"Maybe."

"So what was the outcome of your private chat with him?" Rosie asked while loading up the dishwasher. "I can't believe you've got one of these, I don't know anyone else who's got one."

"That was Paul's doing. You know what he was like, had to have the best of everything. I'd barely used it cos it was just the two of us. Anyway, it was about the scrapyard. I've decided my best option is to take on a partner."

"Oh, I was hoping he'd proposed."

"Rose, what planet are you living on? In case you haven't noticed, we can't stand each other."

"Really, Mil? Cos from where I'm standing, I'd say you're in denial."

CHAPTER 46

Millie unloaded the motor. She'd gone all out on Christmas this year. She had even bought Jasper's wife, Sherry, a rather nice bottle of perfume. She pushed the front door shut with her bum as her hands were full, then placed the last four bags down and stared at them. There were fifteen in all. That was the last of the presents all done. Tonight she planned on wrapping them.

Connie came down the stairs carrying the hoover. "Did you have a nice time at the shops?" she asked, eyeing up all the bags. "How much have you spent?"

"Tommy Lee gave me money for the twins. He hasn't the time to go shopping now he's at the scrapyard all day."

"It's good to hear he's taking his fatherly duty seriously." Connie placed the hoover in the cupboard.

"Mum, you don't have to do the housework for me. Looking after the boys is more than enough help." Millie started to carry the bags into the lounge. "I didn't know what to get Dad for Christmas. I've never known a man so hard to buy for."

"You don't need to buy us anything, save your money."

"As if I wouldn't get you anything, you're my parents, and you've both done so much for me. Hang on, it's here somewhere." Millie checked a couple of the bags. "Ah, here it is. I got him this lead crystal decanter and a bottle of the scotch he likes."

"That's lovely, I'm sure he'll be over the moon with that. He did ring a while ago, needed to speak to you." Connie held the decanter and smiled. "That'll look lovely on the side. Don't think the scotch will last long, though."

"Did he say what it's about?" Millie asked while searching more bags.

"Something to do with a buyer for the scrapyard. I can hear one of the twins, let me just check on them."

"No, I'll go. Can you stick the kettle on, please?" Millie kicked her shoes off and ran up the stairs, delighted that soon her problems would be over.

***

Tommy Lee climbed out of the grab. He was starting to enjoy himself. Never in a million years did he think he'd get used to the dirt and grime, but the place had grown on him. For the last couple of weeks since he'd taken over, he'd learnt all about the yard and the docks. He'd kept a close eye on both, leaving Millie to concentrate on his boys.

He made his way back to the Portakabin. He needed to warm up a bit and grab a cuppa, then he would do his usual safety checks prior to leaving for the night. Duke was behind the desk talking to Millie's brother, Aron.

"Think it might snow," Tommy Lee said, shutting the door behind him. "Yous want a cuppa?"

"Yeah, as you're making one," Duke said. "I phoned Millie, but she was out shopping, I'll talk to her tonight. Aron, go check on the men, make sure they've everything ready for when the copper gets collected in the morning."

Aron jumped up. "I'll have a cuppa, too, I won't be long." He opened the door, and a blast of the bitter cold air hit him in the face. "Dordy, it's cold enough to freeze the balls off a brass monkey."

Tommy Lee laughed. Kids these days didn't know the meaning of cold. He switched the kettle on then turned to Duke. "My brother, John Jo's, fighting Christmas Eve. Reckon there's a fair bit of money to be made if you fancy a bet."

"Where's he fighting?" Duke asked, his interest piqued.

"Romford, that little boxing club near the green." Tommy Lee poured the boiled water into the pot. "I won't be staying late. I'll need to be up early to see my chavvies."

"Okay. I'd only spend the night in the pub, I may as well earn some money instead." Duke grinned. "Who's he fighting?"

"Henry Smith, it's Gypsy's uncle. They've had a feud going since he's been with her." Tommy Lee poured the tea and then handed it to Duke. "I know they got together under unusual circumstances, but they have a chavvie now and one on the way. It's time to let it go."

"Yeah, I know him. Bit of a mouth on the man, he deserves to get knocked on his arse... So it's true then, he won her in a poker game?"

"Yeah, it's true, but John Jo's not to blame, it was her own grandfather who gambled with her life. Right, I'll go check the yard, make sure everything's locked up." He made his way out and started at the front gate. He clocked the motor across the road. It had been there most of the day. Walking towards it, he spotted a man in the driver's seat and one in the passenger. When he stepped across the road, the car sped away.

That wasn't a good sign.

***

Rosie sat glued to the TV, wine in one hand and a handful of crisps in the other. "News is on, Mil," she called out to the kitchen.

Millie walked in and sat next to her, her gaze resting on the giant Christmas tree that stood in the bay window. Its lights twinkled and illuminated the brightly coloured baubles. She glanced at the TV. "I hate the news, it's all doom and gloom." She reached for her wine. "You gonna help me wrap these presents then?"

"You do know this is gonna take us all night," Rosie groused.

"You said you would help. I bought wine and nibbles." Millie grinned, holding up another bag of cheese and onion crisps.

"Fine. I'll—"

"Wait, Rose, isn't that the psychiatric hospital you stayed at?" Millie crawled to the TV and turned up the volume. "Someone's gone missing."

"I know him!" Rosie screeched. "He was the old fella playing chess."

The newsreader described how the elderly man had gone missing in the night. The alarm wasn't raised until a friend came to visit. The gentleman had no family.

"Shit. I should've done something about it, Mil, I'm partly responsible."

"You're not to blame, it's that creepy doctor… Do you think we should go to the police?"

"Who would they believe, the doctor or an ex-patient and gangster's moll?"

"Rose, I am not a gangster's moll. I'm a businesswoman," she said indignantly.

"Okay, whatever you call yourself, we can't do nothing, not now."

Millie tutted. "Fucking gangster's moll. I don't know where you get these ideas from." She leant across the table and grabbed her glass, then took a large gulp. "Now they're under the spotlight, they aren't gonna be able to do anything that might draw further suspicion, so I'm guessing they'll leave it until this dies down, probably at least a month. We'll stake out the place end of January."

"You promise?" Rosie asked, blinking away tears.

"I promise. Now help me get this lot wrapped."

***

Tommy Lee headed back to the Portakabin. The uneasy feeling wouldn't leave him. "I think we may have a problem."

"What sort of problem?" Duke asked suspiciously.

"The unwanted visitor sort. When I was checking everything I noticed a motor parked across the road. It had been there for a few hours, two blokes sitting in it, like they were watching the place." He held his hands in front of the heater.

"Fuck. Do you think they'll be back tonight?"

"Dunno, but I think we should stay here tonight, just in case they do try anything… If we pull the motor out of sight and lock the gates, it they do come back, they'll think we've gone." He reached for the phone. "I'll let Millie know."

"No," Duke said. "You know what my daughter's like, she'll drive straight over here. Let me phone around and get some men here, then we'll tell her tomorrow when we go home."

CHAPTER 47

Millie carried the twins down the stairs, one in each arm. They were coming up to eleven weeks old and now getting to the point where she struggled to carry them both. They had woken at six a.m., and she didn't want to wake Rosie as they'd had a late night wrapping the rest of the presents. She lay them down together in the crib then went to make up their bottles. When she entered the kitchen, Rosie was already sitting at the table sipping tea.

"Morning, Mil."

"What are you doing up already?" she asked.

"Couldn't sleep. Every time I closed my eyes I was back in that place. I could even hear that squeaky trolley."

Millie sat next to her and placed her hand on hers. "I'm sorry, Rose, I should've done something sooner."

"You've had enough on your plate, what with losing Paul, losing Micheal, the fire, the twins, you've gone through so much… This was never your problem, I should've done something."

"Whatever they are up to, we will expose them." Millie stood, ready to make the twins' bottles. "Together."

***

Tommy Lee sat up and stretched. He had managed to get a few hours' sleep while sitting on one end of the sofa. He glanced at Aron who was at the other end still asleep. Duke was in the chair behind the desk with his feet up, snoring.

Without disturbing the pair, he let himself out of the Portakabin and went for a mooch around the yard. He liked to check everything before the men arrived for work.

Everything seemed to be in its place. However, the men who were in that car never came back, unless they knew they'd stayed the night.

"Morning." Duke marched towards him. "Everything all right?"

Tommy Lee nodded. "No sign of anything out of the normal. We're gonna have to have someone here every night."

"We need a couple of guard dogs, too," Duke added. "Don't you find it strange that someone's put an offer in for the place?"

"It is considering we haven't advertised, but then people talk, and word gets around. I think we should only deal with him face to face and not his representative… I need a cuppa, you coming?" Tommy Lee made his way back to the Portakabin. Duke's words had struck a chord with him. Why would you send a representative to do your dealing if you're that keen? Was the man testing the water?

He stepped up into the Portakabin. Aron was slumped back on the sofa, eyes open.

"That was the worst night's sleep I've ever had. I feel like my body's broken," he said.

Tommy Lee laughed. He could sleep anywhere, he had to when he was in the army. "I think we should arrange a meeting with this buyer. Tell them we won't deal with anyone but him, then the ball's in his court."

"I'll phone later and set it up. Would be nice to get it sorted before Christmas Day cos I don't think Connie will like it if I'm here then," Duke surmised.

***

Millie washed up the last bottle and dried her hands. She had sent Rosie up for a lie down, hoping she would catch up on some sleep. She felt uneasy but wasn't sure why. It was like she was waiting for another disaster to strike. There always seemed to be something going wrong these days.

She was waiting for Scott who was going to escort her around the businesses. It had been a while since she had checked on things. Maybe that was why she felt uneasy.

Connie came in the kitchen door. She didn't seem her usual chirpy self. "Morning, Mil, how's the twins been this morning?"

"Morning, Mum. They haven't stopped crying, I've only just managed to get them down for a nap. Do you want a cuppa, I'm just about to put the kettle on?" She studied her face. "Did you sleep all right?"

"A cuppa would be nice... I slept okay, why do you ask?"

"You look a bit pasty. You're not coming down with something, are you? How do you feel?" she asked, nervously wringing the tea towel in her hands.

"Are we alone?" Connie peeked out into the hallway.

"Yeah, Rose is in bed. Whatever's wrong, Mum, you're scaring me."

"Millie, don't say a word to anyone."

"I won't. What is it?" In her mind, her mum was ill. Was she dying?

"Promise me," Connie pleaded.

"Of course. I promise, now spit it out." She watched her mother's face closely. This was going to be bad.

Connie gasped. "I think I'm pregnant."

***

"Meeting's all set, he'll be here at two p.m.," Duke said, slamming the phone down.

THE STEPNEY TAKEOVER

"Good... Right, I'm off to the café. Sausage and egg sarnies all round?" Tommy Lee asked. He felt like his stomach was eating itself. They'd had no dinner the previous night and no breakfast. Just unlimited cups of tea and a couple of whiskeys.

"Sounds good to me," Duke said. "And I'm sure Aron won't say no."

Tommy Lee set off for the café, pulling his jacket up around his neck to protect him from the biting wind, then shoved his hands in his pockets. He walked along the road until he spotted the car that had been watching the scrapyard. Had they been here all night? He opened the café door. A loud ping alerted the owner of his presence. Tommy Lee quickly scanned the room as he walked to the counter.

"I'll have six sausage and egg sarnies, please, mate."

He took a seat at the table and picked up the newspaper that had been left there. With his gaze on the paper, he listened. Two men sat near the door, whispering. He thought he could just pick up a Manchester accent but couldn't be sure.

"Here ya go, sir, six sausage and egg sandwiches. D'ya want sauce?"

"Brown please, mate, on all of them." He handed the money over and then headed to the door. Just as he reached the table the two men sat at, he dropped his change. Swooping down, he apologised to them while he retrieved it.

"Not a problem," one said in a thick Mancunian accent.

Got ya, Tommy Lee thought with a smile.

***

Millie stood on the quayside looking out across the Thames. She was in a trance, her thoughts on Paul. He'd loved this place as much as he'd loved the scrapyard. She wondered what life would have been like if he was still here. Would they still be playing games with each other's lives or would they both have moved on? That was pretty doubtful; he believed she was his property and as such would have destroyed anyone who stood in his way to own her again. She was simply another business that he owned, like here.

The scrapyard and docks were both profitable, but this was the real money earner. Goods could be brought in and out under the guise of legitimate jobs.

"Mil, tea's ready."

The sound of Scott's voice brought her back to reality. A gust of wind hit her, almost taking her breath away, the gentle lap of the water becoming more violent. The spray of saltwater hit her face. It stung.

When she entered the office, her hands were tinged purple.

"What were you doing out there, Mil? Stand in front of the heater and warm yourself up a bit," Scott ordered.

"Has Tommy Lee been here this morning?" she asked.

"No, the men said he hasn't turned up yet."

That was strange in itself. He was always punctual. "We'll go to the scrapyard next. It's time I checked in with him." She wrapped her hands around her cup, the warming sensation comforting.

"Mil, are you sure you're okay? You seem a bit preoccupied," Scott asked, his words full of concern.

"I'm fine, just a lot on my mind." Her first thought was Connie. How could her mum be pregnant? Shit, what would Duke say? Millie glanced at Scott who stared back with a frown. "Did you see the news last night?"

He shook his head. "I was out, why?"

"That manor place where Rosie stayed was on. Apparently a man's gone missing. Reading between the lines, it's someone with no family, which fits with what Rosie said. Someone came to visit him. An old friend or neighbour, I can't remember now. Anyway, it was all over the news and now she's upset. Blaming herself for not having done something about it earlier."

"Shit. We were gonna go down there and watch the place," he said. "Just with everything going on, I forgot."

"She wants to make them pay, and it's up to us to help her. I can't do anything at the moment. I'm being watched by Duke and Tommy Lee. And I can't spare any men while the businesses are under threat."

"How about a private investigator?"

"Scott, you do realise how much they cost?"

"Then what's the answer?"

She thought for a moment. "We do need to do something cos she's not sleeping, and I'm scared this will set her back… Let's have a think and see if we can come up with something. I told her they won't do anything yet until the heat's died down. Hopefully by then I'll have a partner in the scrapyard, and I'll be able to spare some men to watch the place… Anyway, go and tell the men we're going. I want to find out why Tommy Lee didn't come here this morning, but I just need to make a quick phone call."

***

"Motor's coming in," Aron said, stepping into the Portakabin.

"They're early." Duke looked at the clock.

Tommy Lee took a seat behind the desk. "They want to show they won't be told what to do. So now we show them otherwise." He grinned.

Four men entered the Portakabin.

"Please take a seat," Duke offered.

Ignoring him, they spread out around the room.

The smallest man walked to the desk and spoke. "We haven't got time to waste. I've taken the liberty of getting a contract drawn up. Once ownership is transferred to me, I will hand over the money."

Tommy Lee laughed. "Nothing is gonna be signed over until the money's in the owner's bank."

"As I understand it, Paul Kelly's widow owns this place, is that correct?"

"She does, but we are looking after her interests. So it's us you'll need to deal with."

"Have you ever heard the term organ grinder and monkey?" The short man grinned. "Well, I have no time for monkeys, so I'll wait for the organ grinder."

***

Millie marched towards the Portakabin, annoyed she had to park in the street. She had Scott keeping an eye on the road while she came in. Her attention was drawn to shouting coming from the office. Reaching into her bag, she pulled out her gun, slipped the safety switch off, and held it in her pocket. She stood just outside the door, out of sight so she could listen.

The crash of a chair made her jump. It was followed by a deep Mancunian accent.

"Don't do anything stupid, boy, now phone her and get her here or I'll get my men here to start blowing some brains out."
Shit

She turned and motioned to Scott, waving her gun in the air. He quickly exited the motor and ran across the road towards her, grabbing his own gun from his waistband. She placed her finger against her mouth, showing him to be quiet.

"You have until the count of ten," the man continued.

"Scott, go up the end and open the window, the catch is still broken. Wait for me to give you a sign, and then if you get a clear shot, take it."

"What's the sign?" he asked.

"I'll cough... and don't open the window until I distract them." She silently prayed to a god she didn't believe in. And then strode around to the door.

"Good afternoon, gentleman." She stepped in and headed to Tommy Lee. She held the gun to her chest under her coat while putting one arm around his neck. "Take the gun. Scott's outside," she whispered against his mouth. She felt him take it gently from her hand.

"What can I do for you?" she asked, turning towards the man.

"Sign the paperwork. No one has to get hurt," Shorty warned.

"And what if I don't want to?"

"You don't seem to understand, miss, this isn't a request, this is an order." He grinned, showing yellow stained teeth.

"I see." She turned her head slightly. "Are you ready?"

"Yes," Tommy Lee said.

Millie coughed loudly, then she was pushed aside as Tommy Lee started shooting. It happened so quickly, the shouting and noise of the gunshots echoed in her ears.

Tommy Lee reached for her, helping her up. She found herself staring at Duke. He looked angry.

"What the fuck were you thinking?" He ran his hand over his face. "You are grounded... for life."

"I second that," Tommy Lee added.

"Is that the thanks I get for saving you lot?" She caught sight of Aron over his shoulder. "You're bleeding." She panicked.

"Its fine, just a scratch. Thanks, Millie."

"What are you thanking her for, she could've been fucking killed," Duke spat.

Scott entered the Portakabin. "The others are here."

"Better late than never," Millie said. "Search these scumbags, see if they have any form of identification on them, then go tell the boys to find out everything they can about this outfit. Maybe we should pay them a visit."

"Just listen to yourself," Tommy Lee said, staring at her. "You could've been killed, and here you are, planning on taking the fight up north."

"I'm not planning anything, but I need to know who they are and what they're capable of. This is the nature of the business." A knot formed in the pit of her stomach just from the look he gave her.

"I can't do this, Mil, I'm not gonna stand here and watch you get killed. You're on your own." He stormed from the trailer.

The sound of him screeching away in his motor was all she could hear.

CHAPTER 48

It was Christmas Eve. Millie sat on the bed, her heart heavy. Was it because she hadn't seen hide nor hair of Tommy Lee since he'd stormed out of the Portakabin two days previous? Or was it because Duke had secured a buyer for half of the scrapyard? She didn't know. Her emotions were a jumble, all mixed up inside her.

Was she doing the right thing? Duke told her he knew this man personally and he had experience in the scrap game. He also guaranteed that he wouldn't do her over. She would still have an equal say in the business, and do the accounts, but he would run it without her having to worry. Whoever he was, he sounded too good to be true, and in her experience, someone like that normally was.

Tommy Lee hadn't been to see the twins either; that was so unlike him. He loved his boys, she knew that. The worst thing was she felt guilty. Had she enjoyed the drama that day? Yes. Was she turning into a female version of Paul? Yes. Tommy Lee didn't like what he saw, and to be perfectly honest, neither did she.

She walked to the window and wiped the condensation away so she could see out. The sky was white; it could snow.

That would be nice for the twins' first Christmas. It would be nicer, though, if they saw their daddy.

"Millie, we need to go and sign the papers," Duke called up to her.

"I'm just coming," she said back, slipping her shoes on. She descended the stairs. "What time do we need to be there?"

"Eleven-thirty a.m. Con, we're going." He kissed her cheek and smiled. "We won't be long."

Millie kissed the twins goodbye and joined Duke in his pickup truck. "Why don't you buy a newer one, with a heater that works?"

"This works just fine, and besides, it has sentimental value," he said.

"What sentimental value?" She laughed.

"I taught you and the boys to drive in this, so even when it won't work and it's ready for the scrap heap, this little beauty will stay with me, if only to look at, till the day I die."

That surprised her. Who would've thought Duke Lee, the rough-and-ready man who'd fight anyone, was so sentimental? She wondered if Connie had spoken about the pregnancy. One thing was for sure, this baby wouldn't be learning to drive in this heap.

The engine started, and Dean Martin blared out of the speakers.

"Everybody loves somebody sometime," Duke sang along.

She looked at him and smiled. "You really love Mum, don't you."

"Yep, she's the only woman for me... and I loves me children." He smiled. "I told you once before, it's all about family."

Sighing inwardly, she nodded. Here she sat, a single parent to twins and no man to love her. Was she even worth loving, and if she was, would she ever find that again? It was doubtful. Her main priority were her boys and the businesses. She watched the houses and shops whiz past in a blur, all merging into one. Before she knew it, Duke pulled up inside the solicitor's car park.

"You okay?" Duke asked.

"I think so. So what's this man like who's buying half the scrapyard?" She glanced at Duke. "You haven't told me anything about him."

"I've told you all you need to know. He'll be a good business partner, he won't do you over, and more importantly, it will free you up to be a mum."

"You sound like Tommy Lee," she said.

"You can't blame a man for wanting the best for his chavvies, Millie. I never thought I'd say this, but I'm glad he's their dad."

Millie almost choked on thin air. "You've changed your tune."

"It takes a big man to admit when he's wrong, and I was. Come on, let's get this over with. The pub is calling."

***

Connie had just finished tidying up when Millie and Duke returned from the solicitor's. "Kettle's on," she said when they came through the door. "How did it go?"

"The man who's buying it got held up, so we signed as Dad couldn't wait. The money should be in the bank by about two." Millie threw her bag on the sofa and made her way to the kitchen with Connie following her. "Don't you find that weird that he didn't turn up? I mean, if you're buying into a business, wouldn't you want to meet your business partner?" She reached for the wine bottle in the fridge and found a glass.

"If he was held up then he couldn't help it. I'm sure you'll meet him soon," Connie answered.

"I'm off to the pub, I won't be late," Duke informed them.

After the front door closed, Millie glanced at Connie. "You haven't told him, have you?"

"I'll tell him when I'm certain. Do you want a mince pie with your wine?"

"Mum, don't change the subject. You wouldn't have told me if you weren't sure." She took a mince pie when Connie placed a tin on the table. "Homemade, yum. What was I saying, oh yes, you know you're pregnant, so what are you scared of?"

"The boys are now eighteen, that's a big age gap, and I'm a grandmother." Connie threw her hands up in the air. "I don't know."

"So you're the one with the problem. Didn't you tell me babies are a blessing? Well, that means this one is, too." Millie picked up her glass and the tin. "I'm gonna go and watch a bit of TV, come on."

THE STEPNEY TAKEOVER

***

Duke entered the boxing gym. He hadn't been in here for a few years now. It had a new owner, and he'd done the place up, even putting in showers. It wasn't like that when he'd started the bare-knuckle fighting. He'd often gone home covered in blood and guts, and his mother, Darkie, would hose him down. And then, of course, Connie had taken over when they'd run off.

He made his way towards the ring where people were gathering.

"Duke, over here." Tommy Lee waved his hand in the air. He stood with his brothers, John Jo and Sean Paul.

"Who's taking the bets, lads?" Duke asked.

"See that man over there, with the grey cap on, he's taking the bets," John Jo said.

"I'll walk over with you." Tommy Lee pushed through the waiting crowd. "How's Millie?"

"She's okay." Duke pulled out a roll of ten-pound notes. "You still coming tomorrow?" he asked while counting them.

"Don't know if that's such a good idea."

"It's your chavvies' first Christmas. Personally, I wouldn't miss that for the world."

Tommy Lee stood with his hands in his pockets and shrugged. "I don't want to make it awkward for anyone, besides, me mother will want me at hers for dinner."

"Suit yourself, but just remember, you're gonna have to face her sooner or later."

CHAPTER 49

Millie finished laying the table before she made a start on the veg. The turkey had gone into the oven at an ungodly hour, thanks to the twins, and she had a joint of beef and pork waiting to go in.

She had been up at the crack of dawn feeding, bathing, and dressing the twins, and then she had showered and put on a black lace dress. It seemed a bit short to her, but Rosie had assured her when she'd bought it, it was perfect for Christmas. With her hair piled up on top of her head, she finished the look of with a large pair of creole earrings.

The twins had matching pale-blue romper suits on. To a stranger they wouldn't have been able to tell them apart, even Duke struggled at times. She decided it was probably a man thing. But she knew them, she knew their tiny differences which seemed to stand out to her, but not to other people. It was like their personalities. They were beginning to shine through. Baby Duke sucked his thumb and preferred to sleep on his side, where as Tommy boy liked to sleep on his back. He was also more alert than his brother. He was seven minutes older and a few ounces heavier, maybe that made a difference.

Pouring herself a wine, even though it was only nine-thirty a.m., she turned the radio on and smiled. 'When a Child is Born' by Johny Mathis started, so she turned the volume up a fraction before finishing the potatoes. She felt happy, even content. This time last year she had been a mess. Separated from Paul and living here on her own. And let's not forget pregnant with Micheal.

He had, of course, come round with expensive gifts for her. Perfume, gold and diamond earrings and matching necklace and bracelet. He was very materialistic; she'd never really noticed before.

I wonder what he bought his mistresses.

"Fuck you, brain." She groaned. Today was not the day to think about him.

Connie came through the kitchen door carrying presents. "Your father will be over later, he didn't get in until one this morning, totally drunk. He'll be bringing the rest of them."

"Bung them under the tree, Mum, and help yourself to a drink," Millie said. "And don't wake the twins, I've only just got them back to sleep."

'Peace on Earth/Little Drummer Boy' came on next by David Bowie and Bing Crosby. Another one of her favourites. She sang along while preparing the rest of the veg.

"The table looks amazing, like out of one of those posh magazines." Connie entered the kitchen. "I would've prepared the dinner, Millie, you didn't have to do it all."

"You need to rest, Mum, a woman in your condition needs to take it easy… How are you feeling?"

"I'm feeling like I need a cup of tea. Would you like one?" she asked and eyed up Millie's wine. "Don't you think it's a bit early for that?"

"It's Christmas, chill, woman." Millie continued to chop the cabbage and hummed along to the radio. "You can baste the turkey for me."

"Morning, Connie, Mil. Merry Christmas."

"Morning, Rosie, Merry Christmas to you, too." Connie grabbed another set of cutlery.

"What are you doing?" Millie asked. "I've set enough places."

"Ahh, your father bought a visitor home last night." Connie's face flushed. "He'd also insisted that he stay for Christmas dinner."

"Who, Mum, who has he invited?"

Connie swallowed loudly before she answered. "They were out together last night, and your dad brought him home. They were both so drunk."

Millie reached for the wine bottle and poured a large glass. "I knew today was too good to be true." She gulped it back in one and wiped her mouth on the back of her hand. "What's his name?"

"It's Tommy Lee."

After refilling her glass, Millie raised it in the air. "Merry fucking Christmas."

***

It was midday by the time Scott arrived. Millie was still busy in the kitchen, frantically stirring, chopping, and taste-testing. The worktops were piled high with dirty pots, pans, and dishes, and she was starting to get tipsy. The vegetables bubbled away on the stove top, the meats browning in the oven. The smell of Christmas hung in the air.

"All right, Mil. Whoa, it looks like a bomb's gone off in here," Scott said while glancing at the mess. "Who knew you were secretly an unhinged galloping gourmet." He laughed, until she glared at him. "I'll go in the other room and leave you to it." He backed away, then fled.

The back door opened, and Duke walked in with Tommy Lee following. "Morning, Mil, Merry Christmas." He clocked the dirty pots and pans piled high. "I'll send Connie out to help clean this up a bit." Then he disappeared, leaving her with Tommy Lee.

"Merry Christmas, Millie, you look beautiful." His thick southern Irish accent had always affected her, that was how she'd ended up in bed with him in the first place, but today, maybe because it was Christmas, or maybe it was because she was on her fourth wine, it made her tummy do this weird fluttery thing.

"Merry Christmas, Tommy Lee." She looked into his sparkling blue eyes.

THE STEPNEY TAKEOVER

"I'll start washing up," Connie announced as she entered the kitchen. She stopped and glanced between the two. "Not interrupting, am I?"

"No, Mum." Millie turned and continued to mix the stuffing.

"I'll go see the chavvies," he muttered before walking away.

Connie filled the sink with hot soapy water and a splash of bleach. "Is something going on between you two?"

"No, Mum, as you've pointed out, he's the twins' father." Millie topped up her wine. She would need it now her mother had the bit between her teeth.

"That look between you says differently," Connie continued. "Your father likes him."

"Mum, please. Can we not do this now? I've got all these people here expecting to be fed."

"Go and take a break while I clean up. I'll pop this stuffing in the oven." Connie opened the oven door, and the smell of the food filled the kitchen. "This smells wonderful."

"While we're on the subject of things going on, are you gonna tell Dad about the little secret you're keeping?" Millie asked, with a swift change of subject to her mother.

"I'll tell him today. Now go and put your feet up for ten minutes."

Tommy Lee sat holding baby Duke. It amazed him how he seemed to have changed in just a few days. "I'm going to tell Millie today," he whispered to Duke. "I think she should know."

Duke gave him a nod of approval. "Just make sure we have dinner first and there's no sharp objects near her." He looked up when she entered the room.

"Can I get yous a drink?" she asked the room collectively.

"I'll get them, Mil. You sit down, you've been in the kitchen hours," Rosie offered.

"You would never have noticed by the mess." Scott laughed.

"You can give me a hand," Rosie snapped at him in reply.

"I'll have a cup of tea, please, food smells good, Mil," Tommy Lee said.

Her face flushed; she clearly wasn't good at taking compliments.

"You should see the table, it's fit for royalty." Rosie grinned.

"I'll have a beer," Duke told Scott. "Turn the telly over while you're up, I'm not watching this shit."

Millie went back to the kitchen. "Do you want tea, Mum?" The washing up was piled neatly on the draining board. "You could've put that in the dishwasher."

"I like to do it by hand, I know it's done properly then." Connie grabbed a cup and handed it to her. "Meat's just resting for ten minutes before it can be carved. Is there anything else that needs doing?"

"No, go and sit with Dad, he's commandeered the TV and keeps switching channels. Think he's starting to piss everyone off." Millie waited for her mother to leave then opened the back door and headed off down the garden. She carried a tiny blue teddy. When she reached Micheal's memorial, she placed it underneath the tree. "Merry Christmas, Micheal."

***

Everyone sat around the table munching their way through the mound of food. Tommy Lee held Tommy boy and Millie held baby Duke.

"This is bloody lovely," Scott said through a mouthful of food.

"You've done well, girl," Duke added after swigging his beer.

"It's the best meal I've ever had," Tommy Lee said to Millie. "You're a good cook."

"Thanks," she said to them, her face heating up. "Save room for Christmas pud."

"I need a rest first, Mil, I'm stuffed." Rosie rubbed her tummy.

"Ahh, this is their first Christmas," Connie gushed at the twins. "Look how alert they both are… I wish my Jasper and Sherry could've made it. I feel like I haven't seen much of baby Sherry." She sighed.

"You could have gone and spent Christmas Day with them, Mum," Millie told her. "It wasn't compulsory you be here." Did Connie feel obliged to be here?

"I couldn't leave you on your own," Connie grumbled.

"I wouldn't be on my own, I have the twins, Rosie, Scott, and Tommy Lee… Why don't you go see them tomorrow? You could stay a few days with them."

"Are you trying to get rid of me?"

"Connie," Duke growled. "What's gotten into you, woman?"

Millie stood and passed baby Duke to Rosie. "I'll clear the plates away."

"I'll give you a hand," Tommy Lee said while picking his own plate up. "Here, Connie, why don't you hold your grandson."

They headed to the kitchen, arms full of dirty crockery.

"Don't take that to heart, Mil. Families always bicker at Christmas." He laughed. "My family actually fight over who gets the pick of the Quality Street, and when I say fight, I mean there's actual blood spilled."

She smiled. "I guess that's families for ya." Opening the dishwasher, she loaded it and then switched it on. "Shall we go back in for round two?"

He nodded and followed behind her.

"Who would like a refill?" she asked with a cheery smile on her face and another bottle of wine tucked under her arm. "Can you do the honours, Rose, while I put the twins down for a nap?"

She took Tommy boy, and Tommy Lee took baby Duke. "They should sleep for an hour or so before they need feeding," she told him.

Millie glanced at her mum as she sat. Was she going to cry? "Mum, are you okay?"

"I've got something to tell you, Duke," Connie announced.

"Oh God." Millie put her head in her hands.

"What is it, spit it out?" Duke said.

"I'm having a baby," she exclaimed.

Silence followed.

Even Scott looked stunned.

"Congratulations." Tommy Lee grinned.

"Haven't you got something to tell Millie?" Duke grinned back.

Tommy Lee rubbed the back of his neck, the smile dropping from his face quicker than a ton of bricks. Was he nervous?

Millie frowned at him. "Well, I'm sure you're not pregnant, too, so what is it?"

He picked up his glass and necked the remaining whisky. "I'm the one who bought half the scrapyard. We're partners."

CHAPTER 50

Millie threw the hoover in the cupboard and headed to the kitchen to make a cuppa. It was that awful time in between Christmas and New Year when no one knew what the day or date was.

Duke and Connie had headed off to Kent, on Boxing Day, to see Jasper and his baby. Which was a relief for Millie; she didn't want to see either of them, her temper was still bubbling away. Christmas Day soon went downhill after the baby and business announcements. It had taken an hour for Duke to speak — he'd been in total shock at the baby news. And as for her and Tommy Lee, well, that hadn't ended well either.

"Fucking Irish pig," she mumbled while filling the kettle.

The thing that none of them seemed to grasp was the underhanded way he and Duke had gone about it, pretending the mystery buyer couldn't get to the solicitor's in time.

THE STEPNEY TAKEOVER

"I bet you had a good laugh at my expense." She grabbed a cup from the cupboard and placed it down with such force it smashed into pieces.

She would've expected behaviour like this from Tommy Lee but not Duke. He was her dad, shouldn't he have been on her side? Why was it, whenever she let people into her life, they always let her down? Not necessarily straight away, but somewhere down the line something would happen to hurt her.

Just look at her first husband, Levi, and the beatings she'd taken. The black eyes, fractures, and verbal abuse. Then Paul and his betrayal. She wondered just how many other women he'd slept with while they were married. And Connie, who now seemed to resent her, for what Millie wasn't sure, and Duke, who'd lied to her.

She switched the kettle off, instead opting for a small brandy. That would warm her shattered heart.

After she'd poured the brandy, she sauntered over to the window and, squeezing next to the Christmas tree, she peered out. There had been a dusting of snow overnight with more expected today. Rosie and Scott were checking on the businesses for her while she stayed in the warm with the twins.

She jumped at the shrill sound of the phone ringing. "Shit." Was it Duke again? He'd already phoned three times today, leaving messages on the answering machine. Each one had said pretty much the same thing: 'Hello... hello, Millie... Just checking you and the twins are okay... Oh, it's me, your dad, bye.'

Connie hasn't bothered, though, obviously still pissed off with me.

She waited for it to stop and then stood waiting for the light to flash, telling her he'd left another message. No light. Good.

She went back to the lounge and checked the twins who were sleeping soundly. Probably on account that they were up most of the night, wanting to play. She sat on the sofa, resting her head back. Having the babies had changed her life. The downside was she couldn't just up and go out anymore, but the upside far outweighed that. When she spoke to them they smiled at her. They knew she was their mummy, and that was all Millie needed to melt her heart.

A loud knock came from the front door. Cursing under her breath, she opened it. Tommy Lee stood there, hands in his pockets and an annoyed look on his face.

"What do you want?"

"I'm here because your father phoned me. Why aren't you answering your phone?" He pushed past her and marched to the lounge.

"Do you mind, this is my home, you can't just—"

"Oh, I can, Millie. I know me and your dad hurt you, but it wasn't done for that reason."

"What reason was it done for then?" she asked.

"It was done to keep you safe, it was done to give you the freedom to look after our chavvies without having to worry about the scrapyard, and it was done so you wouldn't have to wonder if you were getting fleeced."

"If that's true, why didn't either of you tell me?"

"Truthfully? Because we're both scared of you," he admitted.

"What?" She laughed. "You two are scared of me?"

"You've got a bit of a temper on you…" He sighed. "Look, I want to spend time with them." He pointed to the twins. "And you."

***

Rosie sat playing with the twins on the floor. "Mil, they turn their heads now when you wave the teddy in front of them. "Yous boys are so clever, yes, you are."

"Did you tell Scott dinner's at six?" Millie yelled from the kitchen.

"Yeah, he said he'll be back before then… Do you wanna hand with anything?" Rosie called back. "I feel like I'm not pulling my weight, Mil."

"No, it's all under control," Millie said as she walked back in.

"It smells delicious. What are we having?" Rosie asked.

"Bacon pudding. You know, it's kinda nice Connie not being here. I actually get a chance to cook without her taking over." She held her hand up to stop Rosie from replying. "I know what you're gonna say, and yes, she was a great help since I've had the twins, but she seemed to have trouble backing off."

"I wonder if that's why she was a bit funny towards you Christmas Day, because you cooked and she didn't?"

"I put it down to her being pregnant, but it could be. I guess now the boys are off her hands she's left with no one to care for other than Duke… I think this baby will do her good."

"I think that was the front door, Mil, I'll get it," Rosie said, jumping up.

Millie knelt next to the twins. "Hello, my babies, Mummy loves you both so much, yes, she does."

"So does Daddy." Tommy Lee's voice drifted over her shoulder. He knelt next to her and smiled down at the twins. "These are for you." He thrust a bunch of flowers towards her.

"Thanks, I'll go and put them in some water." She stood and retreated to the kitchen where Rosie stood, grinning.

"What?" Millie whispered.

"He's bought you flowers." Rosie winked. "Are you gonna tell me what's going on, or shall I ask him?"

"Nothing is going on, I simply invited him for dinner, along with Scott."

"So you've made up?"

"Obviously. Stop grinning, Rose, he's the twins' dad, we have to get on."

"Yeah, you keep telling yourself that. I've seen the way you look at each other. You fancy him."

"Of course I fancy him! How do you think the twins got here? They weren't found under a bloody gooseberry bush, were they."

"Is everything okay out there?" he asked.

"Yes, just putting the kettle on," Millie said. "Rose, I'm warning you, do not embarrass me. Now stick these in a vase while I make his tea."

***

Millie placed Tommy Lee's plate down in front of him. "Help yourself to gravy." Then she passed Scott his.

"Thanks. Never had bacon pudding before, smells good," he said. "And it's nice not having to cook, Mil."

"Can you pour the wine, Rose, while I get ours?" Millie disappeared into the kitchen, returning seconds later with two more plates.

"Has there been any more news on that fella's disappearance?" Scott said while stuffing a large roast potato into his mouth.

"No. I think we should consider our stakeout," Rosie said. "I've been following the news, and there's been no more said."

"I can't stay out all night now I have the twins," Millie added.

"Can someone please enlighten me?" Tommy Lee asked. He had an irritated tone to his voice and stared straight at Millie.

"Okay, this is the shortened version," Rosie said. "I went nutty and got put into a private psychiatric hospital. People were going missing in the dead of night. The private doctor told Millie I suffered from psychosis, but Millie knew there was something wrong with the place so she blackmailed the doctor to get me released, and Millie's dodgy doctor reckons they could be selling body parts."

Tommy Lee had kept his gaze on Millie the whole time. "Blackmail and a dodgy doctor, really, Mil?"

"Firstly, he's not my dodgy doctor, thank you, Rosie, and secondly, the psychiatric doctor in that place was crooked. Why else were they worried about me going to the authorities?"

"No wonder Duke's going grey." Tommy Lee sighed.

"He is not. I mean, it's only a few hairs," Millie said indignantly.

"I don't want you involved in this, Millie, understand?" Tommy Lee ordered.

"But I—"

"I said, *understand*?" he spat.

"Fine." She reached for her glass and drank the lot down. "Give me a refill, please, Rose."

"I'll help, I've got a few ex-army mates who will, too. They'll need paying, though."

"Money's not a problem, as long as it's dealt with quickly," Millie added.

"I'll make a couple of phone calls after dinner. Now can we enjoy the rest of the meal in peace?"

CHAPTER 51

January 1978

It had been two weeks since Duke and Connie had left. The New Year had been and gone, and now it was Friday the sixth. Millie had spoken to Duke briefly on the phone a few days ago, after Tommy Lee telling her to act like an adult. He had a way of getting her to do things lately. Annoying, bossy fucker that he was.

Duke had told her Connie wasn't ready to come home yet as she wanted to make up for the lost time with her granddaughter, Sherry. That had stung a bit. Millie had never stopped her from going to Kent, but had Connie felt obligated to babysit? And had Millie just assumed she wanted to? Well, she wouldn't assume anything again.

THE STEPNEY TAKEOVER

She had just finished dressing and doing her hair when Rosie walked through the door.

"Hey, you sure you don't mind babysitting?" Millie asked, running down the stairs.

"Wow, Mil, you look amazing. You sure have gone all out for just a business meeting tonight." Rosie winked. "Are you hoping to get laid?"

"Rose!"

"What? You've already got two kids with him." Rosie giggled. "So come on, how big is his manhood?"

"Big enough to do the job." Millie giggled.

"In inches?" Rosie pressed.

"I don't know, I left my tape measure at home."

"Shall I ask him, Mil?"

"Rose... eight or nine at a rough guess."

"Bloody hell. And I'm guessing he knows how to use it."

Ignoring her, Millie continued. "There's bottles on the side, nappies—"

"I have looked after them before, now stop fussing... I can hear a motor outside."

"Oh shit, where's my shoes?" Millie asked while looking under the stairs.

"They're here. Now go and have a great time, and make sure you wear protection."

***

Duke drew the trailer into place while Connie unlocked the mobile and got the fire started. It had been a crap journey home from Kent, and all Duke wanted was a beer. He carried in the bags of shopping they had bought on the way.

"Do you fancy going to the chippy for tea, Duke?" Connie asked, taking the bags from him.

"There's nothing I'd like more after driving all that way," he moaned.

"I'll walk round there then, you finish putting this lot away." She huffed.

"No, I'll go, woman. You get sorted in here." He reached for his coat and started walking down the lane. As he approached Millie's house, he detoured in and knocked.

"Hello, Duke. Millie's not here at the moment." Rosie smiled.

"Where has she gone and when will she be back?"

"She's gone out to get something to eat, and I don't know, she said she wouldn't be late."

"Who's she gone with?"

"A friend as far as I know. Can I give her a message?"

"Yeah. Tell her I'll see her in the morning. Night, Rosie." He trudged back up the drive and out onto the road. He was hoping to speak to her and smooth things over with her and Connie. He wasn't sure what had happened or why, and to be perfectly honest, he was fucking fed up with it all, but he couldn't have his wife or his daughter at loggerheads.

***

Millie smiled at the waitress as she removed the dirty plates. "Thank you." She glanced at Tommy Lee who was staring straight back. "That was lovely. Thank you."

"Would you like dessert?" he asked.

"No, I'm stuffed." She leant back, the strain on her dress seam from the meal evident. "God, I've definitely eaten too much, I feel like my dress is going to burst off."

He laughed, topping up her drink. "Sounds interesting, but keep it on for a bit longer." He winked.

Is he flirting with me?

Millie's face flushed hot; she knew she was turning red.

Shit.

"So when are we gonna start this surveillance?" She tried to calm herself with a change of subject.

"There's no we, Millie, I will handle it, you worry about the chavvies."

"Look, you need to start treating me as an equal and stop freezing me out. This has been my life for a while now, and I'm more than capable of dealing with it."

Tommy Lee sighed. "And you need to get used to having a man take care of you and our boys… When I get it all arranged, I will tell you. When anything happens, I will tell you, but until that time, why can't you sit back and enjoy your life… with me?"

***

Duke sat in front of the fire, beer in one hand, cigarette in the other. He was agitated. He wanted to know exactly who this friend of Millie's was. Male or female? It was unlike her to go out at night and leave the twins.

"I miss little Sherry girl," Connie said, breaking into his thoughts.

"Don't you miss the twins, or your daughter?" The words came out harsher than he had meant. "You haven't seen them for over two weeks, Con."

"I've seen plenty of them since they've been born. Do you think I'm wrong wanting to spend time with Jasper and my granddaughter?" she asked.

"I'm having a hard time understanding what's going on here. I thought you and Millie were close. What's happened?"

"We are, were, oh, I don't know. I love her, Duke, but she can be selfish. I should've cooked Christmas dinner, I'm the mum."

"Is this what it's over, who cooked Christmas fucking dinner? I tell you what, Con, next Christmas I'm taking myself off and staying away from everyone." He got up and stormed to the door. He looked back before going outside. "Maybe she thought you deserved a rest."

He stepped outside and lit his cigarette. The nicotine hit his lungs and his brain simultaneously. He began walking, and a couple of minutes later, he found himself at Millie's door. He knocked loudly.

"Dad, what are you doing here this late, is Mum all right?"

"She's fine. I just wanted to make sure you got home safe after your meal."

"You'd better come inside out of the cold. Where's your coat?" she asked.

"I'm okay. I'll come in for five minutes." He went through to the lounge, surprised to see Tommy Lee sitting there. "Evening." He nodded.

"Duke. Did you have good time in Kent?"

"Dad, do you want a nightcap?" Millie held up a bottle of scotch.

"Yeah, why not." He smiled. "How's work been?" He sat on the armchair. "Bet it's nicer working knowing you own the place."

"Half the place," Millie called from the dining room.

Duke glanced at Tommy Lee. He was smiling. "So you two?"

"Are business partners," he finished.

"Here, Dad." She handed him his drink. "Why didn't Mum come round?"

"She's putting all the stuff away and cleaning. You know what she's like."

"Yeah, I do, she's still got the hump with me. I thought it was just her hormones, but I must've done something really bad to upset her for this long. Can you tell her I said I'm sorry?"

"I'm sure she'll be over tomorrow, you can tell her yourself then." He necked his drink then stood. "I'd best get back. I'll go out the back door."

Millie waved him off. She was more worried now than she was before. Duke wasn't his usual jovial self. Had they rowed? Millie wasn't good with change or seeing the people she loved fighting. It left her feeling vulnerable.

"I should get going, it's later than I thought," Tommy Lee said. "I'd like to see you and the chavvies tomorrow, if that's okay?"

She shook her head. "I've got a better idea. Why don't you stay tonight?"

CHAPTER 52

It had been a further three days, and Millie still hadn't seen Connie. What hurt her more was the fact she hadn't seen the twins. Didn't she care about them?

"Mil, was it just the accounts you wanted from all the businesses?" Rosie asked.

"I need all the receipts as well, otherwise I won't be able to check the books... Before you go, can you watch the twins for ten minutes, I just want to pop and see Connie," Millie said.

"Are you sure that's wise?"

"She's my mother, I need to see if I've done something, I won't be long." Millie rushed out of the kitchen door, ignoring Rosie's warning. She dashed down the garden, through the gate, and up to the door of the mobile. Taking a deep breath, she opened the door and stepped in.

"Hello. It's only me."

"Millie, in here," Duke called back.

She went into the front room and smiled at Duke. She glanced at Connie who didn't even look up. "You all right, Mum?" she asked in an upbeat voice.

"I'm fine," Connie mumbled.

"I thought you might've come over to see the twins, they miss their nan."

"Yes, well, we all miss someone. I need to put the washing on." Connie stood and moved past Millie.

She could feel her eyes watering up but didn't want to cry, not in front of her parents. "I best get back, Dad, Rosie needs to get off to work." She glided past her mother to the door. "Bye then, Connie," was her parting shot.

She didn't get a reply.

***

Tommy Lee tiptoed up the stairs and stood at the door watching Millie. She was slipping on a clean T-shirt after Tommy boy had puked down her. He wolf whistled, and she spun around.

"You pervert." She laughed, picking up a pillow and throwing it at his head.

"You're only a pervert if you get caught." He winked. "You'll be pleased to know the stakeout's on for this week. I've got two mates coming with me. We'll take an old Escort van down. There's a place we can park out of the way, so they won't see us."

"How do you know that?" she asked suspiciously.

"Because, beautiful, I drove down there today and had a look around." He grabbed her around the waist and pulled her tight to his body. Before she could protest, his lips smashed into hers. He backed up to the door and pushed it shut with his foot.

"Tommy Lee, stop, Rosie's downstairs," she whispered.

"She's watching the chavvies for me, I told her I needed a private word with you. Now are you gonna take that T-shirt off or shall I?"

***

"Connie, you need to go and apologise to her. You acted like she means nothing to you, but I know deep down she does," Duke pleaded.

"Maybe you don't know her as well as you think," she snapped.

"What the fuck is that supposed to mean?"

"It doesn't matter."

"Oh, it fucking does. Tell me or so help me God." He gritted his teeth, fighting to stop his anger.

"Were you in on it?" she asked.

"In on what, woman?"

"It's because of Millie my Jasper moved to Kent, and because of that I didn't get to see my granddaughter. Sherry told me everything." Connie poked Duke in the chest. "I just can't look at her at the moment."

"I'm telling you, it wasn't like that. She asked me to ask them to move their trailer away from the fence because that was all she could see from her window. I asked them, Sherry said no, so Millie put that bloody great fence up. Millie may have asked them to move it, but she certainly didn't tell them to move away. But that's fine, you take Sherry's side and lose your daughter and grandsons." Duke grabbed his jacket.

"Where are you going?"

"Pub, I don't want to look at you at the moment," he bellowed.

"See. That girl's caused trouble between us now."

"Connie, I love you, but you are the one who's wrong." He slammed the door behind him.

***

Millie lay on the sofa. The TV was on, but she wasn't watching it. Her mind was still on Connie. The way she was cold, almost like she hated her.

"So," Rosie began.

Millie turned and stared at her; she had a big smile on her face. "So what?"

"So the talk you had earlier with Tommy Lee, how did it go?"

"It went okay, why?" Millie's face flushed.

Shit.

"Well, it's funny, cos I'm sure I heard your headboard hitting the wall." Rosie giggled.

"Rose." Millie laughed. "I told him we had to be quiet."

"It doesn't matter, Mil, he makes you happy... So is he here permanently?"

"I don't know, we haven't spoken about it. I don't even know what it is." Millie sighed. "I think my mind's taken up with Connie. She won't even look at me."

"Didn't your dad say he was gonna talk to her?" Rosie asked. "Here, have a glass of wine."

"No, Rose, I don't fancy it."

"Bloody hell, Millie Kelly turning down a drink. Shit, you must be upset."

"Very funny. I need to keep an eye on Tommy boy, in case he's sick again."

"Is Tommy Lee coming back tonight?" Rosie refilled her glass. "Because when he's around you seem to be, what's the word...?"

"Happier?" Millie suggested.

"No... Complete, that's it, he seems to complete you."

"For God's sake, who's knocking at this time of night?" Millie complained.

"It's okay, I'll get it." Rosie jumped up and answered the door. Seconds later, she returned. "Mil, it's your dad."

"Can we talk, in private, Mil?" Duke asked.

CHAPTER 53

February 13th

Millie woke to the sound of shouting. She climbed out of bed and walked to the window. It didn't surprise her what she saw. Jasper was pulling his trailer alongside Millie's fence. Duke had told her all about the conversation with Connie and how she blamed her for them leaving, leading to her not spending as much time with her granddaughter. It had been a further few weeks, and Connie still hadn't been to see the twins. It was like they weren't important, perhaps they never were.

"What are you looking at?" Tommy Lee asked. He joined her at the window. "Is this what you were telling me about?"

She nodded. She didn't speak in case she cried.

"I'll go over there." He pulled his trousers on.

"No. Please, just leave it. I'll get a couple of my men to plant the trees along the fence and get the gate boarded up. The only thing that's upsetting me is Micheal's memorial is over there."

"Firstly, I'm your man, so I will be planting the trees and boarding up the gate. I'll phone Scott, he can give me a hand. And secondly, you worry about our boys, and I'll worry about you." He kissed her on her cheek, then went to the en suite for a shower.

Millie returned her focus to the scene unfolding outside. She could see Connie holding the baby. It didn't even bother her. She had stuck that brick wall back up, the one she'd learnt to build when she was with Levi, the one that protected her from his abuse. There was very little chance she would ever knock that down again for Connie.

***

Tommy Lee walked through the gate holding a shovel. Scott stood by his side.

"You sure about this?" Scott asked.

"Yes, I'll not have Millie upset. Here he comes. Duke." He nodded. "Millie wants the memorial moved to her garden."

"If that's what she wants, I'll give you a hand." Duke took the spade from Scott. "Have you dug a hole ready?"

"Yes, it's good to go." He noticed Connie watching from the mobile window. "So her mother doesn't want anything to do with her?"

"Connie loves her, she'll come round in time," Duke said.

"Not being funny, Duke, but Millie's not the type to give people a second chance at breaking her heart." Scott flinched when Duke spun around and faced him. "You can't blame her, all us kids who have grown up in children's homes have a safety mechanism, and when that clicks in, it's the point of no return. Millie might talk to her again, but she'll never forgive her."

Tommy Lee wasn't sure what he was listening to. It was the first he'd heard about a children's home. He wouldn't ask questions here, he'd ask her later. "Ready, boys, lift."

Between the three of them, they managed to get the rose bush into the wheelbarrow. Duke then pulled out the tin, with the shawl and teddy in.

Within the hour, the memorial was done, the gate was fixed so it wouldn't open, and the trees were starting to go in.

***

Duke kicked his boots off at the door of the trailer. They were caked in mud. Connie stood at the stove stirring a stew. Jasper, Aron, and Sherry were in the lounge all cooing over the baby. He loved his kids, but this made him feel sick. Connie playing happy families while her own daughter was one hundred yards away, with two babies and no husband.

Connie smiled. "Dinner won't be long."

"I'm not hungry," he said. "I'll be going to see my daughter and grandsons, so don't dish me up any."

"How are the twins?" she asked.

"I don't think they're any of your concern anymore. Con, Millie won't forgive you for this, and to be honest, I don't blame her." He slipped on his clean shoes, grabbed his coat, and left.

He lit a cigarette while he walked round. It helped him think. His family was falling apart, and he was helpless. Scott's words had played over and over in his mind.

You can't blame her, all us kids who have grown up in children's homes have a safety mechanism, and when that clicks in, it's the point of no return.

He flicked the fag away and stamped on it. It was Connie's fault that she had been taken to that place. Connie should have told him about Millie. Instead, she'd chosen to keep it to herself, and Millie's life went to shit.

He knocked on the door and waited patiently. When it opened, Millie stood there with baby Duke in her arms.

"Dad, come in. I've only just got home, I took the boys to see their gran. She's staying on John Jo and Sean Paul's bit of ground in Wickford."

"Duke." Tommy Lee nodded.

"I'm just gonna take this one up to bed, I won't be a minute." She set off up the stairs.

"Can you not tell Millie about the memorial, I want to surprise her later," Tommy Lee whispered.

Duke nodded. "No problem."

He watched Millie coming down the stairs. "I just wanted to make sure you're okay, after Jasper coming back… I didn't know."

"It's fine, Dad, I'm sure it will make Connie happy. Just remember she's pregnant, so do whatever you need to. Right, would you like a cup of tea?"

She'd called her mother Connie, that wasn't lost on him. "I'd rather have a beer."

"I'll get it," Tommy Lee said. "Mil, go and put your feet up." He brushed a finger along her cheek. A simple show of affection.

Duke watched them closely; they both looked happy.

"Shall we go and sit in the lounge?" Millie asked him.

He followed her through, taking a seat in the armchair by the window. "Mil, I'm going to ask you a question and I want an honest answer."

"Okay, sounds ominous." She frowned.

"Just remember I love you," Duke said.

"Dad, you're scaring me."

He took a deep breath. "Would you be happier if you didn't see us at the end of your garden?"

"Are you sure you love me?" She laughed. "Because if this is your way of saying you're moving, I half expected it."

"No, I'm not moving, but if seeing Connie and Sherry is too much for you, I'd move to make you happy."

"You do what's right for you. Excuse me." She left the room, her footsteps running up the stairs.

Had he upset her, too?

"You know, I only found out about her growing up in a children's home today, and suddenly everything made sense…" Tommy Lee said. "She's not as tough as everyone thinks, you know. Underneath that that rock-hard surface, she'll always be that scared and broken little girl in the children's home. When I first met her, she told me everyone who'd come into her life ended up hurting her. So she made people work for her trust, her love, and her loyalty, but they still ended up letting her down. You and Connie have just proved her right. I think you'd best go, Duke, I need to check on her."

CHAPTER 54

Tommy Lee woke early after a fitful night's sleep. He had listened to Millie crying most of the night and held her until she had fallen to sleep. Propping himself up on one arm, he watched her. Her eyes were puffy and swollen, and still, to him, she was the most beautiful woman on the planet.

She moved slightly and opened her eyes.

"Morning," he whispered.

"What time is it?" she asked sleepily.

"Seven twenty-five a.m."

"The twins." She panicked.

"It's okay, Rosie came in and got them, they're downstairs with her." He pecked her on the lips then threw the covers back. "I've got a surprise for you, it might cheer you up."

That seemed to grab her attention. "What is it?"

"I can't tell you, it's a surprise." He laughed. "Do you want a cuppa?"

She nodded then rolled over, pulling the covers over her head.

He dressed quickly then descended the stairs two at a time. Sticking his head in the lounge, he smiled at the twins lying on the floor with their toys. He then made his way to the kitchen and switched the kettle on. Today could be the day that changed his life for the better.

The phone rang, and Rosie answered it. "Tommy Lee, it's for you," she said.

He took the phone from her and listened. "Good." He placed the phone down. Today was going to be a good day.

***

Duke hadn't slept well. Tommy Lee's words played over and over again as if on a loop.

Underneath that that rock-hard surface, she'll always be that scared and broken little girl in the children's home. When I first met her, she told me everyone who'd come into her life ended up hurting her. So she made people work for her trust, her love, and her loyalty, but they still ended up letting her down. You and Connie have just proved her right.

He grabbed his keys. There was a nice bit of ground for sale in Kent. He would go and have a look before making up his mind.

***

Tommy Lee called Millie and Rosie into the lounge. "Sit down, the news is about to start."

"I don't like the news," Millie huffed.

"Shh, you're gonna like this." He focused on the television. "Here it is."

"That's the psychiatric hospital," Rosie said anxiously.

Millie glanced at Tommy Lee; he was smiling. "You did it, you caught them."

The newsreader stated that there was an ongoing investigation into missing patients. The coverage showed police officers standing guarding the front entrance.

"Rosie, they're going to get what they deserve." Millie laughed. "This is the best news." She grabbed Tommy Lee's hand. "Why didn't you tell us?"

"Because I wanted you to see it with your own eyes," he said.

"Thank you," Rosie managed, her emotions clearly a little all over the place. "I'm going to phone Scott."

"That was a good surprise." Millie smiled.

"I've got another one. Put your shoes on and follow me." He pulled her up. "I think you'll love this one, too."

Millie followed him into the garden. "What are we doing out here?"

"Wait. Close your eyes," he ordered.

"If I fall over I won't be happy," she griped.

"Trust me," he whispered, leading her to the side of the garden. "Open your eyes now."

She opened them and glanced down. Her eyes watered. Micheal's monument was right there, in front of her. "I don't know what to say. Words don't seem enough." Taking a deep breath, she turned to him. "Thank you, this is perfect."

"Your dad helped, Mil. He does love you."

"Maybe." She shrugged.

"Do you know who else loves you… me." He knelt in front of her and held up a diamond ring. "Millie, will you marry me?"

She smiled. "Yes, of course I'll marry you."

CHAPTER 55

June 1979

Millie stared out of the bedroom window. It was strange looking at the empty ground where Duke and Connie had once lived. That had been a hard day, not that she had shown her emotions. She had watched from the bedroom window as the trailers were pulled off. They now lived in Kent. Connie was busy with their nearly one-year-old son, Nelson, named after Duke's dad, Millie's grandad.

She had only seen the baby a handful of times. Once was at her wedding last September. She had invited all her family, mainly because Tommy Lee said it was the right thing to do. She had asked Duke to walk her down the aisle, and he had. He'd even looked proud as he'd done so. It was funny, she was close to him. It was like they had this special bond. Maybe it was because she was his only daughter.

Aron was now married. He ran off with a girl called Prissy, and unlike Jasper's wife, Sherry, she was nice. There was no jealousy or fighting for attention.

Millie's wedding was a big occasion, and Tommy Lee's mum, Mauve, had been a diamond, along with Gypsy, John Jo's wife. Tommy Lee had paid for everything. He wouldn't take Duke's money, although he did let him pay for Millie's wedding dress. He wouldn't let Millie pay for a thing. He was old-fashioned like that.

Rosie had been her maid of honour, and she was now married to Tony. They had a lovely little registry office wedding, simple but stylish. They had moved nearer to the docks, which made sense.

Finn was still a big part of Millie's life. He was probably the one she relied on the most, other than Tommy Lee and Duke. He was getting cosy with some woman he had met at White City dogs. Millie was pleased that he had found some happiness after all the shit with his pretend daughter.

Her relationship with Connie never really recovered. She now kept her at arm's length. Connie was trying, but Millie still had that brick wall up. Would it ever come back down? Who knows. Never say never.

And as for Millie, well, she'd sold the club, she was no longer a Kelly, and the piece of land with the warehouse Paul had owned, both for a tidy sum. The scrapyard, her and Tommy Lee owned, which they'd agreed to sell, and they'd used that money to buy a little boxing gym in Romford. The docks was run mainly by Tony, and the brothel, which she left in Gladys's capable hands, remained Millie's. Scott was left to oversee her interests.

The one secret she carried, she would leave here. The night Paul was killed, she had arranged it. She had gone to see Nicky's husband, Robbie McNamara, and plotted it all with him after telling him how Paul had killed his wife. Then, to make it look good, she'd had him caught, made them chop his tongue out so he couldn't grass her, and got him disposed of. That was the one lesson she had learned from Paul. Always tie up loose ends.

"Mil, are you ready?" Tommy Lee shouted up the stairs.

"Just coming." She glanced around the empty room then closed the door. After making her way down the stairs, she smiled at him.

"Just one more quick check." She gazed at the empty front room with a tinge of sadness. There had been happy memories here as well as the sad. Was she right to be leaving Stepney, though?

"You okay, darling?" he asked, wrapping his arm around her shoulders.

She nodded. "Come on, we've got a lot of unpacking to do the other end."

"You're not doing it, not in your condition." He stared at the huge baby bump.

He had bought a house in Romford, right on the outskirts. It was still four bedrooms but with a much bigger garden. He wanted his kids to spend as much time as possible outdoors, like he had growing up, he had informed her.

"Mummy," Tommy boy called, quickly followed by a "Mummy," from baby Duke. Now they were walking and talking they were a right bleedin' handful.

"Right, are we finally ready, Mrs Ward?" Tommy Lee asked.

She gazed up at the house, then glanced at him. His piercing blue eyes stared back at her. Rosie had been right, he made her feel complete. As long as she was with him, she knew she would be all right. "I think we are, Mr Ward." She grinned. "Off on our next adventure."

The End

ABOUT THE AUTHOR

Carol Hellier was born in Oldchurch Hospital, Essex, in the mid-sixties. When she was in her mid-twenties, she discovered her parents were in fact her grandparents, and her eldest sister was her mum.

She married a Romany and started her married life off living in a caravan/trailer. This has given her a useful insight into the Romany world which shows in her writing.

She has lived in many different counties but now resides back in Essex. She spends her time working for the NHS, writing, and with her large family.

Previous titles:
Book One - *The Stepney Feud*
Book Two – *The Stepney Alliance*

Coming soon: A spin-off from the Stepney series – title to be announced.

Previous books:
Dolly King, The Gangster's Daughter
The Orion Prophecy, in the Shadows - under the author name Carol McDonald

You can follow the author on:

Instagram: author_cahellier

Facebook: https://www.facebook.com/carolhellier

TikTok: carolmc441_author

Printed in Great Britain
by Amazon